P9-CMA-143

Soul Catcher

G.P. Ching

Carpe Luna Publishing

Soul Catcher: The Soulkeepers Series, Book 4
Copyright © G.P. Ching, 2012
Published by Carpe Luna, Ltd, PO Box 5932, Bloomington, IL 61704

This book is a work of fiction. Names, characters, places, and incidents are either products of the author's imagination or used fictitiously. Any resemblance to actual events, locales, or persons, living or dead, is entirely coincidental.

All rights reserved. No part of this publication can be reproduced or transmitted in any form or by any means, electronic or mechanical, without permission in writing from the author or publisher.

Second Edition: May 2014

ISBN 978-1-940675-05-3

Cover art by Adam Bedore at Anjin Design.
www.anjindesign.com

Formatting by Polgarus Studio.
www.polgarusstudio.com

v.2.0

I have no doubt that in the future, the laws that criminalize so many forms of human love and commitment will look the way the apartheid laws do to us now—so obviously wrong. Such a terrible waste of human potential... And never let anyone make you feel inferior for being who you are. When you live the life you were meant to live, in freedom and dignity, you put a smile on God's face.

—Archbishop Desmond Tutu

Books by G.P. Ching

The Soulkeepers Series

The Soulkeepers, Book 1
Weaving Destiny, Book 2
Return to Eden, Book 3
Soul Catcher, Book 4
Lost Eden, Book 5
The Last Soulkeeper, Book 6

The Grounded Trilogy

Grounded, Book 1
Charged, Book 2 (Coming Soon)
Wired, Book 3 (Coming Soon)

Contents

Chapter 1
Taken

"Chevy! Come on, time to go." Chevy's father yanked the cord to raise the window shade, his voice holding more than a hint of frustration.

Chevy Kikmongwi tossed an arm across his eyes to shield them from the offending light. He ignored his father's prodding. Why did he need to participate in this stupid ceremony, anyway? Welcome to modern civilization. Time to evolve beyond believing in rain dances, even if he *was* half Native American.

"I'm not leaving, Chevy. You may choose to live with your mother, but until you're eighteen you will respect and participate in Hopi traditions with the rest of the tribe. Now move!"

With no intention of getting out of bed, Chevy flipped to his stomach and pulled the pillow over his head. He should have realized moving back to Flagstaff from Sedona would mean increased visits from his father, but he'd hoped the year away would dull the big man's desire to involve him in tribal affairs. Unfortunately, his dad was not the type to give up easily or take no for an answer. Robert Kikmongwi was not like Chevy's mother and did not back down from his fifteen-year-old son. Without warning the futon flipped on its side, and Chevy's body crashed to the linoleum.

"Owa! Geez, Dad. What the hell? I could've broken a hip or something." Slowly, Chevy propped himself on his elbows.

"Next time, be ready, and this will be less painful for both of us." In a red T-shirt and jeans, his father didn't look any more Native American than anyone else's dad in Flagstaff, but looks could be deceiving. A member of the Walpi village, he bought into all of the Hopi mythology, hook, line, and sinker. He probably believed the Snake Dance actually brought rain.

No getting out of this. Guess he'd have to get through it. "I need a minute," Chevy said.

"Yeah, I'd say so. Smells like a brewery in here." Oh, he was pissed. He was doing that thing where he closed and opened his fists.

"A couple of the guys came over and, you know."

"Yes, I do. Doesn't your mother have any rules?"

Chevy grunted and ran a hand through his too-long black hair. "If you got a problem with Mom's rules, go talk to her about it. Our rules work for us."

"What you mean is, you like having no rules and Shelly likes not having to worry about parenting you."

The shrug Chevy gave said it all.

His father slapped the doorframe as he exited the room in a huff. With much effort, Chevy stood, head throbbing in time with his heartbeat. *Damn.* The bathroom door wavered in his adjusting vision until he stumbled through to the porcelain sink. He fished a painkiller out of the medicine cabinet and tossed it to the back of his throat, rinsing it down with water from the tap. When he was finished, he spread his eyelids, one side at a time, careful not to tug on his new eyebrow piercing, and dripped some Visine over his chocolate browns. Had to look presentable for the native ladies. A little flirting would go a long way to shorten a slow ceremony. If he was lucky, Raine Nokami might find him in the crowd. She was hot enough to make a day on the reservation worth it.

As he climbed into the shower, the fighting started. Dad must have found Mom, which meant she'd come home last night after all. They'd be rehashing all the ancient history about how she'd promised to raise him the Hopi way. That wasn't going to happen. No way was he going to live in a clay box and farm corn in the desert. And for what? To follow the divine direction of some Great Spirit? Did they even know how people on the outside laughed at their antiquated faith?

Nope, Chevy had bigger plans for himself. Plans to change the world.

Stepping from the shower, he toweled off and tied his hair back into a ponytail. He brushed the taste of stale beer from his mouth and dressed in jeans and a gray T-shirt. Then, as loudly as possible, he exited his room, hoping the stomp of his feet and the slam of the door would shame his parents into giving the argument a rest. The sooner he hit the road, the sooner this would be over with, and he could get back to his real life.

* * * * *

The red dirt of Route 264 billowed up around the tires of his dad's Jeep. The two-and-a-half-hour drive from Flagstaff to the reservation was an exercise in small talk. How was school? Did he have a girlfriend? Like Chevy would share any of his personal thoughts with his parental units. Eventually, the one-word answers and head nods ebbed the flow of questions, and the even hum of the road replaced the forced conversation.

"We'll have to go on foot from here," his dad said as he parked the Jeep in a gravel lot outside the village.

Like Chevy didn't know that. This wasn't his first visit to First Mesa or Walpi, but he held his tongue and obediently followed on the footpath.

"If you were raised here, with the others, it would be time for your coming of age ceremony."

"Yeah?" Chevy internally groaned. Not another ceremony.

"I'd present a challenge, a test of courage, and if you succeeded in overcoming the challenge, you would be invited into the *Kiva* and be part of a ritual. After the ritual, everyone here would consider you an adult."

"Adult enough to decide I never want to come back here?" Chevy snapped.

It was a cruel thing to say. The older man's forehead wrinkled with the grimace that crossed his face, but he didn't say anything to rebuke Chevy's comment. Instead, he raised his proud chin to the pueblos on the top of the mesa, the warmth of the August sun already hot enough to bring a sheen of sweat to the surface of his skin.

This was going to be a majorly long day.

"Cheveyo!" the high voice that called his Hopi name cut through the distance like a bird's caw. Raine. Her straight hair floated behind her, spread like black wings, dwarfing her petite frame as she raced toward him. Dark eyes cut to his soul.

Thankfully, his dad swerved to go talk to a man Chevy didn't recognize and was out of earshot by the time she reached him. Her brown arms flung around his neck and pulled him into a tight hug before backing to a respectable distance. "I'm glad you came," she said.

"Good to see you too, Raine, but don't call me Cheveyo. My name is Chevy."

"Not here it's not." She smiled and the world stopped turning. "When you were born, your mother held you up to the rising sun right over there." She pointed to the edge of the red-rock crag. "And when the first rays touched you, she named you Cheveyo."

Chevy shook his head and laughed. She always pushed this, every time he visited. "Yeah, and because she was white she didn't realize she'd chosen a bad name. She thought it meant spirit warrior, but it doesn't. Cheveyo is an ogre that steals children in their sleep. If you were named after a monster, you might prefer a nickname too."

"I think it sounds tough. Roll with it." Her eyes flashed and she took a half step closer, tossing her hair over her shoulder. Oh, she smelled good, like sweet spices. "Maybe, you'll become such a great man Hopi will have to change the meaning of the name."

Riiiight. Chevy held his tongue. He didn't want to risk making her angry and losing her company.

His father appeared at his side. "Raine, so good to see you. How'd it go yesterday?"

"Good. I think the spirits helped me."

"Helped you do what?" Chevy asked.

Patting her shoulder proudly, his father answered for her. "Raine was chosen as the Antelope Maid. She told the story yesterday and is going to be part of the ceremony today."

"Wow. Congratulations," Chevy stuttered. "Who had the honor of accompanying you as Snake Youth?" *Please don't say Drew.*

"Drew," Raine whispered as if she could sense Chevy's dread.

"That's cool," Chevy responded too quickly. He nudged his father's elbow. "Hey, we should find Grandma before the ceremony starts."

"Good idea. Nice to see you, Raine."

Close behind his elder, Chevy gave Raine a small wave goodbye as he headed toward the plaza. The frown she wore darted straight into his heart. Hell, it wasn't her fault the tribe had paired her with Drew for the ceremony. But Chevy dreaded the ceremony even more, now. Raine wouldn't be by his side, silently poking fun at the festivities. Instead, she'd be a part of the irrational display. It almost made the experience worse.

He battled with himself all the way into the adobe-walled village. Should he be more supportive of her? Of the tribe? No. No, he couldn't allow himself to be pulled into this. Living the Hopi way was a prison. The reservation was literally landlocked, surrounded by the Navajo. Walpi didn't even have running water for God's sake. This was not the life for him.

His grandmother, Willow, emerged from her pueblo and embraced him in a bone-crushing hug, surprisingly strong for her four-foot-ten-inch frame. "Welcome home," she said. "Come. Let's find a place to observe."

Observe. That was all he could do. He wasn't actually part of all this. Sadly, his father and grandmother wouldn't participate either, even though they probably wanted to. His grandmother was a medicine woman, deeply faithful to the traditions. She would observe and explain to him in some weak effort to make him understand. Everyone tried so hard to bring him along. They would be better off when he turned eighteen. He'd never come back here, and his Hopi relatives would eventually forget about him and go on with their lives. For now, he sat between them on the bench on the edge of the plaza, waiting in the hot Arizona sun, under a cloudless blue sky. The painkiller he'd taken was wearing off, and his head began to throb.

"Over there is the *Kisi*," his father said, pointing at a crude shrine of sticks and animal skins. The focal point was an altar covered in brightly colored sand. "That's where they keep the snakes. The snakes carry the prayers of the faithful to the underworld, and if our dance is acceptable, the spirits will send rain."

Chevy rolled his eyes.

"They come," his grandmother said, stating the obvious. He couldn't have missed the drumbeats. The snake priests and their attendants paraded into the plaza, beating drums and shaking gourd rattles. One by one, the priests reached into the *Kisi*, pulling out whatever snake their fingers wrapped around first. The diamond-shaped head of a rattlesnake poked out from one of the priest's fists. *Damn.* He didn't remember them using poisonous snakes in the past, but then a couple of years had passed since his dad had forced him to attend a Snake Dance. With any luck, he wouldn't have to watch anyone die today.

The priests danced around the plaza, the snakes slithering over and under their hands. For the second lap, the priests held the snakes in their mouths, never missing a beat. At the same time, the attendants tried to distract the snakes from striking with their snake whips.

Chevy wiped his sweaty palms on his jeans.

"They use all the snakes," his father said. "The gatherers will keep them in the plaza as the priests drop them during the dance. See? The feathered wand soothes them and then they throw cornmeal to distract the snake before snatching them by the head."

Either brave or stupid, Chevy thought.

By the time the priests had circled the plaza several times, chanting their prayers, fifty or more snakes wriggled around the gatherers' necks and arms. Then, a snake priest found the *Kisi* empty. With a bowl of cornmeal offered by an attendant, he drew a large ring on the ground. The gatherers released the snakes inside the circle.

Raine, dressed in white, joined the dance and worked to keep the snakes inside the cornmeal boundary. *Holy cow*! Chevy's heart threatened to leap out of his mouth as she leaned over and used her snake whip to turn a rattler back toward the center. The diamond head coiled, ready to strike, and wouldn't you know it, there was Drew, swooping in to save the day. He coaxed the reptile toward the center of the circle, away from Raine. Chevy dug his nails into his thighs.

The whole thing unfolded like a train wreck, terrible and mesmerizing all at the same time. The priests scooped up snakes by the armful, returning them to a different shrine as the gatherers and attendants kept any stragglers from reaching the crowd.

"The snakes are released into the pit to carry the prayers to the underworld," his grandmother whispered.

Chevy didn't even realize he was holding his breath until the last snake slithered into the shrine. Thankful no one was hurt, he gasped in relief. The priests accepted bowls of liquid from the women of the village. Chevy cringed as they drank, then heaved onto the red dirt near their feet.

"The vomiting cleanses them of the snake charms." His grandmother smiled as if induced vomiting was an ordinary occurrence.

It was all so disturbing: the rhythm, the dancing, the chanting, beautiful Raine in danger, and then the vomiting. Chevy's head throbbed. A war waged within him, his brain telling him the ritual was archaic and ridiculous, but a deep, unused part of him desperately wanting to be part of this, to understand and participate next to Raine. As if those feelings weren't confusing enough, at that moment the previously clear blue sky opened up. Hell if he could explain why, but rain began to pour in sheets over Walpi village. The Hopi people shouted praise and gratitude toward the heavens and the Earth.

Chevy cracked. He leapt up and raced toward the footpath, hurling himself down the mesa.

"Chevy, wait!" his dad called from behind him.

He didn't wait. The rain soaked him to the bone, but he didn't care. He had to get away. If he didn't get a handle on this thing inside of him, this part that wanted to believe, he'd never save his sanity.

Near the car, Chevy stopped short of a grouping of juniper trees, their twisted branches oddly at home in the rain. An enormous winged snake with a white plume of hair stared at him through the leaves. His breath hitched. A *Kachina*, a Hopi spirit! He fell to his knees, quaking.

The snake stepped forward, transforming into a tall redheaded woman in purple stiletto boots that paused in front of his prostrate form. What the hell? Was he hallucinating? Dehydrated from his hangover?

"Well, now this is interesting," the snake woman said in a low, breathy drawl. "You are quite the offender. Kind of kicked the 'honor your ancestors' thing to the curb, didn't you?"

Chevy bowed his head.

"There, there. Take my hand and I'll give you exactly what you deserve." The snake woman extended her long fingers, her sharp tapered nails reminiscent of a bird's talons.

Gaze lifting to her bright green eyes, he extended his hand.

"Cheveyo!" Raine barreled down the mesa, not stopping until her hand gripped his shoulder from behind. She locked eyes with the snake woman. "Who are you? Are you here for the ceremony? You're too late."

Chevy wanted to explain to Raine what the snake woman was, but before he could utter a single syllable, the spirit clasped his wrist violently. A growl emanated from deep within her chest, and her thin lips peeled back from abnormally long, sharp teeth.

Raine cried out and pulled back on his shoulder.

Snake Woman did not release Cheveyo. Her other hand shot out to grip the twisted trunk of the juniper tree beside her.

Everything slowed. For once in his life, Chevy saw things with absolute clarity. The tree bark shingled the snake woman's arm, climbing toward him like a predator. The tree was swallowing the spirit and would eat him too. *Oh no, Raine!* He yanked against the *Kachina's* clutches, but Snake Woman wouldn't let go. Locked around his wrist, the spirit hissed through clenched teeth. Every cell in Chevy's body resisted. Counting to three in his head, he pulled away with everything he had in the opposite direction. The effort paid off. His hand slipped from hers, and he dove into Raine, trying his best to protect her from the bad spirit.

But something was terribly wrong. As he collided with Raine, he entered her skin, sliding inside her body like an overcoat. He blinked twice, staring down at the feminine arms and hands lifted in front of his face.

Then, he gaped in horror as his own body disappeared inside the bark of the juniper tree.

Chapter 2
Harrington Enterprises

Malini straightened her skirt and pressed the button for the elevator. This had to work. She'd been trying to get an audience with Senator Bakewell for weeks, to find the Watcher who was influencing him and take the dark angel out of the equation before the next vote.

"What's the bill called again?" Jacob asked, straightening his tie.

"S. 5109-International Economic Assurance Act. If I read it to you, I'd give you a headache, but the bottom line is the legislation would legalize the employment of slave labor in the United States as long as the slaves were not American citizens."

The elevator doors opened, and the two stepped inside the privacy of the compartment. Jacob grunted. "That would effectively decriminalize human trafficking. Who would ever vote for that?"

"No one with a clear head, but the council and I think Watchers have been influencing Bakewell for years and possibly a few other representatives. The legislation itself is confusing. Sounds like a boon for the economy to most people. If I wasn't privy to Fatima's loom, I probably wouldn't understand the consequences."

Fatima was Fate, the immortal who lived in the In Between, weaving the destinies of every living soul on the planet into fabric. Malini alone, as the Healer, could read patterns in the fabric and use her gifts to interpret possible futures.

"We might not fully understand the consequences, but the Watchers do. Lucifer's up to something. I can feel it," Jacob said, eyes darkening. The Lord of Illusions always seemed to have a plan B. After the Soulkeepers had forced Lucifer back to Hell that summer, when Abigail botched his human sacrifice, they'd thought they would get a break to regroup. No such luck.

"Yep. I can feel it too."

"So, we end the Watcher and let Senator Bakewell get back to his usual philandering ways?"

Malini giggled. "That's the general idea."

"How are things with the council going, anyway?" Jacob asked.

The new Soulkeepers' council consisted of Malini, because she was the Healer, Abigail and Gideon, as administrators of Eden, Lillian as the head of field operations, and Grace and Master Lee as Helpers. The point of the council was to enhance the communication and coordination of the small team of Soulkeepers. The Watchers outnumbered them. Always would. Even with Mara slowing time in Nod and Hell, the Soulkeepers had to work smarter to thwart the evil Lucifer inflicted on the world.

"Just okay," Malini said honestly. "Sometimes I think the adults don't take me seriously as their leader."

"I thought we'd moved beyond that."

"Me too. But it's still there, Jake, festering under the surface. Some of the things I bring to them are hard to accept. Like when Bonnie and Samantha couldn't return to Nebraska." Her eyes darted down to her tangled fingers. "They lost the restaurant. I thought Grace was going to blow a gasket."

"They're not chained to Eden. If Grace would rather take her chances with the Watchers, she can be my guest. That goes for the twins too."

"Jake!"

"I'm just saying, Malini, they should consider the alternative before taking their frustration out on you."

The elevator stopped, and the doors opened. Malini and Jacob stepped into a vast, pale space, all steel, glass, and ivory sandstone floors. Malini's heels click-clacked as she crossed the foyer to the front desk. Shiny metal letters on the dark wood read *Harrington Enterprises.*

A slender blonde with a French manicure ended the call she was on and fixed them with a hard, green-eyed stare. "Can I help you?"

"We're here to interview Senator Bakewell for our school newspaper. His assistant told us he'd be here meeting with Mr. Harrington and would have a few minutes to talk with us."

"One moment, please." Abruptly, the woman stood and power-walked down the hall.

"That was weird," Jacob said.

"Did you smell her?"

"Yeah. Eau de Watcher with a core of human. Not even masked with illusion. Possessed or influenced?"

"Influenced. Long term by the strength of the aroma." Malini rubbed her nose. "I'm texting Lillian for backup. I'll have her wait in the lobby, just in case." Her fingers flew and then she tucked the phone back into her pocket.

Jacob reached out with his power. If the blonde was influenced, he might need a weapon. "There's a pitcher of water in the conference room to your right, a bathroom down the hall, and a jug of it this way. Maybe some sort of break room," Jacob whispered. "You're covered."

"Let's try to do this without making a scene. She's human. She probably doesn't know what we are. Keep this low profile, less to clean up later."

Jacob nodded.

Click-Clack. The blonde returned, a cardboard smile on her face. "Right this way."

She led them along the windows overlooking the magnificent mile to a door labeled Conference Room D. She rapped lightly.

"Come in," a man's voice drawled.

The woman opened the door. "I have your twelve o'clock. School interview."

"Send them in, Amanda."

Amanda stepped aside, directing them inside with a swing of her arm. A stoic man in a crisp gray suit raised a cup of coffee to his lips before standing to welcome them.

"Senator Bakewell?"

"The one and only." Bakewell's smile lit up the room.

Malini walked around the conference room table and politely extended her hand.

Bakewell stared at her offered handshake and cleared his throat. "Sorry to be rude but I've had a bought of illness recently. Amanda should have explained, I can't touch you. Call me a germaphobe!" He gave a deep laugh. "Truly, it's as much to protect you as me, darlin'."

Malini lowered herself to the chair next to him, flashing Jacob a pensive look. If she couldn't touch the senator, she couldn't heal him of his Watcher influence. Of course, if they didn't find and kill the Watcher responsible, there was no point anyway. He'd be influenced again in no time.

Jacob pulled out a chair across the table and sat down.

"I'm Mandy Witherspoon from St. Scholastica High School. Thank you for agreeing to this interview."

"Always interested in helping the future of America," Bakewell said. "And who are you?" he asked Jacob.

"Oh, I'm Fred." Jacob held the man's stare for a second. "Er, I'm just her ride."

Bakewell laughed. "Behind every successful woman is a man who can parallel park."

Jacob chuckled, but Malini's mouth pressed into a flat line, silencing them both. "Why don't we get started? Your assistant said you only had a few minutes."

"She would know." Bakewell nodded.

Malini pulled a pen from her purse and opened her notebook to a blank page. "How did you get your start in politics?"

"My father was a politician. You could say serving the American people is in my blood. As soon as I'd earned my law degree, I pursued a career in politics. My first position was mayor of the little town of Pointer, Ohio."

Malini cut him off. "I have a history of your career. It's very impressive."

He tilted his head. "Thank you, young lady."

"Can you tell me what legislation you're most excited about right now?"

"Sure. I've sponsored a bill to increase the penalties for illegal drug possession and another to increase our investment research into biological energy alternatives."

"Biological energy alternatives?" Jacob asked.

Malini shot him a sharp look. He shrugged apologetically.

Bakewell chuckled. "The driver speaks! There's a professor at UCLA who thinks he can genetically modify bacteria to produce petroleum. If his research pans out, we could put the little buggers in our landfills where they'd eat our garbage and poop out oil. I think that idea's worth some government funding, don't you?"

Jacob nodded.

"What can you tell us about S. 5109?" Malini asked.

The smile faded from Bakewell's face and his cheek twitched under his left eye. He took another drink of coffee, his eyes rolling in his head as he tilted the cup back. At the same time he set the mug down, he checked his watch.

"I am awfully sorry; it appears we're out of time. I hope you've got enough for your interview. If you want any other information, feel free to ask Amanda at the front desk."

"But I've only asked you three questions!" Malini protested.

Bakewell stood and pushed in his chair.

"I can see you're busy." Malini stood and motioned for Jacob to do the same. She held up a finger and flashed a charming smile. "Please, Senator, one more thing. Your coffee smells delicious. Would it be okay if we grabbed a cup before we go?"

"Of course. Down the hall and to the right." Bakewell gave her a curt nod and rounded the table, holding the door open for the two of them.

"Nice to meet you, Mandy and, uh, Fred." He poked his head into the hall. "Amanda!"

The blonde came click-clacking from the front desk. "Yes, Senator Bakewell?"

"Please show Mandy and Fred to the refreshment area and then show them out. Let Harrington know I'm ready for him."

"Yes, sir." Amanda pointed a hand in the direction she came from. "Right this way."

Malini followed her directions, Jacob sidling up next to her.

"What now, Mandy?" Jacob asked.

"Now, we get a drink," she said.

Amanda stepped ahead of them and opened the door to a small kitchenette area with three vending machines, a microwave, and a coffee pot next to the water cooler. "Help yourself," she said. "Cups are in the cabinet. Let me know if you need anything. I'll be back to check on you in a moment." She took off toward her desk, no doubt to inform Mr. Harrington the senator was waiting.

Malini reached into the cabinet and pulled down a Styrofoam cup. She poured a half cup of coffee.

"Care to share what we're doing in here?" Jacob said.

Raising the cup to her nose, Malini sniffed. "It's in the coffee," she said.

"What's in the coffee?"

"Watcher elixir. Here, smell."

Malini held the cup under Jacob's nose, the scent of cinnamon, sulfur, and spice growing stronger with the movement.

Jacob sniffed, then gagged. "Yep. That's the stuff. Doesn't make sense though. He spends most of his time in Washington, D.C. Do you think the Watcher is here?"

She dumped the coffee down the sink and stared at the wall. "I'm not sure. Amanda has been influenced for quite some time, and she lives here. Bakewell is here regularly but not frequently enough to maintain the type of influence I suspect. The Watcher must be reaching him in D.C. too."

"Huh," Jacob said. He leaned up against the counter and sighed.

Healer or not, trying to think like a Watcher was never easy. With a deep breath, she rinsed the cup out and poured herself some water. She raised the Styrofoam to her lips.

Sniff-sniff. She lowered the cup and stared down into the water. "What business is Harrington Enterprises in, Jacob?"

"I don't know."

"Can you Google it?"

Jacob pulled out his phone and typed the company's name into the search bar. "A bunch of things: pharmaceuticals, energy, water purification."

Malini held the cup under his nose.

Jacob took a deep breath and let it out slowly. "It's in the water."

"Gives new meaning to drinking the Kool-Aid," Malini said.

"Looks like Lucifer is up to his old tricks again."

"Yeah, and there's nothing we can do. The Watcher might not even be here. It's wherever this water is bottled."

They both stared at the water cooler as if it would sprout lips and start giving them answers. Out of the corner of her eye, Malini glimpsed a man in a sharp navy suit pass by the open door to the break room. Something about the way he moved was too graceful, inhuman. She turned her head to get a better look. Dark wavy hair, a smile that could sell toothpaste, and navy blue eyes. He straightened his red tie, and then moved beyond her line of sight. The saccharine sweet, sulfur scent of Watcher hit her full force. Jacob narrowed his eyes at the pull of evil from the doorway.

"He's—"

Jacob was already around the corner. Malini followed, kicking off her heeled shoes and running down the hall at breakneck speed. As she turned the corner into the long stretch of hallway to the atrium, she saw the Watcher tapping the button for the elevator frantically. Unnatural eyes locked onto hers, and a knowing, nervous smile twitched across the demon's face. Without missing a step, Jacob's hand moved toward his ankle, calling the water from his flask. He hadn't counted on Amanda. She leapt around the desk, blocking their target with her body and distracting Jacob.

"Hey, you can't run in here," she said.

He shoved her out of the way in time to see Blue Suit disappear into the stairwell. Malini cruised around Amanda, kicking off the desk to pick up speed and corner into the stairwell. Luckily, bright light filtered through windows lining the small space. Sunlight limited a Watcher's power; they might have a prayer of catching him.

In defiance of gravity, Jacob cartwheeled over the stair rail, dropping to the landing a floor below. The move would be dangerous for an ordinary human, but Soulkeepers developed superhuman agility and strength over time. The Watcher wasn't smiling anymore.

Down, down, she pursued, floors flying by, hot on the demon's heels. The male frantically tried a doorknob, a gold lion's head ring flashing in the bright sunlight. Locked. Malini smiled. Jacob succeeded in reaching his flask and his broadsword of ice formed in his palm. They had him!

With suicidal resolve, the Watcher dove over the railing, twisting out of reach of Jacob's stabbing blade. Malini watched the demon drop to the landing below, forcing her feet to move faster down the stairs. Only, they'd reached a lower level of the building, and the topography changed. This floor housed a spa with a tranquil atmosphere, partially drawn curtains decorating the stairwell. The Watcher grinned at her one last time before sinking into a sliver of shadow. Navy blue eyes, suit, and golden lion's head ring disappeared in a plume of smoke, leaving behind only a wisp of sulfur stench.

"Damn!" Malini rolled her eyes at the ornate doors to the spa with contempt.

Jacob channeled his sword back into his flask. "Do you think he was the source of contamination?"

"I don't know. The elixir was inside the bottled water. If that was the Watcher responsible, he contaminated the bottle at the source. Senator Bakewell spends most of his time in Washington. If he's influencing him there too, we've got a very busy Watcher on our hands."

"Still, it's possible."

"Yeah, but did you notice his suit? He's posing as an executive. There's something else going on here, Jacob."

"We could go back upstairs and grill Amanda for more info."

"She's influenced too. She won't tell us anything."

"Then what do you suggest?"

"We need to collect ourselves, talk to the council, and do our homework on Harrington Enterprises. My gut tells me this is bigger than Senator Bakewell."

"Shoes?" Jacob asked, glancing at her bare feet.

She shook her head.

"You're the boss." He led the way toward the atrium to meet Lillian.

"And I can parallel park too," Malini said under her breath.

Chapter 3
The Council

The next day, Malini arrived in Eden alone with two things on her mind: Harrington Enterprises and Cheveyo. She needed to ask Abigail and Gideon for help researching where the infected Harrington water was produced and distributed. Until she understood the connection between Senator Bakewell and Harrington, she was putting out a fire with an eyedropper.

Cheveyo was another story entirely. He'd been missing far too long. With two experienced Helpers on the case, finding him should have been easy, but every lead came up empty. She'd even visited the In Between and searched for his thread. Maybe he'd been taken by the Watchers? She hoped not.

They needed every Soulkeeper left alive to stand any chance of keeping Lucifer at bay.

Abigail met her at the door. "No Jacob today?"

"Laudner family brunch."

"Ah yes. How is Aunt Veronica doing?"

"Ninety-six and still gripping to life with both crotchety hands." Malini laughed.

"Same as I remember then." Abigail led the way through the jeweled foyer of The Eden School for Soulkeepers.

"How are things with you and Gideon?" Malini asked.

"Oh …Uh … Good, I suppose. Settling in."

"You don't sound thrilled exactly. Is married life not what you expected?" Immediately, Malini regretted the all-too-personal question.

She dipped her head. "Oh, marriage is fine … perfect actually. Eden, on the other hand…"

"What about Eden?"

"Honestly, sometimes this place feels like a prison. Both Gideon and I would rather be working alongside the other Soulkeepers."

First Grace and the twins, now Abigail. Didn't anyone appreciate the safety of Eden? Malini paused outside the hallway. "I'm sorry, Dr. Silva. It's just too dangerous for you right now."

"Yes, of course. After Lucifer's threat at our wedding, we should be thankful for Eden." She didn't sound thankful.

Malini nodded and let it drop.

"How long do you have today?" Abigail asked.

"A few hours. My family thinks I'm studying at the library. I should be, of course. Senior year, you know."

"That's right! Have you applied anywhere?"

"Your alma mater."

"University of Illinois? They'd be fools not to admit you. What will you study?"

"Journalism."

Abigail turned away but not before Malini caught a flash of skepticism. Everyone assumed she'd study medicine because she was a Healer, but the idea of having to allow people to die on a regular basis when she had the capability to heal them didn't appeal to her. Life and death were a delicate balance, so easily thrown off by the most benevolent of actions. No, she would be an observer, ferreting out evil and bringing it to light.

At the stairwell, Malini noticed the halls had been conspicuously empty. "Where is everyone, anyway?"

"The rest of the council is waiting for us in the conference room, and the students are studying in the dining hall. We haven't made the curriculum easy."

With a snort, Malini declared her support. "Better hard now than hard later when they're fighting for their lives."

"My sentiments exactly." Abigail hooked right at the top of the stairwell.

"Are Grace and Lee back from Sedona?"

"Not exactly." Abigail flashed a knowing smile and opened the door to the room next to her office.

The conference room consisted of a long wooden table in front of an arched window overlooking the jungle. When Malini walked in, Lillian and Gideon tilted their faces up to greet her. So did Grace and Master Lee, although Malini could see right through their bodies to the chairs they sat in.

"Wha—" she said as her mouth dropped open.

"Warwick's stones," Abigail explained. "We figured out how they worked. They project the image of the person calling to the other stones in the set." She motioned toward the rough, blue gemstone on the table. "Ancient cell phones."

"Handy," Malini said.

Inside the blue tint of his transparent image, Lee's hologram smiled. "Good morning, Malini."

"Good morning," Malini took a seat across from Grace's hologram "Any new clues on Cheveyo's whereabouts?"

Grace spoke up first. "We found an apartment in Sedona with residual traces of Soulkeeper energy. Only, no one lives there anymore. Building manager says a woman and her son moved out over a month ago."

"Did they leave a forwarding address?" Malini asked.

"A place in Flagstaff. The son's name was Chevy."

Gideon shifted in his seat. "Surely a nickname."

"Presumably. We're headed to Flagstaff tomorrow to confirm he's our Soulkeeper."

"Excellent," Malini said. "So, why do you both look so worried?"

Lee sighed. "The residue was faint, Malini. I am an experienced Helper. I've been tracking Soulkeepers for decades. Either he is in transition, or he has never used his power. He is going to be vulnerable."

"Crap. Do you think Lucifer has him?" Malini asked.

Abigail shook her head. "Lucifer may have his name from the list, but if we can't locate him, chances are Lucifer can't either. Something about this boy is making him hard to find, both for us and for the Watchers."

"We need to get to him first," Malini said.

"Obviously." Grace pursed her lips.

What's with the attitude? Malini scowled.

Master Lee made his best attempt to diffuse the tension. "We will find him. Before we leave for Flagstaff, we are visiting his old school and interviewing neighbors. A picture would aid our search efforts."

"Makes sense. Thank you," Malini said.

With nothing left to share, Abigail reached for the stone. "Thank you for being with us today. I'll keep the stone with me in case you find anything."

Grace nodded, reaching for the sister stone. Her image flickered and then disappeared, along with Master Lee's.

"That was disappointing," Lillian said, turning a paperclip between her fingers.

Malini couldn't argue. Discouragement hung heavy in the air between them. "How are the new Soulkeepers coming along?" she asked, hoping for better news.

"Good. Bonnie and Samantha are tougher than they look, and Jesse was already good as gold after training with Master Lee," Lillian said.

"And Ethan?"

Lillian's eyes flicked to Gideon's. They both made a sound like a soft groan.

"What is it?"

"He's, um, challenging," Lillian said.

"What does that mean?"

"Well, he has trouble following the rules," Gideon said.

Abigail tilted her head in agreement. "He's late for every class, has been caught trying to cheat several times, and is otherwise annoying."

"Annoying?" Malini laughed.

She bit her lip. "He loves to be the center of attention. Yesterday, he burst into song, some obnoxious rap melody, and started grinding against one of the gnomes. We had to give the poor fellow the day off."

As much as she wanted to keep a straight face, Malini couldn't, overcome as she was by a fit of giggles. Soon the others joined in as well.

Lillian shook her head. "He is funny. A joy to have around most of the time. But can he be disciplined in the field? We're not sure how much we can trust him."

"Hmm. Yes, I can understand why that could be a problem."

Abigail cleared her throat. "He has a past. The night I picked him up I think he was running from the mob. He admitted to stealing some money."

"Ah. Trust is a major issue then."

"Next time you're in the In Between, can you follow his thread?" Abigail asked. "Give us something to go on?"

"Of course." Malini nodded.

"Good." Abigail scribbled a note to herself.

"Well then, Lillian filled us in on yesterday's mission. What is your plan with regard to Harrington Enterprises?" Gideon asked.

"None yet. I need your help with some research. Maybe one of the helpers can bring you resources."

"No need. We have all the resources necessary. Follow me." He gathered his notes and headed for the door.

Confused, Malini said her goodbyes to Lillian and followed Gideon into the hall. Abigail joined them at her side.

"Where are we going?" Malini asked.

Abigail smiled mischievously. "We have something to show you, something I believe you will find quite interesting."

"Interesting like The Huffington Post or interesting like a hive of Watchers trying to decapitate me?"

"The first."

"Excellent!"

Through a door at the end of the hall, Malini followed Abigail into an antechamber.

"I don't remember ever being in here before," Malini said.

"This room wasn't accessible." Abigail pointed toward the door they'd just entered. "That used to be a solid stucco wall."

Malini lowered her chin and raised her eyebrows.

Gideon paused to face her. "I was lamenting the lack of outside information in Eden when Archibald, the good gnome that he is, asked if there was anything he could get for me. I said, 'Yes, a New York Times.' And, without leaving Eden, he brought me one."

"What? How?"

"As we've come to expect here, there's more to this place than meets the eye. Turns out Warwick sealed off this room with magic when he left. I don't blame him. The content is worth protecting."

"Show me." Malini was smiling now. She suspected what might be behind the double doors and crossed her fingers, hoping she was right.

Abigail grasped the carved wooden handle and pulled. Behind the heavy door was a golden, three-story, round room from a fairy tale.

"A library!" Malini said, stepping inside. A winding staircase led to the second and third floor, where curved shelves stretched floor to ceiling, laden with tomes.

"Oh yes, a library. An enchanted library. Come, a demonstration is in order."

"Please!" Malini said excitedly.

"We'll start with the fiction section. What are you in the mood to read?"

Malini grinned. "Romance."

Abigail led her to a shelf of books labeled with a hand-carved plaque in a language Malini didn't know. "Choose a book," she said.

"But the spines have no titles," Malini said, confused. She lifted a leather volume off the shelf and flipped it open. "The pages are blank."

"You didn't tell it what to be," Abigail said. "Close the book again."

Malini did.

"Now concentrate on the book you want to read." Abigail waited. "Open it again."

Delighted, Malini opened the book and read the words that appeared on the page. "'It is a truth universally acknowledged that a single man in possession of good fortune must be in want of a wife.' Holy magical library, this is Jane Austen!" Malini gaped at Abigail, who was laughing as if she still couldn't believe it.

"And that's just the beginning," Gideon's voice boomed from above. He hung over the gold railing on the second floor. "Come check out the Google section."

Malini jogged up the stairs to his side. "Google section?"

"My nickname for this section." He pointed to a row of black tomes. "Ask these books a question—out loud. It seems to work better that way."

Rubbing her hands together, Malini asked the question weighing on her mind. "Where is the Soulkeeper Cheveyo?"

The spines blurred and then filled with print. "Arizona Live Births, the History of Hopi Civilization in America,

Flagstaff Arizona visitors' guide. Looks like Grace and Lee are searching in the right place!"

"Incredible, yes? Anything we need is at our fingertips." Gideon lifted the first tome and started flipping to the section labeled "C."

"What does it say?"

"There isn't a Cheveyo listed," Gideon said.

"Figures. But like anything else here, it's a matter of asking the right questions."

Gideon nodded.

"I wonder…" Malini ran her fingers along the spine of a book. "Do you think this place is connected to my power somehow? Where does the information come from?"

Contemplative, Gideon rubbed his chin. "Anything is possible, I suppose, although these books mirror what's available in the outside world and nothing more. They can't predict the future or focus on a specific soul any more than a biography."

"I see."

"I hate to disturb you, Malini," Abigail called from below. "I know there's more you'd like to do here, but the gnomes are expecting to see you before you go, and I think, the students too. It means a lot to them."

Malini nodded. Part of being a leader was being *there* for people. It was something she'd had to get used to, a part of growing up she'd never expected. Her presence, her attention, brought comfort to others. Even on days she didn't believe in herself, she had learned others did with an almost mystic reverence, and it was important that she uphold the responsibilities of her station.

"Gideon, would you mind researching Harrington Enterprises for me? And continuing to dig for more information on Cheveyo?" she asked.

"Of course not. I'd be happy to," he said.

Thank goodness. Malini descended the stairs, straightened her spine, and cleared her head. At Abigail's side, she prepared to give her full attention, her full self, to whoever needed her.

Chapter 4
Strange Expectations

In the small town of Paris, Illinois, Dane Michaels adjusted his bright orange tray on the brand-new folding table in the remodeled cafeteria. After the disaster at prom last year, an act of violence the town labeled domestic terrorism, reconstruction had taken an entire summer, but Paris High School was fully operational again.

"Are you guys going to the school dance?" Dane whispered across the table to Jacob and Malini. Not that anyone was listening anyway. The rest of the school had long since decided the three friends, who always sat in the far corner, had nothing interesting to offer. Better they never knew the truth.

Jacob glanced at Malini. "Considering the last dance we went to resulted in Lucifer blowing up the school, I wasn't planning on it. Plus, Malini and I have work to do."

Malini lowered her fork and huffed in his direction. "Jake, yes, okay. There's always work to do. But it's our senior year. We can't miss homecoming just because the devil wants us all dead. I'm not letting him get the best of me."

"Sorry," Jacob said, leaning away from Malini's tantrum. "You wanna go to homecoming?"

"Yes, thanks for asking. I'd love to." She forced a tight smile.

Dane leaned forward in his seat. "Actually, I was talking about the *other* school dance. Although I am on the Paris homecoming committee, and it is going to be fabulous."

His two best friends exchanged glances. Malini raised an eyebrow. "Other school? How have I not heard of this? The Healer should be the first to know." She laughed.

"It's something Ethan's been organizing."

"Ah." Malini poked her baked beans with her fork.

"I guess since there are so few of us, you could just call it a back-to-school get-together," Dane said. Maybe he shouldn't have told Malini. He hoped Ethan wouldn't get in trouble because of him. Dane liked the school in Eden better than Paris. He felt safe there. Unlike Malini and Jacob, he didn't have Soulkeeper powers to protect him if the Watchers returned for a replay of prom night. He was vulnerable to any demon who wanted him dead. Worse, the time he spent in Hell gave Lucifer an imprint of his soul. Outside of Eden, the devil had constant supernatural GPS on his ass and could demand his astral projected presence on a whim. He was a sitting duck.

"You've been spending a lot of time with Ethan, huh?" Jacob said softly.

Malini elbowed him.

"Ow! What the hell? Just making an observation." He rubbed his arm vigorously.

Dane pretended not to catch that Jacob's inference had to do with Ethan's sexual orientation. He didn't want to go there. "Well, uh, he doesn't have many friends here, you know, and he's not allowed to leave Eden much. He's been helping me on the farm a little. It gives him something to do. Probably boring considering he's from California and used to work in a club, but he doesn't seem to mind." *And he makes me feel safe.*

"Yeah," Malini said. "He needs you, Dane. You've been a great friend. He and the twins are probably going stir crazy. When is this dance?"

"Friday night. After training. Everything's cleared with Abigail." *Damn*, he sounded too excited. He had to remember Eden wasn't *his* school. As lucky as he was to be included, he didn't belong. Not really. When they all graduated, he'd go away to college, hopefully, and then what? He wouldn't be hanging out in Eden every weekend, that's for sure. Or he could do things his dad's way and take over the farm. Not much time for battling evil when there's corn to grow.

A soft brown hand landed on his pale one. How did she know?

"We wouldn't miss it, Dane. We can all go together. Sounds fun. Plus, maybe while we're in Eden, you and I can talk," Malini said.

Warmth infused his arm, and an easy calm settled over him. "Okay." The bell rang, but he couldn't look away from her soothing topaz eyes.

Jacob groaned and swiped her hand from his. "All right, that's enough healing for the time being. Come on, Malini. We'll be late for English." He placed a protective arm around her shoulders and steered her body toward the exit.

Dane followed them from the cafeteria, rolling his eyes at the theatrics. Jacob knew as well as Dane did that he had nothing to worry about when it came to Malini. Those two were destined for each other.

What was his destiny? He frowned as the image of himself dressed in overalls and carrying a pitchfork slid across his mind. Panic shot through his abdomen, and he was reminded of why he needed to concentrate on his studies. Melding into the hallway traffic, he hurried to his next class.

* * * * *

The hinges of the screen door screeched as Dane entered the farmhouse, his bulging backpack weighing down his shoulder. Homework in every subject. So much for easing into the school year. Still he'd have to buckle down to get it all done if he wanted his Friday night free to spend in Eden.

"That you, Dane?" his dad called from the family room.

"Yeah. I'm home."

"Good. I need your help in the grain silo. Problem with the blower. Need to get 'er fixed before harvest." The old man rushed into the kitchen with long, quick strides and rubbed his forehead with the back of his thumb. As always, he was in a hurry. A farmer's work was never done.

"Can't today, Pop. I've got tons of homework." Dane eased the backpack off his shoulder and dropped the weighty cargo on the kitchen table for effect.

His dad stopped abruptly, a rarity in the Michaels's household; the man was never still. "Can't you do it tonight, after dark? Only so much daylight left."

"Like I said, I've got hours of homework, and I've got to be awake. All AP classes, remember?"

Plugging his burly hands into his pockets, he shook his head. "This is ludicrous. There's only so much education a boy needs. You've got responsibilities 'round here!"

"Luke, you heard the boy!" Dane's mother yelled from the hall, a basket of laundry on her hip. The miserable expression on her face said what her words didn't. There'd be hell to pay if his father pushed it.

His father grunted and turned his head away, like he couldn't stand to look at Dane a moment more.

"I can look at the blower on Saturday. I'm sure Ethan would help me if you can wait a couple of days."

"Ethan, huh?" His dad shook his head and stomped through the squeaky screen door. "I'll check if Walter can do it." Dane hoped he'd go easy on his younger brother; his dad was in a mood, again.

Robotically, his mom entered the kitchen, her thin lips pursed. She'd aged this year. New wrinkles carved out the path her frown took on her face, and her hair was gray at the roots. "You haven't helped 'round here much since you've been home," she said, her voice heavy with disappointment.

"I help when I can."

"Which ain't often."

"It's not what I want to do." The words were out before Dane could consider the implications of the admission.

His mom scooted the basket off her hip and onto the table near his backpack. She started forcibly folding the laundry. "Sometimes a thing grows on a body once they try it."

"I spent the first seventeen years of my life trying it," Dane murmured, then immediately regretted it. Tears gathered in his mom's eyes. He hated to hurt her. None of this was her fault, and he'd put her through so much this summer when he disappeared.

Of course, it wasn't *his* fault either. He'd been captured and held prisoner by Lucifer. But he couldn't tell his parents the truth about what happened. Instead, he'd said he didn't remember anything, and the town assumed his fate was the same as Stephanie Westcott's, who also couldn't remember anything. Dane was told he was abducted, drugged, and kept in a warehouse, a victim of a human trafficking ring. He was freed, just in time, by an FBI sting operation. While a good story, there wasn't a grain of truth to it. Nevertheless, his family welcomed him home and eventually stopped asking questions.

Things hadn't been the same since,because Dane wasn't the same. Not only was he still a bit thinner, his mind was constantly elsewhere. He couldn't force himself to pretend anymore that he wanted anything to do with the farm.

Now his mother stared at him with dull eyes as if she didn't know who he was anymore. "You may not remember anything about your abduction, but I do. You left a gaping hole in our family. It broke my heart."

"I'm sorry—"

She held up one bony hand. "You're eighteen, a legal adult, and I suppose you'll do what you want to do. But we need you, Dane. Whatever happened to you was traumatic. Your father and I've let you do your own thing for a while so you could recover. But I'm beginning to think this isn't about recovering. Don't you want to be part of this family anymore?"

"Mom." Dane shook his head. "I *do* want to be part of this family. But why does that always mean corn and soybeans? Isn't it enough I'm here, and I'm healthy? I'm not the only one who can work the farm. You've got Walter and Jenny."

"Walter's only fourteen and doesn't have half the brains for business you do. You know that. And Jenny will never be able to handle the physical demands."

"You underestimate both of them. Give them a few years." Cracking his neck, Dane shuffled to the cabinet to pull down a mason jar. He opened the fridge and reached for the lemonade.

"We may not have a few years," his mom said from behind him.

He abandoned his quest for a beverage and turned back toward her. "What is that supposed to mean?"

"Your father isn't well."

Dane closed the refrigerator door.

"He's had some tingling in his toes for a year or so now. It's advanced recently. Sometimes he can't feel his leg at all. Now it's started in his fingers. Doc doesn't know what it is. After harvest, he's got to see a doctor at Mayo clinic for more tests. Of course, he should go now, but he won't. Not with a full field."

Suddenly nauseous, Dane swallowed hard and pressed a hand to his stomach. His father, sick? He'd always thought his dad was practically invincible. Nothing ever slowed the man down. An ongoing joke in their family was how his dad was back in the field the same day Dane was born. He'd never spent a morning in bed his entire life. What if it were true? If his father needed him, genuinely needed him, he'd have to help, at least until Walter was old enough to take over. That meant no college, no Eden. Not for a long, long time.

"So, after harvest? In December? That's when he goes to Mayo?"

"Yes." His mother's face paled.

"Give me until then. I need time. I'll start in the spring, if he's not better, if he really needs me. I'll help out more."

For the first time in what seemed like forever, his mother smiled.

Chapter 5
Ethan's Eden

Ethan circled the hooded figure, ready for anything. From under the cloak, a knife appeared and whipped at his head with blinding speed. He pushed with his telekinesis, and the weapon dropped harmlessly at his feet. A barrage of throwing stars came next, sailing at his chest from the folds of her cloak as she spun closer to him. This was more difficult. As fast as possible, he concentrated on one at a time, deflecting each with his mind and attempting to dodge the rest. The last one grazed his shoulder.

He spun away, trying to distance himself from his assailant, but she was too quick. She executed a front flip over his head, an admirable feat considering the long, flowing cloak she wore, and pressed the tip of her dagger into his

back. He tried to dive roll forward, but she dropped to the
floor and swept his legs with one of hers, causing him to
topple to the sanded wood.

The dagger plunged toward his heart. With everything he
had left, he held her off, gripping her wrist with his hands
and prying the blade from her fingers with his mind. The
knife clanked to the floor beside them, but not before she
thrust her hands forward, cutting off his eye contact with the
sleeve of her cloak. Her knee pressed into his chest, pinning
him to the floor, and with his face covered he couldn't use his
power to get her off. In three lithe moves, she flipped him
onto his knees and bound his hands behind his back, all with
her bell sleeve tightly wound around his head.

"Do you know what you did wrong?" Lillian asked.

"I let you get too close," Ethan said from under the
cotton.

"Correct."

The black cloth retracted, and he took a deep breath.
Lillian freed his hands and lifted him to his feet, tossing the
cloak to the floor in frustration.

"You're not concentrating, Ethan. You are powerful, but
you lack focus. You can't allow yourself to get distracted."
She smoothed her straight black hair back from her face and
crossed her arms over her chest.

"Kind of hard to concentrate with a knife in your face."

She sighed. "I know it's not easy, but your telekinesis is
useless if you can't see your target. For you, maintaining
distance is essential."

"Not always possible," Ethan complained. "What if I'm overcome from behind? What if there's more than one assailant?"

Lillian smiled, approaching him. "That's why we learn martial arts. If you didn't have your power, where would you strike me?"

He jabbed, stopping short of touching her. "The eyes, nose, solar plexus, kidneys."

"Correct. So when an attacker has a knife in your face, don't use your power to disarm him. Use your power to blind him."

Ethan's mouth dropped open. Of course, she was right, but the thought was brutal. Using his telekinesis to push in an eyeball or thrust a person's nose into their brain seemed almost like cheating. He laughed through his nose at the irony. Usually, cheating wasn't a problem for him.

"In a real fight with the damned, they won't play fair. Demons will maim you in a heartbeat and eat your flesh while you're still alive. Strike early and leave no advantage for the sake of fairness." She smiled. "I'd hate to lose such a talented Soulkeeper."

He nodded. "Thank you, Ms. Lau."

"You're welcome, Ethan. Your skills are coming along nicely. It's obvious you've been practicing."

"I want to be ready. Next time I want to fight." During the last major battle, Ethan was left behind in Eden to nurse Dane back to health. Not that he'd minded. Not at all. But he wanted to be useful. The Soulkeepers were his family now.

She slapped him on the shoulder. "It's good to be brave. Even better to be prepared."

"Yeah." He grinned. "I think you just proved as much to me."

"Good. Clean up this mess and you're done for the day." She nodded her goodbye and slipped out the rice paper door.

Hands on his hips, Ethan eyed the sanded wood floor apprehensively; knives, swords, stars, and even nunchakus littered the dojo. The spoils of war. As exhausted as he was, he was also pleased with himself. When he'd first arrived in Eden, he couldn't have defended himself against a wooden staff. Now Lillian required the entire room's arsenal to bring him down. Ethan focused on the dagger closest to him. The blade soared from the floor into the rack on the wall, followed by the throwing stars and the long sword. A wooden staff and a chain were next, the last wrapping itself neatly on a spool. Brass knuckles fit into a small drawer, and the cloak hung itself on a hook. He turned circles, using his mind to clean up the remainder.

When everything was righted, he stared at the rack on the wall, proud of how far he'd come. Every day he grew stronger, more confident. More a Soulkeeper. Lately, that was all he wanted to be.

"This some kind of new training method," a disembodied voice said into his ear.

Ethan whirled around as Jesse formed behind him out of thin air. He might never get used to the way the guy could break apart and hang in the air or his electric violet eyes, so unsettling. But his particular gifts were damn useful and frighteningly powerful. Ethan was glad Ghost, as he liked to be called, was on his side.

"Nah. I was just thinking about how far I've come since I've been here. Lillian is an amazing instructor."

"True that." Ghost stepped to his side. "Bonnie needs help hanging the decorations in the dining hall. She says she wants you to do it, so she doesn't have to use a ladder." He chuckled.

"What's so funny?" Ethan led the way through the door and into the hallway.

"Isn't it obvious, Ethan? If she wanted to, she could meld with Sam and easily reach the ceiling. She wants you to do it because she thinks you're hot, or as the twins say, haaawt."

Ethan snorted. "I *am* haaaawt, but I'm also gay. She knows this. Everyone knows this. I've known I was gay since I was twelve."

"Maybe she thinks she can change the flag you're flying." Ghost laughed so hard he came apart a little at the edges.

Ethan stopped abruptly in the hallway. "You can't even say that with a straight face. Look at me, Ghost. Is there one heterosexual cell in my body?"

Ghost stepped back and rubbed his chin for a moment. "No. Absolutely not. You came out of the womb singing *Somewhere Over The Rainbow* with jazz hands."

"Thank you," Ethan said, spreading his fingers on either side of his face for effect. "It's taken me a long time to be happy and proud of who I am. I don't need anyone trying to change me. Hell, I get enough of that from my parents." He continued toward the dining hall.

"Aww, consider it a compliment. Let's face it, there's a limited pool of Soulkeeper genes, and since Sam and I are sort of, you know…"

"Heavily flirting with a side of occasionally making out."

"Um, yeah. You could put it that way. Anyhow, maybe Bonnie feels like you're what's available." Ghost shrugged.

A shiver traveled the length of Ethan's spine, and he tightened his forehead. "Worst reason to like someone ever. Just because we're Soulkeepers, doesn't mean we need to breed with each other. Hell, it would be better to spread out the genes. You know what? I'm not even going to go there. It's stupid. I'm gay. Bonnie needs to find someone else to set her sights on."

Ethan continued toward the dining hall, noticing with the lull in conversation only his own footsteps were audible even though Ghost was right beside him. The guy was unreal. He paused at the door and took a deep breath.

"Hey, I could tell Bonnie there's always Dane."

Wincing as if he'd taken a blow to the gut, Ethan gaped at Ghost in disbelief.

"I'm just kidding, dude, but you seriously need to sort that one out. The guy has no idea what flag he's flying. Might not even own a flag pole," Ghost whispered.

"Do me a favor and don't talk about Dane or his flag pole," Ethan said. "It's none of your business."

Ghost flared his hands next to his shoulders and smirked. "What if I'm interested?"

"Hah! If I was born with jazz hands, you were born winking at the nurse who caught you."

"Yeah, you're probably right."

"Listen, I have feelings for Dane, true. But I don't want him to change for me. Being homosexual is no cup of tea in this world. Part of me hopes he's not. And, honestly, it doesn't matter because I accept him for who he is, unconditionally."

"That's beautiful, man."

Ethan flashed a lopsided grin. "I have my moments."

"But what if he just needs, like, a push. You know, he grew up in *Paris,* not exactly an open-minded metropolis. Maybe if you just grabbed him and showed him how you felt—"

"Worst idea ever." Ethan shook his head. "No, if Dane wants something more than friendship, he'll have to figure that out for himself. I'm not going to force him into anything. I'll wait."

Ghost sighed. "You might be waiting a long time, bro."

Ethan shrugged. "Come on. Let's get this over with." He pushed open the door and entered an enormous room that reminded him of a cuckoo clock. Circular and constructed of intricately carved wood, the open space welcomed him in. All of the Soulkeepers ate here when they were in Eden at long wooden tables with high-backed chairs that stretched across the room.

Bonnie looked up from her spot at the head of the center table where she strung nuts, pinecones, and dried fruit into a garland. Everything in Eden had to be handmade and natural. Even the power was solar. And the diet? One hundred percent vegan. While a challenge to get used to, Ethan had to admit he'd experienced clarity here he'd never had in the outside world, an inner peace that made him want to be a better person.

"Ghost!" Samantha sang, skipping from the place where she arranged flowers on the table to Ghost's side. He pulled her to his hip and kissed her cheek.

"It's about time. Could use some help here. Party's supposed to start in an hour," Bonnie said, annoyed.

Ghost laughed. "Relax, Bon-bell. It's just us coming. No one is going to say a word if the garland isn't up."

"Hey!" she yelled. "This is important. If we're stuck going to school here, we might as well make the best of it. Plus, this garland is a pain in the butt. Respect my skills, or else."

"Or else, what?"

"Or else, I'll get Archibald to hang it."

Everyone groaned. The school gnomes were exceedingly useful when it came to keeping up the grounds, cooking, and cleaning, but they were terrible at odd jobs. The problem was you had to be ridiculously specific to get what you wanted. They had to know when to start and when to stop. Ethan had asked Sage, a two-foot-tall female with a beard, to fold his laundry and found her three hours later, folding and unfolding the same shirts. Not only were his clothes permanently creased from the pressing, but Sage was irate. She huffed from the room, rubbing her sore hands. Abigail ordered her to take two days off to placate her and berated Ethan for not being more careful. None of the Soulkeepers liked to use them for fear of making a mistake and damaging one of them.

Ethan sauntered to Bonnie's side, accepting the end of the garland from her. She flushed when his fingers brushed hers. *Ugh*. He stepped backward, a little too quickly, and cleared his throat. Full attention on the garland, he lifted it with his mind to the ceiling beam, tying off the end. As strong as he was now, the dexterity required to split and cross the force he created in order to tie a knot was challenging. He hadn't perfected the skill yet, but somehow he managed, even under the scrutiny of Bonnie's stare. He moved on to the next strand, draping the garland in swags across the timbered ceiling.

"It's beautiful," Bonnie said into his ear. When had she moved so close?

He finished tying off the last strand and dusted his hands as if he'd had to use them. "Yeah. Looks great. I like what you did with the pomegranates." He gave her an efficient smile, trying his best to bleed all warmth from his expression. Somehow, she'd gotten the wrong idea about him. He didn't want to be rude or presumptuous, but he also couldn't lead her on.

Her eyebrows knitted together. "I'm going to go get the music," she said softly.

To Ethan's relief, she left the room, but the way she grinned at her sister as she passed through the enormous wooden doors made his stomach sink. *Oh hell!* Why couldn't anything be simple?

Chapter 6
The Quota

With a flick of her well-manicured hand, the redheaded Watcher, Alexandra, opened the gate to Nod and dragged the Hopi boy into the city of the damned. Her dark purple, stiletto boots trudged over the filthy street, past a group of Watchers stripping flesh from a newly captured human. *Yum!* As soon as she made her deposit with Auriel, she was joining that party. This little number made her quota for the week.

She yanked her quarry into line behind the ten or so other Watchers bringing in their souls. Ahead of her, Xavier had an old woman in his clutches.

"Please, please let me go. I need to take care of my grandchildren." She struggled helplessly against his talons.

"Oh, dear woman," Xavier said, pressing a nail into her chin, "I'll take care of your grandchildren. The young are so much sweeter."

The woman burst into hysterics, weeping desperately.

Alexandra eyed her captive and gave the boy a little shake. He was still breathing, and his eyes were open, but he wasn't panicked like the other humans. As quiet as if he were sleeping, he stood next to her, facing forward, with a vacant expression. Aside from an occasional blink, she could barely tell he was alive.

"There's something wrong with my human, Xavier," Alexandra said.

The dark-haired mass of muscle turned around, flexing his navy blue wings. "What's wrong with it?" he asked.

"It's not crying out like the others. No fight whatsoever."

Xavier poked the boy in the chest, hard enough to knock him off balance. Alexandra kept him from falling but was sure the force of the jab should elicit some sort of response. "Odd," Xavier said. "Don't mention anything to Auriel or she might not count the soul toward your quota."

"Right. I'm not doing this again today. I hate going up." Since the last battle with the Soulkeepers, Lucifer had increased the Watcher quota of souls, partly as a punishment for his failed plan and partly out of undiluted evil. She could appreciate the latter, but it was more work than she liked. There wasn't enough room in Nod for all the souls, which meant some had to die, and the dead didn't bury themselves. It was exhausting.

"Maybe she won't notice," Xavier said.

Alexandra growled, showing a bit of fang. "So what if she does? A human is a human. It should count."

The line advanced toward the entrance to the steel and glass building where Auriel waited to sort deposits. Xavier pushed his soul forward by the neck. The old woman screamed, begging for her life anew. Alexandra dragged her boy roughly behind them. The human stepped forward but didn't make a peep. Maybe his brain was damaged. Auriel wouldn't be pleased. Watchers usually didn't take physically or mentally damaged humans because their usefulness in Nod was limited, and often their souls were too clean to take comfortably. There had to be sin or the skin would burn when touched.

This boy didn't burn, and he'd better count.

Xavier entered, and Alexandra shouldered the door open behind him. Elbowing into the room, she jockeyed for position in the crowded lobby. "You ten," the bored-looking blond Watcher behind the desk said. She pointed a baby-pink wing toward the elevator. "Level three."

Alexandra sprinted for the elevator doors. As luck would have it, her dormant human proved to be an advantage. She was the first onto the elevator and hastily punched the button. The doors closed before anyone else could get on. She grinned, hearing the snarls of the Watchers stuck in the lobby. *You snooze, you lose.*

The doors opened on level three, the throne room. She rolled her eyes. Only Auriel would require such pomp and circumstance to drop off a soul. She missed Mordechai's more pragmatic approach. But so be it. Alexandra dragged the boy's body down the red velvet runner to the platinum-blonde Watcher on the golden throne.

"I have one, fifteen-year-old Hopi boy for deposit," she said.

Auriel glanced up from her manicure and sniffed the air. Her face tightened, stretching her lips into a hard line. "Where did you find this one?"

"On the Hopi reservation in Arizona."

Jumping off her throne, Auriel lifted the skirt of her ivory gown and paced down the steps of the raised platform until her face was inches from the boy's. "What's wrong with it?"

"Nothing, Queen Auriel. He took my hand. Clearly an offender."

Again, Auriel sniffed the air, lifting the boy's hair to her nose and whiffing the strands directly. "I know that scent," she said with a start. A smirk spread across her face, more teeth than lips. "Alexandra, you dimwit. You've taken a Soulkeeper."

"Wha-what?"

"Can't you smell it? He reeks of kindness and self-sacrifice. It's subtle but unmistakable." She shook the boy by the shoulder. "What is your name, Soulkeeper?"

The boy stared vacantly at Auriel.

She dug in her talons and shook harder. "Answer me!"

"Queen Auriel, he bleeds," Alexandra said. It would be her head if the boy truly was a Soulkeeper and died before Lucifer could question him. "We should call Lucifer."

Auriel retracted her talons from the boy's skin. "What sorcery is this? Has he been responsive?"

Alexandra dropped her head and shuffled her purple boots. "Not since I brought him through the tree."

Whirling toward her throne, Auriel screamed loud enough for the other Watchers, who had gathered in the doorway of the throne room, to take a step back. "Lucifer. Lucifer!"

Dark smoke swirled near her feet, changing into oily droplets that tornadoed from the red velvet carpet. The drops squeezed together into a sharply dressed blond man who straightened the lapels of his gray Armani suit jacket. The Watchers at the door broke into applause, as did Alexandra. She noticed Auriel clapped the loudest in an obvious attempt to curry favor, and her nostrils flared.

"This better be important, Auriel. You took me from a meeting with the board of directors."

"My lord." Auriel tore the boy from Alexandra's talons. "I have found the lost Soulkeeper."

Alexandra placed her clenched fists on her hips. Auriel shot her a warning glance.

The Lord of Illusions pinched the boy's chin between his thumb and forefinger and stared into brown, vacant eyes. "Finally, the long, lost Soulkeeper." Lucifer tipped his head to the side, examining his catch. He inserted his hooked finger into the human's chest cavity and pulled out ... nothing. "He's not in here."

"My lord?"

Lucifer's dark laugh echoed through the room. "This is his body, but his soul is somewhere else."

"Can they do that?" Auriel asked.

"Never before. Tell me, Auriel, what happened. I need every detail."

Auriel fidgeted with the corner of her gown.

"Auriel!"

"Alexandra was the Watcher who actually pulled him through the tree," Auriel sputtered.

With a smug grin, Alexandra stepped forward and snaked her arm into the crook of Lucifer's elbow. "I would be happy to give you all of the details, my lord."

"Good." He waved a hand in Auriel's direction. "Auriel, see that the boy's body is stored in the zoo." Lucifer's eyes locked solely on Alexandra. As they strolled from the room, past the other waiting Watchers, she began to tell her story, not leaving out a single detail.

* * * * *

Auriel drummed her talons on the arm of her throne. With the abnormally large intake of souls and finding the lost Soulkeeper, she should have been in a better mood. Instead, her black blood boiled. She'd have Alexandra's head for the way she'd looked at Lucifer. There was a reason they called her Queen Auriel. While Lucifer could have anyone he liked, he most often chose *her* to share his company, and Auriel intended to maintain her position by his side.

"Oh relax, Auriel. Do you give me no credit?" Lucifer stood in the center of the otherwise empty throne room, Alexandra's purple wing dangling from his bloodied hand. "She angered me." He tossed the wing aside and approached her.

"Did you find out about the boy?" Auriel asked, easing off the throne and lowering herself to her knees in front of him.

He ran his fingers through her hair and cupped her cheek. "Always on task," he murmured. "Yes. It seems our Soulkeeper, Cheveyo is his name, can possess another human's body. When Alexandra took him, he jumped into the girl with him. She was a bitch to find. Raised the Hopi way, simple and sweet. I found her thanks to the boy's soul. The echo from his body was easy enough to track. Her name is Raine Nokami. She's missing. Her Hopi parents are beside themselves with grief." He chuckled.

"He couldn't have gone far with her. Alexandra just took him this morning," Auriel said, then cringed when she realized her mistake. The look he gave her. How embarrassing. "Mara," she said with disgust. "Time is slower in Nod. The witch is messing with us still. How much of a delay?"

"Two weeks, but she changes our clock often. It's impossible to say from below." Lucifer's eyes drilled into her.

"What is it you wish me to do?" she asked hesitantly.

"It has come to my attention Cheveyo could be useful to us. Alexandra mentioned the boy was confused about what she was, thanks to a convenient resemblance we have to Hopi spirits."

"What do Hopi spirits look like?" Auriel asked. With the right illusion, she could look any way he pleased.

"Some look like winged snakes. They call them *Kachinas*."

"Fascinating."

"I don't believe Cheveyo knows he's a Soulkeeper. You will find him, pose as a *Kachina*, and convince him to join our cause."

"Our cause?"

"The Soulkeepers have been hiding. I didn't know where at first, only that their souls would conveniently disappear. When Abigail dropped off the map, things became painfully clear. I think they've found Eden."

"*The* Eden? How?"

He scowled. "The Great Oppressive Deity, of course. It must be Eden, the one place I can't follow. The one place they are safe from us. But I have a plan to end their bothersome sanctuary."

"Please, share your brilliance with me, my lord," Auriel gushed.

"The human we captured, Dane, is somehow able to join them there. He disappears at the same time as Malini. If we can convince Cheveyo to help us by possessing Dane, he can infiltrate Eden and slaughter the Soulkeepers from the inside out." Lucifer's lips peeled back from his teeth.

"A Trojan Horse. Your magnificence astounds me. But why can't one of us possess him? Call Dane's soul now and I will do it."

"Eden is guarded by two cherubim and the Great Oppressor's own power. You wouldn't be able to see it, let alone enter. The power would filter you out of Dane's body. But Cheveyo has the mark of a Soulkeeper. He'll be allowed to enter hidden inside the human's body."

Auriel tapped her bottom lip with her finger. "Tricky. I must make him believe killing the Soulkeepers is the right thing to do, and the only way to get his body back. It will take a beautiful, elaborate lie."

"You are the best liar I know, besides myself," Lucifer said. He offered her his hand and lifted her to her feet. "We can't allow Death, Time, or Fate to interfere. You'll have to live among them until our cause is achieved."

The idea of walking in the sun didn't appeal to Auriel, but she nodded anyway. Lucifer would reward her well if she accomplished this. Living above ground wouldn't be pleasant, but she would do it to cement her place as Mordechai's successor.

"I won't fail you, my lord. The boy is as good as mine."

He yanked her into his embrace. "Good girl. For once, we've gotten lucky. Let's find a way to tell the Soulkeepers we've found Cheveyo. We'll need them to deliver our precious cargo."

"With pleasure."

"Excellent. Before you go, I have another need for you, Auriel." Lucifer laughed wickedly before delivering a sharp kiss to her throat.

What Lucifer wanted from her would be painful and humiliating, but she welcomed him with open arms. This was the price she paid for her position. Not that she had a choice anyway. The day Auriel decided to follow Lucifer from Heaven was the last day she chose anything for herself.

Chapter 7
Jump

C *heveyo? Please don't do this. I need to call my parents.*
They must be so worried.

"Raine, I've told you a million times, call me Chevy." The
noise from the soda machine masked his words. He just
couldn't get used to talking to her inside his head, but
speaking out loud to no one had its drawbacks. Like, people
generally stared at the crazy woman talking to herself.
Possessing Raine's body was highly inconvenient.

She started weeping again. He hated when she cried.
Besides being much louder inside his head than in real life, he
couldn't put his arm around her to comfort her, making her
sobs a special kind of torture. If he wanted to, he could cut
her off, lock her behind the steel door he'd discovered at the

back of his brain, but he was afraid. Her voice had grown
steadily weaker the last few days, and he was concerned
severing their connection might hurt her. For the first time,
his Hopi name seemed apropos. Cheveyo the monster who
steals children.

He flipped open the can and raised the soda to his lips,
noticing Raine's hand wrapped around the aluminum. How
disconcerting to be inside *her* body, but remain in control.
She was locked inside his head, not the other way around.
But no matter how much she fought or screamed or cried, he
couldn't go back to the reservation, not until he figured out
why this had happened. A curse of the *Kachina*? A
punishment for not believing?

Walking back to the motel room, he stomped on a roach
as he entered the door, gagging at the smell of stale smoke
ever-present in the faded orange decor. He wanted to crack a
window but couldn't risk someone overhearing what he
needed to say to her.

"Raine, please stop crying."

She sobbed harder.

"I'm not sure why the spirit stole my body or why I'm in
yours, but we can't go home until we figure this out. What
would I tell your parents?"

*You could tell them the truth! The spirits are punishing you
for not taking them seriously. This is your fault, Cheveyo. We
need the priests to help us.*

"You don't know that, all right? You don't know why my
body was taken and you certainly don't know how to fix this.

If the priests get me out of you, where will I go? Until I find my body and we figure out how to put me back, I'm stuck."

What about your parents? They must be so worried. And how is sitting in this pit of a motel room helping to find your body?

Chevy didn't know how to answer her. He wasn't sure what to do. But he was afraid to go back, afraid the priests would judge him and cast him out to roam the Earth for eternity as the evil spirit he was. He had to try to find another way.

"There has to be a way to get my body back from the spirits," he said sternly.

The door smashed open, bouncing off the interior wall and washing the room with afternoon light. A weirdly cold breeze circled inside. Chevy jumped up and poked his head into the outdoor corridor. There was no one out there. It must have been the wind. He closed the door again.

When he turned back around there was a woman in the room, blonde, tall, and heart-stoppingly beautiful. He gasped. How did she pass without him noticing?

"Hello, Cheveyo," the woman said. How did she know his name? Especially considering he was inside Raine's body.

He shook his head like he didn't know what she was talking about.

"Oh, Cheveyo, don't you recognize me?" The woman shivered, transforming into a snake with a shock of white hair and menacing leathery wings.

Chevy collapsed to his knees, tears flowing. "However I have offended you, please forgive me."

The snake slithered forward, transforming into a blonde woman again. "Yes, Cheveyo, you have offended me. But you can make everything right again. I have a mission for you from the Great Spirit. If you help us, you can prove your worth again, and your body will be returned from the underworld."

Shaking so hard his teeth clacked together, Chevy forced himself to look up at her terrible presence. "What do I need to do?"

"First, something to drink." The snake woman waved her hand, and a small table appeared with a cup of steaming tea. "Sit."

He did as he was told. The tea tasted of dark spices and smelled of cinnamon. The warmth from the liquid coursed over his tongue, down his throat, and infused every muscle in Raine's body. At the back of his skull, he could feel her slip away, rendered insentient by the concoction. Completely relaxed, he slumped in the chair, his eyelids sagging.

"That's better," Snake Woman said. "Now, listen to me very carefully. In this world, there are good spirits, like me, who keep the world safe from evil ones. But evil is everywhere, and I need your help to stop it."

"How?" Cheveyo mumbled.

"There is a boy, slightly older than you, who is destined for great evil." The snake woman removed a disk from her pocket and projected the image of a muscular boy with brown hair and gray eyes. He looked about eighteen. "He is part of a group of humans who call themselves the

Soulkeepers because they exist to ruin human souls. You must possess this boy as you have possessed Raine, and follow my instructions. Once you have destroyed the Soulkeepers, I will return your body to you."

"I don't know how to do it," Chevy stuttered. "It just happened. Raine was touching me, and my soul jumped into her body."

The snake woman smiled. "That is how it is done. You touch someone, skin to skin, and will yourself into the body. You'll see, with practice it will become second nature to you."

"Can you show me?" Chevy asked, reaching for the snake woman's hand. He hoped he could free Raine with her help.

The spirit jerked away. "Don't ever touch me!" she snapped.

Chevy recoiled, bowing his head. A red flag of warning rose inside of him. His father always said never to trust a man who wouldn't shake your hand. Did that apply to spirits?

"The evil you are made of is incompatible with my purity," the snake woman hissed. "If you touch me, you will die. Only human beings."

Of course. He nodded his head and wiped his sweaty palms on his thighs. He was no better than a worm, groveling at her feet. His heart ached to set things right. "How do I find this boy?"

"His name is Dane Michaels. I will call him to you. You will know him when you see him, and you will possess him."

"Yes."

"But first, you need practice. Can't have you freezing up when the time comes. Besides, I think Raine has had enough."

Chevy's tears started anew. She did understand and was showing him mercy. He needed to try his best to please her.

"What can I do?" he asked.

"Downstairs, there is a small restaurant where a boy named Jaden works. You will find him cleaning tables. The boy has no family, few friends, and lives in room twenty of this motel. Go to the restaurant, jump into the boy, and wait for my instructions. No one can know you've taken control. Keep working at the restaurant and don't call attention to yourself. Go. Do it now."

I don't trust her. Raine's voice was an unwelcome interruption. *The elders have never told stories of good Kachinas using people like this. She's a bad spirit, Cheveyo. Don't listen to her.*

Chevy nodded and pushed himself up to his feet, wiping the tears from his cheeks. He turned from the snake woman and exited the room.

Don't do this. Please. I have a bad feeling.

"Sorry, Raine, you just don't understand," he said, closing her out behind the steel wall.

Chevy jogged down the concrete stairwell, past the pool, and into the Prickly Pear Diner. The place was practically empty, aside from an elderly couple in a booth near the back and their mousy-haired waitress. It was easy enough to find

Jaden; there was only one boy bussing tables. He looked up when the bell above the door rang.

"Can I help you?" Jaden asked politely.

Chevy strode forward and grabbed Jaden's wrist.

"Hey? What the hel—"

The snake woman was right. The jump was almost instinctual. He willed his soul out of Raine and into Jaden, sliding easily into the boy's skin. The first thing he noticed was the weight of the bin of dirty dishes in his hands. He rested it on the table in front of him.

Raine's hand still gripped his wrist, only she had power over it now. From inside Jaden, Cheveyo could see what he'd done to her. Dark circles loomed beneath her eyes, and her hair was a rat's nest. The clothes he'd put her in were wrinkled and dirty.

"Don't do this, Chev—Chevy," she whispered. "We can go home. The elders will know what to do."

"Al, you better get out here!" the waitress called.

Chevy gazed at Raine, the girl he'd grown up with, his good friend, and understood what he had to do. This was his problem, not hers.

A large man in an apron appeared behind the counter. "What's going on out here, Jaden?" he asked.

Chevy didn't hesitate. "This is the missing girl, Raine Nokami. I don't think she's right in the head."

"No. No!" Raine protested. She backed up, shaking her head. "Don't do this. It's wrong. She's a bad spirit."

The man behind the counter fished a phone from his pocket. When it was obvious he'd called 911, Raine made for the door, but the stout man leapt over the counter and blocked her path. The police responded almost immediately, the spinning red cherry lights lighting up the diner. Soon Raine was ushered into the back of an ambulance, shaking her head and uttering the truth, which sounded like nonsense to everyone else.

"Wow, that was something. Good job recognizing her. I've seen the flyers but, man, she was in bad shape."

Chevy nodded. "Lucky, I guess. I just saw the flyer this morning. Scary though. Did you see how she grabbed my arm?"

"Yeah, a real head case. Okay, enough excitement. Back to work. Maybe we'll get some tourists in here curious about the drama."

Sure enough, a few diners appeared in the doorway. The mousy-haired waitress began seating them at the booths, telling the story over and over about the found girl with the messed-up head. He grabbed the rag off his shoulder and began to wipe down the nearest table, telling himself this was for the best. Raine was safe now.

What? What's happened to me? Jaden's panicked voice woke up inside Cheveyo's head. He ignored it, slammed the steel door shut, and kept working. He'd explain it all to the boy tonight, safely behind the locked door of room twenty. And then, he would wait. He'd follow the spirit's instructions. He'd find this Dane and keep him from doing whatever evil thing he planned to do. Raine would see. This was the only way. Soon, he'd have his body back and be able to explain everything. Soon.

He hoped.

Chapter 8
Party in Paradise

Dane climbed off the boat and stepped onto the path to the Eden School for Soulkeepers, oddly nervous. Odd because he'd spent enough time here to be comfortable with the path through the jungle, the stately white adobe mansion, and all of the people who lived here, but for some reason, waves of anxiety had been plaguing him since morning. Heart racing and head swimming, he was afraid to think too hard about what his body was trying to tell him. He suspected his nervousness was due to Malini's request to talk with him alone. He'd heard somewhere bad news came in threes. His father's illness had been number one. Was this the night the council would kick him out of Eden because he wasn't a Soulkeeper?

He glanced over his shoulder at Malini as she followed hand in hand with Jacob through the jungle trail. She smiled just like always, not giving him any indication of foreboding news. He picked up the pace, pushing aside wide palm leaves and branches of trees he couldn't even name. Tropical birds cawed overhead, and a legion of lemurs stared at him with round, reflective eyes as he broke free of the vegetation and crossed the yard to the entrance of the school.

"Master Dane! Welcome back to Eden." Archibald, the head garden gnome, stood near the door, pointy green hat in hand.

"Good to see you again, Archibald. Are you working tonight?"

"No, sir. Ms. Bonnie gave me the night off and said I could do anything I like. I like watching guests arrive. Your clothing is unusual."

Grinning, Dane looked down at his favorite plaid shirt, jeans, and work boots, comparing them to Archibald's green lederhosen. He guessed it was all in what you were used to.

The gnome reached a hand tentatively toward his shirt.

"Would you like to touch it?" Dane asked.

Archibald's lips pulled back from his ragged teeth. He waddled forward a step and stretched a grubby, green-stained hand toward Dane. He rubbed the gray plaid between his fingers, and then ran his chubby touch down the outside seam of his jeans. Dane disguised his groan as a cough, when he noticed the streaky grass stain the gnome left in his wake.

"The fibers are strange, Master Dane. Does the fabric itch?"

"No."

The gnome rubbed his chin skeptically.

Malini came to his rescue. "Please excuse us, Archibald. We don't want to be late."

The gnome bowed his head and backed into the shadows. "Of course, Healer. Enjoy your evening." His body twisted, and he was gone.

She brushed the excess dirt from Dane's side. "I don't think this stain is going to come out."

"It's just a smudge, Malini. No big deal."

"That was cool of you. Archie kinda gives me the creeps," Jacob added.

Dane shrugged. "You've got to think he's never been outside of Eden. I can buy a new shirt, but how many chances will he get to see one like this?"

"You are a sweetheart, Dane," Malini said, pecking him on the cheek.

Jacob growled.

Dane followed the two of them to the dining hall, placing a hand on his flip-flopping stomach. Behind the ornately carved doors was a natural wonderland. Candelabras lit the carved wood interior between crossbeams draped in evergreen, red fruit, and pinecone swags. Fir trees lined the walls, branches laden with berry sprays and additional candles. Pushed against the windows, the dining tables sat loaded with large bamboo bowls of popcorn, chips, and cookies. A glass punch bowl bubbled with a tropical blue drink. Where the tables used to be, a dance floor was squared off, and music played from a small but powerful battery-powered speaker someone had obviously brought in from the outside world.

Bonnie and Samantha swayed casually to the music, sipping cups of the blue liquid. The girls were all dressed up in black mini-dresses and jewelry. Now that he thought about it, Malini was wearing a dress too, a casual emerald number. Maybe he should've worn a tie? No, Jacob was wearing jeans and a black button-down, and Ghost appeared near the girls in his usual faded T-shirt. Guess it was come as you are.

Dane's eyes flipped around the room. Why did he feel so antsy? Maybe because Jacob and Malini had crossed the room to talk to Bonnie, leaving him standing alone awkwardly at the entrance. He approached the snack table, hoping no one would notice his accidental abandonment. That was when the door creaked open.

Ethan entered the dining hall in the black T-shirt and jeans he almost always wore. His eyes found Dane immediately, and he smiled. An easy calm overcame Dane as he smiled back. Maybe this was the problem; he needed a friend. Jacob had Malini, Jesse had Sam, and Bonnie almost always hung with Sam too. Dane was a third wheel until Ethan was around. Ethan always made him feel important, part of the group, even when he obviously didn't belong. The guy had seen him at his worst, when he'd first returned from

Hell nothing more than a skeleton, but somehow he still treated him as an equal. He was such a good friend.

"What's in the blue juice?" Ethan asked as he approached the table.

"I'm not sure," Dane said. "Looks like some kind of berries or something."

Ethan poured a glass and took a sip. The corner of his mouth pulled to the side, and his eyebrow arched. "I think it's alcoholic." He handed over the glass.

As he reached for the punch, Dane didn't think twice about drinking out of the same glass, but when his fingers brushed Ethan's, a wave of heat passed through him. His mouth dried up, or maybe his tongue swelled, he wasn't sure. He caught himself staring at the point of contact like he couldn't pull his hand away. With magnetic accuracy, his eyes flicked up to Ethan's dark ones. His mind drifted while his visual cortex fixated on the way Ethan's bangs swept across his brow and his lips curled around impossibly white teeth.

He didn't analyze the experience; he just pulled away, turning so he could distract himself with the jungle outside the window. He took a long swig, emptying the glass. "I think you're right. There is alcohol in this."

"Don't get too excited," Ethan said. "Like everything else in Eden, I'm sure it's rated G. You can drink the alcohol, but it won't make you drunk."

Dane gave a breathy laugh. "Yeah, I think I'm safe from getting too excited." The words came out sounding defensive even though he didn't mean them that way.

Ethan didn't seem to notice. He just poured himself another drink. "So, how are the Ps?"

"My parents … not great actually. My dad isn't feeling well."

"Sorry to hear that. Something going around on the outside?"

"Yeah, something like that. Hey, would you mind helping on the farm tomorrow, just for a few hours?"

When Ethan didn't answer right away, Dane pivoted toward him, and the magnetic thing happened again. Right to the chestnut browns.

"Of course I'll help," Ethan said. "You know, every time I talk to you, you say how much you hate the farm. Yet every time you invite me to do something with you, it's on the farm. Are you trying to tell me something?" He chuckled softly.

"No. Ah, maybe. It's hard to explain."

Bonnie appeared beside them, swirling the liquid in her cup. "Did you guys know, in Eden, alcoholic beverages won't make you drunk? Something about the nature of the place."

Dane glanced at Ethan and laughed, then took another drink.

"Ethan, would you like to dance?" Bonnie asked.

He shifted uncomfortably, glancing at Dane, and took a drink in an all-too-obvious attempt to delay giving her an answer. Didn't Bonnie know Ethan was gay? Duh. She was making him uncomfortable. He decided to save the guy the embarrassment of turning her down.

"I'll dance with you, Bonnie," Dane offered. "I think Ethan was just about to get something to eat."

Bonnie looked at Ethan impassively, then gave Dane a hint of a smile. "Of course. Thank you."

He offered his hand and led her onto the dance floor. When they reached the center, Bonnie's arms wrapped around his neck, and Dane noticed Ethan looked less than happy about the situation. Of course, now he was alone without anyone to talk to. Dane hadn't thought of that.

"So how is life outside of Eden?" Bonnie asked flatly as they swayed between the other couples.

Dane raised his eyebrows. "Boring and shallow. I'd rather be here any day."

"You've got to be kidding? Sometimes I'd like to chew my own arm off to get out of this place."

"Honestly? You'd rather be studying for a calculus final than learning how to mix an herbal cocktail capable of blowing a demon's head off."

Her lips parted and a tiny laugh lightened the air between them. "Well, Abigail's class is pretty interesting. Sorry to be such a butt about it. I think I've just caught cabin fever. Not for long though. Lillian says she thinks Abigail is going to send us on a mission."

"Us?"

"Well, all of the Soulkeepers."

Dane's ears grew hot. Not him. She was talking about the real Soulkeepers. He swayed silently, staring at the wall behind her shoulder.

"I'm sorry. How rude of me. I know you want to be part of this," Bonnie said. "But honestly, I'd like to switch places with you sometimes. I miss having a normal life. School and … boys." Her eyes darted toward Ethan, who was leaning against the snack table watching them.

Clearing his throat, Dane decided to broach the subject with her. "Are you, um, interested in Ethan? Because I'm pretty sure he's gay. I mean, he's told everyone."

"I know he *says* he's gay, but he's only, like, nineteen. Maybe he just hasn't been introduced to anything else. People can change, you know."

He frowned. "I don't think that's how it works."

Her fingers toyed with the back of his hair. It tickled a little. "Here's what I think. Sexuality is a spectrum. You've got heterosexuals on one end and homosexuals on the other, but then there are people kind of in the middle."

"Aren't they called bisexual?" Dane asked.

"Yeah, I guess. Well, those people can change, right?"

"I guess." Dane shrugged.

"So, maybe Ethan has just limited himself. Maybe, if the opportunity presented itself, he'd, er, change his direction."

"Huh. Okay. Well, good luck with that."

He pushed a strand of her red hair behind her ear. The way her freckles peppered her nose was cute. The sprinkling of brown dots reminded him of a doll his sister once had, which made him think of his mother and how disappointed she was when he took off that evening.

"How about you?" Bonnie asked. "Is there anyone special in your life?"

Dane took a moment to answer. "No, not really. I used to date this girl named Amy, but there wasn't a hell of a lot there to work with. I'm not sure why we dated each other, exactly. I guess because people in town expected it."

"Oh, how sad."

He shrugged. "Not really. I don't think about her at all anymore. We never, um, you know, got very serious, so."

She nodded. "Yeah, Sam and I haven't dated too much either. It's hard for guys to understand that we are two different people, but we never want to be apart. Our condition is weird for outsiders."

The song ended. Dane lowered his arms. "Thanks for the dance."

She nodded. "I think I'll go get a drink." Her eyebrows waggled. She wandered off toward Ethan, who glared at Dane expectantly.

"Sorry, buddy, I tried. You're on your own," Dane said under his breath.

Malini appeared in front of him, shaking her head in Bonnie's direction. "That's a disaster waiting to happen."

"I know, right?"

"Well, since you are without a dance partner anyway, how about that talk?" she asked.

Dane bobbed his head. Oh, man, here it was. Might as well get this over with.

He followed her out of the room, to the end of the hall, across the veranda, and out into the garden. Night shrouded the tropical plants as they entered the jungle, the full moon's light glinting off the tops of shiny leaves but not strong enough to reach the path below. Monkeys leapt from tree to tree, and a flock of fluttering wings erupted to their left. The scent of banana and coconut thickened the air. She led him deep into the greenery by touch or instinct, to an overgrown place where the trees pressed in around them, exposing only a sliver of the night sky. Pivoting, she halted and looked up at the stars visible between the branches.

"I like it here. It's peaceful," she said.

"Me too." Dane's voice sounded small and weak. No hiding his apprehension.

"I've wanted to talk to you for some time now about how you were able to come to Eden."

He nodded, although she might not have noticed in the darkness. Even with the light of the moon, she was barely more than a silhouette under the branches.

"When Dr. Silva traded herself for you, she knew you would die if she didn't get you to me fast. She carried you to the boat, risking her own life in the process. No one knew how close a fallen angel like Abigail could come to Eden. She wasn't exactly a Watcher because she'd never eaten flesh, but she definitely wasn't a Soulkeeper."

Malini placed a hand on Dane's. He cringed. Now was the part when she would tell him Abigail had broken the rules and he couldn't come back after this. He braced himself for the bad news.

"She placed you in the boat, but she wasn't sure how it worked. With only a few moments before she must return to Lucifer's side, she left you. Do you remember what happened between the time she placed you in the boat and the time Jacob and I found you?"

"No," Dane said, but his answer sounded uncertain, even to himself.

"What do you remember? Please." Malini reached out and touched his hand.

Rubbing his eyes with his finger and thumb, Dane considered his options, and then decided he had nothing to lose by telling the truth. "I remember dreaming."

She tugged at his hand. "What did you dream about?"

He took a deep breath. "A spider." Malini didn't laugh or comment or anything, so he continued. "There was a spider in the boat. A massive spider, bigger than me, and she had one of those bug sacks, all wrapped up in her web."

"You called the spider 'she.'"

"Yeah." He laughed. "When she was real close, she had a face like a woman, long black hair, and big dark eyes with the whole universe inside them. Thousands of twinkling lights." Dane shook his head. "I must sound crazy. I've never told anyone this before."

"Your secret is safe with me, Dane, but please continue. It's important."

"She asked me if I'd like a drink and offered me the web sack. I was disgusted, you know, because I thought it was a bug or something, but I was so weak and thirsty. I nodded my head, and she raised the side to my lips." Dane's voice broke and his breath caught. He was remarkably close to crying. "It tasted good, Malini. I don't know what she gave me. It could have been some half-masticated bug for all I know. I drank it. I think she saved my life."

"Oh, Dane." She pulled him forward by the hand and wrapped her arms around him as the tears began to flow.

How could he tell her how scary the dream was? No words could describe his helplessness, or the horror of imagining himself entombed in a spider's web. "I wish I could forget, just forget the whole thing. Do you know how hard it is to go to counseling once a week to 'work through my abduction' and not be able to talk about what really happened? I don't want to waste my parents' money, but I can't possibly tell the truth. I'm probably crazy."

"You're not crazy." Malini clasped his shoulders. "I know the spider."

"What?"

"I think Fatima—er, Fate paid you a visit. She'll never admit to it, of course. But I suspect the water she gave you to drink came from the river outside of Eden. The water is blessed. All Soulkeepers are descended from someone who saw and drank that water. Only those who truly have a heart to rid the world of evil can see or drink it. Abigail and Gideon are the only exceptions. God knew the choice they would make to sacrifice themselves for all of us, and when He made them human, He gave them the ability to enter here as a reward for their self-sacrifice. But I think Fate helped you drink the water, Dane, and now you are here."

"I don't understand."

Malini tilted her face toward the moon. She sighed. "I think the water changed you. I think you might have the Soulkeeper gene now."

Dane had to catch himself against the trunk of a tree. A lump formed in his throat. Did she just say what he thought she did?

"Either you are the only exception the cherubim have ever made or…"

"Or I have a latent Soulkeeper gene inside of me?"

"Yes."

"So how do we find out?"

"We don't." Malini squeezed his hand.

"But I have to know."

"Believe me, you will know if the gene switches on."

Dane pulled his hand out of hers. "You don't understand, Malini. This whole time—I thought you were going to say I didn't belong here. And now, to learn I might be one of you! I have to know who I am."

"You do belong here, Dane. God let you through the gate for a reason, Soulkeeper or not. You are human now, and you might always be human but, no matter what, you belong here."

He shook his head and turned back toward the path to the school. He couldn't put his feelings into words. In one way, this was more than he'd ever hoped for but, in another, to be this close and not know for sure was frustrating.

"Dane," Malini said softly.

He turned around to face her. "Yeah?"

"I want you to take this." A leather strap dangled from her fingertips, a red stone at the end of it. He'd seen the stone before. Jacob used to wear it, and then Malini. The chain was different. "I had it reset for you. I want you to wear it until we figure this out."

"Why?"

"This stone is connected to me. Not physically but metaphysically."

"Huh?"

"If you need me, hold it up to the light and clear your mind. I'll help you."

"Okay." Tentatively, he reached out and hooked his fingers in the strap, pulling it over his head.

"No matter what, it's okay to be what you are," Malini said. "It's okay to be who you are. The people who love you will love you no matter what. All you've got to do is be true to yourself."

"Yeah," Dane said absently.

Just then, a violent rustling heralded Archibald's arrival on the path. "Ms. Malini!" he called. "You have to come.

Something's happened. Ms. Abigail needs to talk with you, right away."

She took off toward the school at Soulkeeper speed, leaving Dane alone in the jungle with the garden gnome.

"Uh, Archibald, I know it's your night off and everything, but would you mind showing me the way back to the school?"

"Oh yes," the little guy said. "On the way you can tell me all about the exotic city of Paris, Illinois."

Dane grinned in the darkness but didn't deny him. He followed the gnome through the garden, telling stories about his everyday life while trying his best to process what Malini had told him. A new truth. A truth that could change everything.

Chapter 9
Calling Card

Malini burst into the conference room where The Soulkeepers' council had already assembled. At the head of the table, Abigail wrung her hands, while Gideon and Lillian flanked her with equal unease. Backs to the entryway, Master Lee and Grace huddled together, staffs leaning against the table. When had they returned? The news must be urgent if they came in person instead of using the stone again. Maybe they'd found Cheveyo?

"What's going on?" Malini rounded the table to an empty chair positioned between the two groups. She didn't sit. The despair radiating from the two Helpers froze her in place.

"We found something," Grace said, her voice shaking. She pushed a folded newspaper across the table, the Arizona

Gazette. The headline read: 12 DEAD IN BAR MASSACRE.

Malini scanned the article, noting the mutilation of the bodies. Master Lee cleared his throat.

"Definitely Watchers. The flesh was stripped off while they were still breathing." He shook his head. "And there was something else."

Abigail passed a large photograph around the table to her. The first thing she noticed as she accepted the picture from Gideon was the blood. On the mirror behind a dark, blood-soaked bar, words were scrawled across the glass in dripping, sticky red. *He is ours.*

"God help us, they've taken Cheveyo," Malini said.

Abigail rose from her chair and paced toward the window. "I'm suspicious. Obviously, the Watchers left this message for us to find. Why are they taunting us? What do they want if they already have him?"

"We searched everywhere," Grace whimpered, meeting Malini's eyes. "But we didn't know what we were looking for, not exactly. After interviewing everyone this kid knew in Sedona, the description we put together was frustratingly vague. He moved around a lot, and he looked like half the population of Arizona." She clasped her shaking hands on the table.

"Every Soulkeeper I've ever encountered has left a trail," Lee interrupted. "Helpers learn to see the signs, detect their aura. It's how Bell originally found Mara. But Cheveyo left almost nothing. When we left Sedona, we searched Flagstaff again and again. We'd been in that bar. Nothing."

Rubbing her chin, Malini stared at the photo, discouraged. Her own abilities hadn't been much help. She'd searched her threads in the In Between for any hint of where to find Cheveyo, but every lead had turned up empty.

Gideon reached for the photo, and Malini gladly handed it over. Glancing from Abigail to the picture, his mouth pulled into a straight line. "Abigail, when you conjured the list, what did you know about the Soulkeepers on it? Obviously, all those with the gene were not included, or the list would have been much longer."

"Yes, the gene had to be active. A true Soulkeeper," Abigail said.

"Lee, last week you mentioned Cheveyo might be in transition because he left such a faint trace in the apartment. Is it probable Cheveyo has an active Soulkeeper gene but has never used his gifts?" Gideon asked.

Lillian's eyebrows shot toward the ceiling. "When I came into power, I walked into Master Lee's dojo. He didn't find me, I found him."

Lee nodded. "Exactly. This is what I suspect. If the Soulkeeper gene has been triggered, but he hasn't had the opportunity to use his abilities, he'll be more difficult for us to detect. I suspect that's what we are dealing with."

Abigail drummed her fingers on the table, her face taking on an icy quality reminiscent of her days as a Watcher. "Here's what we know. Cheveyo is in transition, which means he probably doesn't understand who he is. Unfortunately, the Watchers are not as ignorant, and they have him. They want us to come. They are using him as bait. But how did Lucifer get to him first?"

The council members exchanged glances, then all eyes settled on Malini. She was just shy of her seventeenth birthday, but she was their Healer, expected and responsible for directing the course of action for the greatest good. She knew what must be done, just like she knew they weren't going to like it. The path they must take was clear to her, although the outcome wasn't. "We need to send a team of Soulkeepers to look for him."

"Didn't you hear what Abigail said? We'll be playing into their hands," Grace said. "Besides, we've already been there."

"It's not you they want," Malini said. "We need to send Ethan, the twins, Jesse, and Dane."

Grace gasped and worked her jaw like a fish out of water. "You are not sending my daughters to slaughter!" she yelled, shoving back her chair and standing. "Did you see what they did to those people? And Dane? Preposterous! He's *human*. They'll eat him alive."

"It's what has to be," Malini said, lowering her chin. She should have broken the news more gently. She should have foreseen Grace would react like this.

"You should send Jacob," Grace seethed. "He's got the most experience."

Malini cringed.

"Grace," Abigail said. "Malini has put Jacob in harm's way again and again. She wouldn't put the twins in danger if it weren't the only way."

"It *is* the only way," Malini said solemnly. "If any of the Soulkeepers would do, I *would* send Jacob. Or I would go myself. But what I've seen on the other side indicates the best course of action is to send these five. They need this experience, and we need them."

Grace harrumphed loudly. When a quick glance around the table found her supporters lacking, she stormed from the room, flashing Malini an accusing look that cut her to the bone. Malini shook the exchange off and turned toward the other council members.

Abigail stood. "All those in favor of following Malini's plan and sending Jesse, Dane, Ethan, Bonnie, and Samantha to Arizona to look for Cheveyo say, aye."

Gideon was the first to speak up. "Aye!"

Lillian followed suit. "Aye."

Lee hesitated, sizing up Malini with a guarded expression. "Aye," he finally said, but he didn't seem happy about it. He rose and excused himself from the room. Unlike Grace, he didn't glare at Malini on his way out. In fact, he didn't make eye contact at all.

"Then the decision is made. Let's pull together the team and make a plan of attack," Abigail said. "Lillian, would you mind briefing the five? I think it should be done tonight."

Lillian nodded and gathered the folder of evidence into her arms along with the notebook and pen she was using.

With long strides, she left the room. Abigail closed the door behind her.

"Are you sure about this, Malini?" Gideon asked from his place at the table. As an angel, he'd doubted Malini's abilities, but as a man, he was her staunchest supporter. He would never question her if anyone other than Abigail was present.

"Yes, I'm sure."

"Why Dane? We don't even know if he has the gene. It doesn't make any sense." Abigail spread her hands. It wasn't a challenge. It was a plea for understanding.

Malini ran her fingers along the wood grain of the conference table, then walked to the window. "There are some things I can't share with you."

"I know," Abigail whispered.

"What I can say is this. I have seen a future where Dane is the key to Lucifer's undoing. He's not just one of the five; he's the most important of the five." A deep hush came over her, even the jungle seemed in on it, and she could hear her heart beating. She had to be careful. The future was a delicate thing, easily upset by careless words. Easily open to misinterpretation.

"Well then, maybe he'll have better luck finding Cheveyo than Grace and Lee," Gideon said.

Malini pivoted slowly to face him. "He doesn't have to find Cheveyo."

Swallowing hard, Gideon licked his lips, seeming almost afraid to ask what was on his mind. "What do you mean?"

"All he has to do is let the Watchers find him."

Abigail placed her hand on Gideon's shoulder and sighed heavily. "So, he's the bait."

"He survived Hell," Malini said. "Don't underestimate him. In this case, the rat might eat the snake." A whisper of a smile crossed her face.

After a moment of awkward silence as Gideon and Abigail exchanged glances, letting Malini's words sink in, Gideon jostled out of his chair. "Since that's settled, on to door number two." He lifted a manila folder from the top of a credenza against the far wall. "I have the information you asked for on Harrington Enterprises."

Malini brightened, taking the research from his hands. "Their water processing plant is relatively new and based in Chicago. There's only one bottling plant, but they distribute all over the country."

"Great," Malini deadpanned, wondering how many tainted bottles might be circulating.

Tightly muscled arms crossed over his chest, Gideon leaned a hip on the credenza, overtaking the substantial piece of furniture with his presence. He might not have been an angel anymore, but even as a human, he was larger than life. "There's more."

"What?"

"They only distribute large bottles, the type used for office water coolers. And all of their orders go to major corporations and government offices." His green eyes flashed with indignation.

Abigail inhaled sharply. "So Lucifer is trying to gain control of the most powerful people in the nation."

Gideon nodded. "This is bigger than Harrington or Bakewell. Hundreds of companies, thousands of people. We've been chasing his right hand while his left has been priming Earth for invasion."

Malini flipped through the folder. "But how can they influence this many people? There can't be this many Watchers topside. We'd know."

With the enigmatic twist of her lip evocative of her days as a fallen angel, Abigail ran her hand across the backs of the chairs, pacing around the conference room. Part of her, the memories left behind, would always remember how to think like a Watcher.

"He's not concerned with influencing them all right now," Abigail murmured. "Lucifer simply wants them to be vulnerable. Senator Bakewell is the exception. A Watcher is here for him and to taint the water. But if I know Lucifer, and I do, it's just the beginning. This smacks of a setup. He's positioning his pawns."

Nodding, Malini leaned against the windowsill to get a better view of the full moon. "Which begs the question, how is he positioning his queen? We need to anticipate his next move. If we don't, we'll be playing into his hands."

Chapter 10
Mission

Heavy with the implications of Malini's conjecture, Dane said goodbye to Archibald at the entrance to the school and paused before going in. What did it all mean? He might be a Soulkeeper, or not. Didn't she understand his presumed future was a life toiling over corn and soybeans? This was his one chance to be something important, to have a bigger life than Paris, Illinois. Being a Soulkeeper would mean everything to him.

For some reason, Ethan popped into his head just then. He took a deep breath. If anyone could help him make sense of this, it would be Ethan. But how much should he share? Malini hadn't said it was a secret, per se, but then again, if she was wrong or his powers never came to fruition, he'd feel worse having told his friends. No, best to keep the revelation to himself, at least for now.

Back inside the dining hall, he found Ethan slow dancing with an overly ecstatic Bonnie while Jacob and Samantha engaged in a lively discussion next to the snacks. For his part, Ethan barely moved and looked like he'd rather be on the receiving end of a root canal than holding Bonnie in his arms. Dane chuckled.

"So, should I ask how the talk went?" Ghost asked, the words out before he fully formed at Dane's side.

"Gah! Stop doing that. Can't you just walk up to someone in a normal way?" Dane placed a hand over his thumping heart.

"Not half as fun as watching you jump. So, out with it. What did the Healer have to say to you?"

"Malini and I have been friends for years. What makes you think it wasn't a friendly conversation?"

Ghost raised an eyebrow over one mischievous purple eye and shook his head.

"I don't think I'm supposed to tell anyone," Dane said, taking an unnatural interest in his work boots. "There's nothing to tell anyway. It was a strange conversation."

"You don't say." Ghost peered at him expectantly.

The song ended and Ethan wasted no time freeing himself from Bonnie's clutches. He stalked toward them. "So what did she say?" he demanded, placing a hand on Dane's shoulder. Dark clouds gathered in his eyes. "They can't make you stop coming here. You made it through the gate."

"She didn't say I couldn't come here. In fact, she said the opposite; I'm always welcome here." Dane shrugged. He was about the same size as Ethan, but somehow, just then, his friend seemed bigger, intensity billowing his presence to twice its natural size.

"Well, good." Ethan took a step back, removing his hand deliberately from Dane's shoulder and stuffing it in his pocket. "Because that would be completely unfair."

For a few painfully awkward moments, Dane shifted from foot to foot under Ethan's penetrating stare. What had just happened? Ethan was being so ... protective.

He didn't have a chance to broach the subject. Lillian charged into the room, snapping up everyone's attention. "I need to see Jesse, Ethan, Samantha, Bonnie, and you too, Dane. Blue room, now."

Questioning glances bounced between them. Samantha tapped the screen of her phone and the music stopped. Jacob approached his mom cautiously.

"You mean Jacob, right? Not me," Dane said on his behalf.

Jacob nodded and turned hopeful eyes on Lillian.

She shook her head. "Not this time. I need you, Dane." With an empathetic glance in Jacob's direction, she held the door open for Bonnie and Samantha. They exited hand in hand, Ghost fading out behind them. Hands on his hips, Ethan didn't follow but glared at Lillian as if she was out of her mind. Paralyzed with uncertainty, Dane didn't either.

This had to be a mistake. Regardless of what Malini had said, he wasn't ready.

"Go ahead, Dane," Jacob said. "Malini doesn't make mistakes. Trust her judgment on this."

Lillian nodded her encouragement.

"Okay," Dane said, finally finding the nerve to cross the threshold.

"No mistakes, my ass," Ethan muttered to Jacob on his way out the door.

"Ethan! Hold the commentary," Lillian scolded.

She led them into a small classroom next to the lecture hall, aptly named the blue room after its cerulean blue decor. The desks were the small kind with chairs attached. She turned one around and slid into the seat. The others jostled into position around her, Dane taking the desk between Lillian and Ethan.

"There's been an incident with the last Soulkeeper, Cheveyo. We have reason to believe Watchers are holding him hostage and need the five of you to go to Arizona to find and rescue him."

"Yes!" Bonnie said, pumping her fist. "Finally, a mission."

Lillian grimaced at her display of enthusiasm. "This isn't a vacation, Bonnie. You need to know what you are dealing with." She opened a manila folder and passed the contents around the circle of desks. Each Soulkeeper paled as he or she saw what was inside the file. Bonnie and Samantha reflexively reached for each other. Ghost faded. But when the information reached Ethan, he stared at Dane and slapped the folder shut as if he were protecting him from the contents.

Dane grasped the manila file, attempting to extract it from Ethan's white-knuckled fingers with an unswerving effort that ended in the quick release and subsequent rebound of Dane's body into his chair. With a grunt, he opened his quarry and perused the picture within. The bloody scene inside made him nauseous. This wasn't just a murder scene; it was a massacre. Dane didn't even bother trying to count the bodies. It was impossible to tell which parts belonged to which human being. This was a rescue mission and finding Cheveyo would mean facing the Watchers. He pressed his eyes closed and passed the folder back to Lillian. An icy chill permeated the room.

Samantha stared accusingly at Dane. "Why isn't Jacob here?"

"This team was chosen by the Healer," Lillian said by way of explanation.

"But—"

Lillian held up her hand. "Please be packed and ready to leave by Friday morning. Dane, you'll need to clear this with your parents. The Helpers can aid you in coming up with a suitable excuse to travel. Perhaps a college visit?"

"By Friday?" Dane's head started to spin. "One week?" Sure, he'd applied to several colleges and had a stack of other applications ready to mail. The story was viable. But after the conversation this morning with his mom when he'd promised he'd be around more, could he lie to her again? Disappear again? This wasn't a dinner cruise. He could die. And what would happen to his family, then?

"Dane? Are you with us?"

"Yes," he said. He couldn't say no; Malini needed him. Besides, this might be his chance to become one of them. The right situation might trigger the change.

Ethan was staring at him again. In fact, the guy seemed downright agitated, as if he was about to bust out of his seat. "I don't like this. It doesn't make sense. He's human. They could *eat* him."

Lillian didn't deny the conjecture. "We are all human. They could eat any of us."

"But we can defend ourselves. Dane will be a lamb to the slaughter out there. It's too risky." Ethan clung to the edge of his desk as if it were a life raft.

"I can decide for myself what risks are worth taking, Ethan." The venom in Dane's voice surprised him. He hadn't meant for his words to have the wallop they did, but Ethan recoiled against the back of his chair like he'd been pushed. He was just trying to help, maybe save him, but Dane couldn't stand to be the helpless human any longer. The more he thought about it, the more he needed to do this. The challenge would make or break him. Either he'd become a Soulkeeper, or die trying.

Without further verbal objection, the other Soulkeepers looked at him with a mix of emotions: pity like Ghost, or contempt like Bonnie and Sam, or pleading dread like Ethan. Dane ignored them. Instead, he focused on Lillian as she opened a different folder and told them everything the council knew about Cheveyo.

Chapter 11
Pride, Prejudice, and Soybeans

In Paris, Illinois, it was universally acknowledged that a first-born son in possession of good farmland must want to farm. Despite this practical wisdom, Monday morning found Dane Michaels at the breakfast table inside the farmhouse his family had owned for over one hundred years, thinking it was time for a change. He'd put off telling his parents about his trip long enough. The letter from Michigan State, provided by Master Lee, weighed down the pocket of his shirt to the point of affecting his breathing.

"You were out late last night," his father said accusingly. He'd propped open the door of the fridge with his shoulder while he poured a tall glass of orange juice. No matter how many times his mom said it wasted the cold, his dad was always doing that.

"I was home by curfew." Dane accepted another pancake from his mom. He offered no further explanation. Thankfully, the long-sleeved shirt he wore covered the black and blue evidence of his evening training session with Lillian.

"I don't wanna hear about you sleeping in class again."

"Dad, that hasn't happened since freshman year, and it had nothing to do with staying up too late. I had mono."

"Hmm." His father gulped his juice, finally closing the fridge door.

Dane swallowed another bite of pancake and folded his hands. "I need to talk to you two about something."

Just then, Jenny jogged down the stairs, backpack slung over her shoulder. "Gotta go to school early today. See you tonight." Her long, brown ponytail bobbed past the table and blew out the door.

"Bye, honey," his mom called from the stove, where she was busy producing additional pancakes doomed to go uneaten.

Dane turned in his chair and caught a glimpse of Jenny climbing into the passenger side of an unfamiliar silver Honda. "Mom, do you even know where she's going?" he asked incredulously.

"She said school. Didn't you hear her?" His mom stared absently out the kitchen window at the retreating Honda.

"It's not even seven. Why does she have to be to school so early? And who was that picking her up?"

"I don't know. I bet it's the Barger boy. They have a class together." His mom flipped the pancake she was cooking.

Flashbacks to his sophomore year tore through his brain, hanging out with Phillip Westcott in the woods behind the school, smoking dope and drinking. Phil used to call it "warming up for class." And the fights—it was how he met Jacob and opened himself up to Auriel.

"I think you should be more careful with her. She's getting to a really impressionable age. Where's Walter, anyway?" Dane asked.

"Sleepover," his dad replied.

"What? You lecture me about staying out too late, and you're letting Walter sleep over on a school night?"

His mom abandoned the frying pan and sat down at the table. "What's this all about, Dane? Jenny and Walter aren't doing anything you didn't do at their age."

"Have you ever considered you should have been stricter with me? Look what happened, Mom. I was abducted. There's a crazy person out there who bombed our school. They never found who did it. You've got to be more careful with them." He tapped his fist on the table.

Both her bony hands wrapped around his closed fingers. "The therapist says it's natural to be paranoid after what happened, but it was a crazy, isolated incident. It's not going to happen again."

"You don't know that." This wasn't the conversation he'd wanted to have with them, but damn it, they needed to get their heads out of the sand. What if Lucifer tried to use one of them to get to him? How would he protect them?

"Everything is fine now, son," his dad chimed in, returning to his chair at the table. "It's all over. We can't live our lives in fear."

Dane extracted his hand from his mom's and scrubbed his face. "You're right," he finally said. "I need to let it go, which is why this is as good a time as any for me to tell you I'm taking a trip."

"Trip? Where do you think you're going?" his father asked.

"Michigan State has invited me for a campus visit." Dane pulled the envelope Master Lee had given him from his pocket and handed it to his mother. His father snatched the letter from her fingertips before she could even open the flap. "I guess my grades were good enough to attract some attention. I leave Friday."

"You can't go," his dad said. "No way am I letting you drive that far alone, and a plane ticket is much too expensive at this point." Scowling, he pulled the folded paper from the envelope and made a show of reading it.

"I'm driving, but I'm not going alone. My friend, Ethan, is coming with me. He's been invited too."

"Ethan? The boy who helped you with the silo Saturday?" his mom questioned.

Dane had to stop himself from rolling his eyes. Ethan had been over more than a dozen times. How could they not remember who he was? "Yeah, he's the one. So, I won't be alone. We'll take shifts driving. I leave Friday morning."

"Ethan." His dad leaned back in his chair, shaking his head. "There's something funny about that kid. I'm not sure I like you hanging around with his type."

"What's wrong with Ethan?"

"He puts off a certain vibe. Like he's a little light in the loafers." His dad made a rude gesture with his hand.

Dane stood up, knocking his chair back from the table. "You mean it bothers you Ethan is homosexual. That's the word for it. Yes, he's gay. He's also one of my best friends." *And maybe more.*

His father's mouth fell open. "What's gotten into you? Listen, boy, you don't want people thinking you're a faggot."

With a small gasp, his mother shot his father a piercing look.

A sudden rage washed through Dane. He leaned forward, resting his fingertips on the table, until his face was close to his father's. "I'd rather be a faggot than a bigot."

Bam. His cheek stung from his father's slap, but not as severely as it might have. Either he was holding back, or whatever illness he had was weakening him. Judging by the expression on his face, it was the latter.

Rubbing his jaw, Dane tossed his backpack over his shoulder and stormed out to the sound of his mother's sobs. He didn't care, he couldn't. He slammed the door behind him and leapt into the cab of his black Dodge Ram. Good thing there wasn't much traffic in Paris at that hour because

Dane cruised to school on autopilot, trying his best to calm down. He turned a sharp corner into the parking lot.

"Whoa!" Jacob's muffled yell filtered through the windshield as he dodged the advancing vehicle.

Dane slammed on the brakes and rolled down the window. "Crap! Sorry."

Jacob chuckled, although his face looked more annoyed than he was letting on. "Where's the fire?"

"My parents are giving me a hard time about Friday."

His friend's face fell. "Do you think you'll be able to convince them?"

"I don't know." He rubbed his cheek where his dad had slapped him.

"We really need you."

"That's just it. I don't think you do. But it doesn't matter because I need to go. I need to get away from here, and I'm eighteen, so…" Dane shrugged.

"So, you're going whether they like it or not."

"Yeah."

"Are you sure you want to do that? I can tell you from personal experience a solid family is hard to come by."

Staring straight ahead, Dane's jaw tightened. "I can't be who they want me to be."

Jacob shook his head. "Sorry, dude, I don't open for identity crisis convos until nine. Want to park and get something to drink before class? The cafeteria has a coffee machine now."

"What are you doing here so early, anyway?"

"Malini helps me with my homework since our evenings are pretty much shot and she knows everything."

Dane lifted a corner of his mouth. "Yeah. She does."

"Ahhh, those are loaded words. Are you going to tell me what your talk with her was about Friday night?"

"Nope."

"She won't tell me either." Jacob backed up a few steps.

Dane parked in the closest spot and climbed out from behind the wheel. Abruptly, he stopped in the middle of the parking lot to stare at a patch of concrete.

"What's going on? Looks like you've seen a ghost."

"This was where Auriel beat the crap out of me, and you saved my life." Dane tipped his face up. "Did I ever say thank you?"

"Like a million times."

"Then, did I ever tell you I'm sorry? For putting you at risk by giving Auriel the information I did."

Jacob laughed. "Um, also like a thousand times."

With a deep sigh, he joined Jacob on the sidewalk and started toward the school. "Well, here's one I don't think I've told you. I'm sick of having everyone else save me. I'm sick of having nightmares every night and feeling powerless to defend myself against the evil I know could be lurking around every corner." As they reached the door, Dane turned to look Jacob in the eye. "Do you know I can't even look at an attractive girl anymore without thinking about Auriel and how she tortured me? How she drugged me?"

For a moment, Jacob didn't do or say anything, just stared at him with the wide-eyed look of someone who'd just been dumped on. Then, he yanked open the door and pointed into the hall. "See that?"

"What?"

"That is the hallway where you kicked my ass. And yes, I was already a Soulkeeper. If it weren't for the water fountain and Principal Bailey, I'd probably be a smear on the tile." He grabbed Dane's shoulder and whirled him around to face the parking lot again. "This is not just where shit hit the fan with Auriel. It's where you slayed, what? A half-dozen Watchers at prom?"

"It wasn't that many. Mostly, I just helped other people kill theirs."

"All I know is, Soulkeeper or not, you are one badass human being. Don't ever think you're helpless. Malini wouldn't be sending you to Arizona if she didn't know for sure you could handle it."

Dane nodded his head and pulled the door back open. "You know what? You're right. I could kick your ass."

With a whack on his shoulder, Jacob led the way inside. The halls were empty as they headed for the cafeteria to meet Malini. All Dane could hear, besides the echo of their footsteps, was the tiny voice at the back of his head that said he was a fraud and a liar. There was a time when he'd believed what he'd said to Jacob. Not anymore. He'd spent days in Hell, trapped on a brimstone slab, inside a ring of unholy fire. The pain had been unbearable, but the worst part was the isolation, the certainty he'd never be in the light again, or loved again. He'd spent what felt like an eternity at Lucifer's mercy. He couldn't go back there. Not for anything. Sure he could talk big, but it wasn't true.

He'd never be that brave again.

Chapter 12
From Here to There

By Friday morning, the tension in the Michaels's household had reached DEFCON 1. Jenny and Walter conveniently made themselves scarce to avoid the likely Armageddon while Dane finished packing. He was waiting in the kitchen for Ethan, who was supposed to pick him up and drive him to the rendezvous point. He still didn't know how he was supposed to get to Flagstaff. As a human, he didn't think he could travel by enchanted staff, or maybe he could. Who knew?

"You can still change your mind," his mother said. She'd slipped into the room without notice, her face tracked with old tears.

"I don't want to. I think Michigan would be a good choice for me. I want to see the campus."

She shook her head, lowered her voice, and checked over her shoulder. "We talked about this. You can't go. You have to help with the farm. I told you about your father's health."

Dane looked her straight in the eye. "And I told you, I'd help in the spring while you guys figured out what to do, but I'm going to college. I'm eighteen and I don't expect you to pay for it. But this farm, this life, isn't for me. I don't know how to be clearer about that."

Tears flowed down his mother's cheeks anew, triggering his heart to make a guilt-driven swan dive into his gut. He placed a hand on her shoulder to comfort her but wasn't sure what to say. Any retraction would be a lie.

"Seems like you've got it all figured out, boy," his dad drawled from the door. Behind him, Ethan waited on the porch, jaw clenched against the tension the old man was putting off. "Get gone. Can't stand looking at you, making your mother cry. Maybe some miles'll snap your head on right. Otherwise, don't bother coming back. If you don't think you belong here, you don't get to be here."

His mother gasped. This wasn't a threat, but a promise. Dane grabbed his bag off the table and squeezed through the door his father propped open. His old man didn't budge, and Dane was forced to brush against his chest to fit past him. At the contact, his dad narrowed his eyes and shot Ethan a dirty look. The screen door slammed as he disappeared inside.

"So, I take it your family isn't supportive of our trip?" Ethan said as they strode down the porch steps.

"Blatant statement of the obvious."

"How bad is it?"

Dane climbed into the truck Ethan was driving, Jacob's blue monster, and leaned his head against the seat. "Bad enough that I might have to find somewhere else to live when I get back." A stifling pause eventually caused him to turn his head to face Ethan.

The guy grimaced at the steering wheel. "It's because of me, isn't it? They know I'm gay and think I'm a bad influence. I should have sent Bonnie to get you. No, then they might think you were fooling around with her. I should have sent Jacob—"

"Stop." Dane shook his head. "This isn't your fault. Let's get out of here. Please." He glanced through the windshield at his mother's scowling face framed in the kitchen window.

Ethan turned the key and pulled out of the driveway, then headed south, away from town. "Okay. Talk."

"I'm not going to lie to you. It's true my dad is a total homophobe, and he didn't love the idea of me traveling with you."

Ethan slapped the steering wheel. "How did he know? Am I that obvious? It's not like a wear a sign around my neck."

"Ethan, my dad thinks any man who isn't actively chasing the nearest female tail is gay. Believe me, it's not obvious, but I did tell him because it was important to me that he knows the truth."

"Why? Why would you do that?"

"Listen, that's not why they're angry, just a stupid excuse." Dane fussed with the radio but none of the stations soothed his temper. "My ancestors have farmed this land for over a century. My parents are upset because I'm the oldest boy and I have no interest in taking it over. None at all."

"You don't want to be a farmer."

"No."

"What do you want to be?"

Dane laughed. "I have no frickin' idea."

"Oh."

"When I was younger, I just assumed I didn't have any other choice. Then after Auriel and Hell, well, you might say the rest of my life is more important to me now than it used to be. I'm not as willing to fall on my sword to preserve the family plot. I was honest about my feelings, and my parents didn't like it. They think if I go away to college that I'll never come back, and they're probably right."

"They won't take no for an answer, huh?"

"Or any other words, including 'maybe after I get my degree.'"

"So it's more about the freedom to choose than the choice."

"Well said."

"What's the big deal, anyway? What about your brother and sister?"

"My dad still thinks a woman can't run a farm and Walter … let's just say he's not the sharpest tool in the family shed."

"So that leaves you."

"It gets worse. My dad's sick. This 'Who's going to take over the farm?' question may need to be answered sooner than later."

Ethan leaned his elbow against his window and whistled. "That's heavy, Dane. What are you going to do?"

Running his hands through his hair, Dane sighed deeply. "I'm going to find Cheveyo and help you Soulkeepers bring him home. When I get back…" He shrugged. Maybe things would blow over. Or maybe he'd be looking for a new place to live.

The hum of the engine filled the space between them. Ethan opened his mouth as if to say something, then closed it again. Good. Dane was done talking about it. It was a hopeless situation. He closed his eyes and rested the side of his head against the window.

Ten minutes later, Ethan announced, "We're here."

He turned up the driveway to a farmhouse that looked like a strong wind might knock it over. Holes peppered the roof, and weeds hadn't quite conquered the junkyard-worthy machinery abandoned in the front yard. A porch swing dangled precariously from one chain, the other long since rusted through. Jacob sat on the porch, feet dangling over the side, while Bonnie and Samantha huddled together near the front door, and Ghost, in his sunglasses, waited almost imperceptibly in the shadow of an elm tree at the front of the pebble drive.

"It's about time," Jacob said to them, jumping from his perch. "I was beginning to think you crashed my baby."

Ethan looked offended. "Not a scratch." He glanced at Dane expectantly, as if *he* were going to explain why they were late! No way. No one else needed to know how messed up his home life was.

"What are we doing here?" Dane changed the subject, hitching his backpack higher on his shoulder.

Jacob seemed to measure his reluctance to expound on their lateness and didn't pursue an answer. "Some of you may have heard that my great-great-grandfather kept some unusual stones in his office. As you know, the small blue ones are used for communication. But we'd never understood the larger geodes' purpose, until now. Seems Abigail finally asked Archibald the right questions. Come on." He picked up a weighted velvet sack near his feet and led the way through the unlocked front door.

The team filed into the farmhouse after him, Dane and Ethan entering the dingy interior last. The living room was a yard sale gone wrong with a threadbare woven rug and mismatched chair and sofa. The house stank like the inside of a rotting stump.

Jacob led them into a bedroom, empty aside from a bed frame with a water-stained mattress. He opened the closet door. A couple of wire hangers clinked together from the draft. Setting the bag down, he reached into its velvet folds and produced a large purple geode. He placed the stone on the floor inside the closet.

"Turns out that Warwick Laudner didn't just stumble on the cavern under his flower shop. He created it. Of course, he used his special abilities to make that one permanent. We, on the other hand, need something more temporary." He placed his hands on the rough back of the stone and closed his eyes. "This part takes a bit of effort."

Purple light filled the tiny space, growing brighter and brighter until Dane had to shield his eyes. The other Soulkeepers crowded in around him, maybe to get a better look at what Jacob was doing, but Dane couldn't see anything to know for sure. Moments passed. When the blinding force faded to a manageable glow, an icy breeze blew through the small room. He lowered his hand.

"Whoa," Samantha said. "I hope everyone knows how to ski."

The floor of the closet had extended another twenty feet. Two large racks of ski equipment, jackets, and goggles lined the walls. Beyond the wood planks, a snow-covered slope dropped steeply, disappearing into a cluster of evergreens.

"I skied once when I was eleven," Dane said.

"The stones create a different challenge every time," Jacob said. "But they are all equally daunting. I think it's meant to keep non-Soulkeepers out."

Everyone stared at Dane in various states of unease. Ghost piped up some encouragement. "If it makes you feel any better, Dane, I've never skied before, ever. Grew up in Hawaii, remember?"

Ethan crossed his arms over his chest. "It helps if you can break apart when you're about to hit a tree."

"Uh … yeah." With an awkward shrug, Ghost wandered farther into the closet and started checking sizes. The girls followed.

Jacob slapped Dane on the shoulder. "Don't worry. Malini's seen you in Arizona and you're not dead. It's easier than it looks … probably."

"You can still change your mind," Ethan said softly.

Dane shook his head. "No. I can't. I'm part of this." Resolved, he stepped in behind Ghost, grabbing a navy blue jacket off the hook.

"*Into* the closet," Ethan said. "This feels wrong on so many levels."

Everyone laughed except for Bonnie, who was overly absorbed with putting on her ski boots. Both girls were fully dressed and ready to go in a matter of minutes. "Our family takes a ski trip to Vail every year," Bonnie explained, then added under her breath, "Well, we used to before we were prisoners of Eden."

Jacob rolled his eyes but didn't justify her complaint with a response. "Go ahead." He gestured toward the slope. "Your mom's waiting on the other side."

Bonnie didn't waste any time. Pulling down her goggles, she smiled and leapt over the threshold. "Woot!" She traversed the slope and slipped behind the trees.

Samantha glanced toward Ghost, who was snapping on his last ski. "Catch me if you can!" She launched herself over the edge, laughing as she zipped into the trees.

"Well, comrades, I'm not the type of man to keep a woman waiting." Ghost's purple eyes flashed before he lowered his goggles. Slowly, he walked his way over the edge and let the pull of gravity drag him down the hill. "Oooooh crap!" he yelled, pushing his heels out to slow his momentum. Still, he fell on his butt twice before reaching the tree line.

"Are these boots supposed to be this stiff?" Dane asked Jacob, who was helping to guide his boot into a ski. It felt like his feet were molded into blocks of concrete.

"Yeah. Just try to snowplow all the way down. Do you know what that is?" Jacob asked.

"Not a clue."

Ethan demonstrated. "Toes together, heels out. Like this. Keep your knees bent; it's easier. Here, I'll take your pack. You've got enough to worry about." He lifted Dane's backpack to his shoulder.

Dane tried the snowplow a few times in the white dusting at the edge of the closet. "Got it. I think."

"You go first. I'll follow behind in case you run into trouble."

Dane nodded and looked over the edge. Icy wind stirred the powder at the top of the ridge. His cheeks stung from the bite of blowing snow while his hands began to sweat inside his gloves. He gripped the ski poles until his fingers hurt.

Heart pounding in his ears, Dane searched his brain for options but came up short of producing any useful scenario other than plummeting down the hill. Mechanically, he bent his knees and leaned forward.

The tips of his skis lowered onto the slope, and the force of gravity tugged him forward. Gradually, he picked up speed. Not so bad. A rush of adrenaline had him crouching lower, driving faster and faster down the slope. But with the trees approaching, he had to gain control. He pressed his heels out into a snowplow like Ethan had shown him. That slowed him slightly, but at his current speed, he was still going to taste pine bark if he didn't change direction. Shifting all his weight to his right edge, he steered around the first evergreen onto the narrower trail. Still too fast. At this rate, he'd cross the slope and collide with the opposite bank of trees in a matter of seconds. He shifted forward and cut on his left edge to correct, turning sideways so that his skis threw up a whopping plume of powdery snow. That slowed him down significantly. He tried it again, shifting his weight back and forth, to stay within the limits of the slope. His knees and hips absorbed the shock as he dashed down the winding terrain.

The trees opened up. A gigantic pile of snow blocked his path. *Holy hell!* Too late to go around it, he braced himself for impact. *Whoosh!* Up, up, and he was airborne. For two glorious seconds, he flew over the snow before gravity defeated exertion. He crashed into the hill, poles flying, and lost his skis as he curled into a ball to protect himself.

Toppling down the steep incline head over ski boots, he somersaulted until he thought he might hurl. All he could see was bright white. Just when he couldn't take it anymore, his momentum slowed. He flattened out and skidded to a stop on his back in snow-angel position.

Ethan's face appeared above him, lips twitching. "Anything broken?"

Dane tested his arms and legs. Stiff, but everything worked. "No. I don't think so."

"Good, because that was *epic!*" Ethan extended his hand and helped him to his feet.

To the sound of applause and appreciative howls, Dane limped the remaining distance to a ski lodge a few feet away. Shedding his equipment inside the wooden corridor, he emerged from the closet of a motel room where the rest of the Soulkeepers waited. Ethan was right behind him.

Grace pulled a cell phone from her pocket, tapped a button, and raised it to her ear. "They're all through."

A geode, identical to Jacob's, rested on the floor. She slipped it inside a red velvet bag. In a swirl of purplish light that extinguished itself within the sack, the closet transformed from the bottom of a ski slope to a normal, everyday, motel closet.

"Welcome to Arizona," Grace said. "Take a moment, if you need it. Then we have work to do."

Chapter 13
The Wrong Direction

Grace unrolled a map across the bedspread, plucking the cap off a sharpie with her teeth. "The bar where the murders took place is next door to this motel." She drew an X on the intersection of two road lines. "Stay within a five-mile radius." With her thumb and forefinger, she measured out a crude circle representing the correct distance.

"Why so close?" Ghost asked. "They could be anywhere by now."

"Because they want you to find them." Grace retrieved the picture Lillian had shown them from a bag on the side chair and tossed it on top of the map. Dane jerked at the macabre sight. The bloody message that dripped down the mirror seemed more real so close to the location of the murders.

"What's the plan?" Ethan asked.

"We break into teams and spread out. Obviously, Bonnie and Samantha have to stay together. They'll go south."

Dane eyed the twins. He'd seen what they could do, melding together and changing form to imitate others or gain strength. While truly an astounding gift, the girls' power was useless if they were separated.

"Ethan, I want you to take Dane north. Since your telekinesis works best at a distance, it should provide him with some protection." Grace handed out copies of the map. "Jesse, that leaves you and me. We'll start to the west. Everyone circle back to center in a clockwise direction and meet back here at five. If we don't find Cheveyo today, we'll get him tomorrow. Text me for backup if you see Watchers before they see you."

Grace slid a large duffle bag from under the bed and started handing out weapons. "From Eden. They've been blessed and will burn any Watcher they touch. Please use discretion." Knives, chains, a pipe, and throwing stars were passed around the room and disappeared inside the Soulkeepers' layered clothing. How were they so good at this? Was this what they learned in school?

Swoop. Without asking permission, Grace had lifted his shirt and affixed a wide band of Velcro to his middle. Two shiny silver blades glinted from elastic bands near his ribs. She bent his arm at the elbow, presumably to check that he could easily withdraw the knives, then smoothed his T-shirt back over them. Dane blinked at her in disbelief. She couldn't possibly expect him to use these against those monsters.

Everything was happening so fast. The armed group headed for the door, Samantha and Bonnie leading the way. Dane stayed put, staring fearfully at the map. For some reason, he couldn't make his feet move.

"Dane?" Grace prompted.

"What do we do if we find them?" he asked in a ghost of a voice.

The others paused, gawking at him.

She raised her chin. "Our goal is to retrieve Cheveyo. If you find the Watchers, follow them if you can. Fight them if you must. And most importantly, come back alive."

Dane nodded, swallowing hard, and trailed outside, making note of the brass number nine on the door. He tried to commit their home base to memory. A garbage can at the end of the walkway read Desert Days Motel. Sweat gathered in the pits of his T-shirt and the back of his neck, but it wasn't from the heat. Flagstaff was cooler than he expected for a city in Arizona. Must be nerves.

"Don't worry. I got your back," Ethan said. He pointed toward the stairwell. "We've got north. Although, chances are we're headed in the wrong direction."

"When you say wrong direction, do you mean the one with or without the Watchers?"

Ethan grinned. "Depends on your perspective." He took the lead, jogging down the stairs and veering around the back of the building.

* * * * *

On her side in the dimly lit pueblo, Raine heaved into the gourd that her grandmother held next to her face. The sick was getting better. This time, only a small amount of black dropped from her lips. She inhaled the incense her grandmother burned. The fragrant smoke soothed her, a little.

"You are healing." Grandmother placed her hand on Raine's head. "Your skin is no longer burning beneath my touch. Drink this." She lifted a gourd of tea from a nearby mat.

Raine obeyed, swallowing the herbal concoction the old woman raised to her lips. It tasted bitter, but was the only thing keeping her alive.

"I need to see the medicine woman," Raine said. It was the most she'd said since she'd been back, but then again this was the longest she'd been awake. "It's about Cheveyo."

"Cheveyo? You know what happened to him?"

Nodding, she tried to push herself up to a sitting position but failed. Thankfully, her grandmother's arm was there to break her fall. "Shhh. You rest. I'll find the medicine woman."

Raine closed her eyes for what seemed like a moment, but must have been much longer. When she opened them again the light through the small window was higher on the opposite wall, and Willow Nitewytewa was standing in the doorway. Her familiar, aloof manner filled the dwelling as if she had seen the end of time and thought it was nothing to get too excited about.

"Your grandmother says you have something to tell me about our lost Cheveyo." She walked into the house and lowered herself to the woven mat next to Raine's head. The old woman stroked her temple. "Tell me what you know about my grandson."

Summoning her strength, Raine told of the snake woman and how Cheveyo's body had gone with her through the tree, but his soul had taken refuge within her. As unbelievable as the truth sounded, she explained how she was trapped inside of her own body, helpless against his will, and then finally freed when he jumped into the boy at the diner. With trembling lips, she confessed everything about the bad *Kachina* who'd threatened to keep Cheveyo's body if he did not do as she commanded.

When all was told, the medicine woman sat back on her heels and stroked the beads around her neck. "I have dreamt of this."

Raine's eyes widened. She'd expected Willow to think she was crazy like the men in white uniforms who'd taken her to the hospital.

"I dreamt that Kótyangwúti, Spider Woman, the creator of all things, crawled down her web into my home. She has the body of a spider but the head of a woman. Kótyangwúti wove me a story from her web. First, she fashioned a child, then tore him in two. Half she put under a basket woven from bad spirits and the other half she put on top of the basket. The one on top she made whole again, a new child. I saw others, strange *Kachinas* I'd never seen before, join hand in hand with the child. Together they faced the bad spirits, battling under the basket. I saw a great uprising and many lost souls. Spider Woman told me to pray, for the fate of many people lies in the hands of a few, including the torn child."

"What does it mean?" Raine asked.

"I think Cheveyo is our torn child, body from soul. If your story is true, I think his body is in the underworld and his soul is wandering. Spider Woman is our intercessor between the heavens and the underworld. I believe the rest of the dream means we cannot intercede. Cheveyo has an important role to play. If he saves himself, he'll save others as well."

"But, Willow, we can't just leave him out there. He needs to know how sick he made me. He has no idea the damage he's doing to the boy he's in."

The old woman shook her head. "Rest now, Raine. Trust me. What Cheveyo needs is space to make mistakes and to learn from them."

"But—"

She rose to her full height, which wasn't impressive. "If you want to help, pray for the good *Kachinas* to come to him, for guidance."

Raine watched Willow leave, heart heavy for Cheveyo and the boy he possessed. She hoped the medicine woman was right. But she also prayed for her own health because as soon as she was strong enough, she planned to find Cheveyo and try to help him.

For now though, the sickness was overwhelming. All she could do was sleep.

Chapter 14
Dead and Gone

Cheveyo needed a doctor, or else the boy he'd possessed did. In the bathroom mirror of room twenty, Jaden's puffy face reflected his internal turmoil. His stomach churned ominously. Throat red and swollen, each breath was painful. After the first few days possessing his body, Cheveyo rarely heard from the boy. Jaden seemed to sleep more and more at the back of his skull, but Cheveyo needed him to wake up now because, as sick as he was, he worried the boy had caught the flu, or worse, might be going into anaphylactic shock from the peanut butter sandwich he'd had for lunch.

"Jaden! Jaden, wake up!"

Grmph

"Are you still in there?"

Why ... are you ... doing this? the small, raspy voice bubbled groggily at the back of his brain.

"Thank God. Listen, dude. Are you allergic to something?"

No.

"You don't look so good."

Tired...

"Jaden?"

Gone again. Cheveyo frowned and pulled Jaden's lower eyelid down to inspect the red rim. Definitely something wrong with this body.

"He's dying." The snake woman's voice came from outside the bathroom.

Cheveyo poked his head through the door, swallowing his apprehension. On the dingy brown bedspread, the beautiful blonde woman perched in a golden gown, her pearly white wings curled angelically behind her. As frightening as her snake form was, this one was equally disturbing. Too attractive. A terrible beauty.

"What's happening to him?"

Crossing her arms over her chest, the corner of her mouth lifted. "You're killing him, idiot. A human body isn't built to house two souls. All of his metaphysical connections are frying like eggs on a Phoenix sidewalk."

"Should I jump?" he rasped. His throat protested, blazing with every word.

She uncrossed her legs, rose, and paced the small room. "There's been a shift in the air. The Soulkeepers are close."

"The evil ones?"

"Yes. The boy we seek is among them. Dane. Once you possess him, let the others take you home with them. Then you strike."

"Strike. What do you want me to do?"

"No questions!" she snapped. She waved a hand and the table and tea appeared again, the scent of cinnamon rising from the steaming cup. "All will be revealed in time."

Cheveyo lowered Jaden's aching body into the chair.

Too tired to lift the cup, Snake Woman brought the brew to his lips for him. "You will do as I say or you will never have your body back. You will spend eternity cocooned in rotting flesh. You must trust me."

Cocooned in rotting flesh. So, he *was* killing Jaden. Guilt plowed into him. What had he done to Raine? Would Jaden even live through this? Great Spirit help him, he was confused.

"Drink." Snake Woman raised the cup to his lips again.

The familiar warmth spread through him, warming him to his toes. "Thank you," he said.

She set the cup down and rubbed her hands together. "I'm afraid your host is not long for this world," she said. "But we can't waste time finding a new one. I'll have to lure Dane to you."

"Should I go to work at the restaurant?"

Snake Woman snorted and shook her head, gesturing toward his arm. "You won't make it."

From fingertips to wrist, the boy's arm had taken on a grayish hue. Cheveyo tried to wiggle the fingers, but nothing happened. Jaden was dying, and Cheveyo would be locked inside. He widened his eyes in panic.

"Imagine if he died, and they buried you inside his rotting body." She chuckled.

Cheveyo gasped. "No. Please no."

As if his fear gave her pleasure, she cackled even louder. "Don't worry. You're no use to me buried. Dane and I go way back. You lie down on the bed, and I'll bring him to you." Grinning wickedly, she turned toward the door, and as she did, her dress transformed into a tight Devil's Canyon T-shirt and short shorts. She tucked her wings away inside her back and pulled her hair into a high ponytail.

He collapsed on the ugly comforter as the door clanged shut behind her. Jaden's body weighed a thousand pounds. What if she left him here to die? What if he couldn't get out? He closed his eyes, and held perfectly still aside from the warm tears that flowed easily down Jaden's cheeks.

* * * * *

"Flagstaff is a quaint little town for a place teeming with demons." Dane peered into the window of a fudge shop, thinking the smiling face on the sign was pitifully misinformed about the day.

"Yeah, I highly recommend a return trip when we're not hunting flesh eaters. Do you want some? I'm sure evil can wait for peanut butter fudge." Ethan's lopsided grin reflected in the glass.

"Who could eat at a time like this?"

"I don't know, the turtle bars look delicious." He shrugged and continued down the boulevard, discreetly scanning a woman waiting for a bus for signs of the unholy.

Dane pulled his sunglasses from his back pocket and put them on, catching up to Ethan on the sidewalk. What should he look for? The rumor was Soulkeepers could sense Watchers. Could he?

"You never really answered my question in the car. Why did you tell your parents about me? That I was gay?" Ethan didn't pause or make eye contact. The question was casual, matter-of-fact.

Dane cleared his throat. "Why wouldn't I? It's the truth, right?"

"Yes. It is the truth. I would never lie to anyone about being gay, but that doesn't mean I offer that information to everyone. If you knew your parents wouldn't be receptive, why tell them?"

Rubbing the back of his neck, Dane tried to answer honestly, but the truth, when it came to Ethan, wasn't entirely clear to him. "I guess I just wanted them to know. It's important to me that they accept you as you are."

"Why?"

"You're my best friend, Ethan." Dane rubbed his neck harder. "You shouldn't have to hide who you are … from anyone."

Ethan stopped short. "You did grow up in Paris, right? You do understand that your parents will never accept my sexual orientation. If you think they will, you're dreaming."

"It's not okay. They shouldn't feel that way."

"Yeah, but now that they know, they won't want me around anymore, Dane. They probably think I'm corrupting you, trying to lure you into my dark and wicked ways." He shook his head and groaned. "You should have just let them go on believing what they wanted to. If you hadn't confirmed it, your parents might never have known for sure."

Dane rolled his eyes and continued down the sidewalk. "Who cares, anyway? My dad effectively kicked my ass out of the house. I'm eighteen; I can be friends with whomever I choose."

"Hmm."

"Hey, stop analyzing it. We've got work to do."

"Don't put me off."

"It really doesn't matter, okay. It was just the truth, and I was offended for you by what my dad said. He's hateful. I was retaliating." They walked on in silence, although he hoped Ethan was still looking for the Watchers because he wasn't seeing anything through his fog of emotions. Mind racing with unexamined thoughts, Dane followed robotically.

After a good six blocks, Ethan stopped short again. This time, he turned so sharply that Dane almost walked into him. He lifted his sunglasses and grabbed Dane's upper arms.

"I'm only going to say this once, so listen up," he muttered.

Dane swallowed, blood pounding in his ears.

"I think you told your parents because you wanted to gauge their reaction. Now, you might have done that because you don't want to be a farmer when you grow up, or maybe you don't want to deal with your father's illness, and you wanted to push them away. But there's another reason you might've done it."

"What?" Dane's voice cracked.

Ethan seemed to notice for the first time that his fingers were digging into Dane's arms. He took a small step back, releasing his shoulders. "I'm your friend. We've been friends since the day I nursed you back to health in Eden. I'll always be your friend. But God help me, Dane, if I have to find out you're gay from someone else, I'm going to kick your ass." He gave him a push in the chest and turned on his heel.

"Wha—?" Dane started quietly, but Ethan was half a block ahead already. Of course he wasn't gay. He couldn't be gay. No Michaels in history had ever been homosexual. Why would Ethan think he was gay? Unless, Ethan was attracted to him. It made sense. They'd spent a lot of time together, and there were feelings, special feelings. Feelings he didn't really understand. But Dane couldn't think about that because being like Ethan wasn't an option. It wasn't who he was supposed to be. Not that it was wrong. He wasn't a homophobe or anything. He supported Ethan, after all.

He tried to catch up with Ethan to explain but stopped short when he realized he wasn't sure what he would say. His brain was filled with half sentences. How could he make him understand?

"Going somewhere?" the voice of his worst nightmare rained down from above. Auriel dropped from a fire escape onto the sidewalk beside him.

Dane tried to scream. Nothing came out but air. He turned to run, but her hand snatched his wrist, holding him to her. Ice water pumped through his veins. Auriel was the Watcher who'd influenced him sophomore year and tortured him in Hell. Not again. "Get away from me." In a panic, he twisted his weight, forcing her backward into the sun. Watchers hated the sun; it drained their powers.

To his horror, she didn't release his arm. Instead, she paused in the light, basking in the golden rays. "I've eaten well recently. Even the sun can't bring me down."

"Ethan!" Finally, his voice cooperated.

Out of the corner of his eye, he glimpsed Ethan's horrified expression, too late. Auriel folded him into her body and raced down the alley away from Ethan. She was ridiculously strong. Within her grasp, buildings flew by in a blur, her superhuman speed making him all but invisible to the passersby on the street. When the Desert Days Motel came into view, he thought he must be hallucinating from the terror. Was it possible she was taking him back to the same motel they'd started from, the one place no Soulkeepers would be because they were all out looking for the Watchers? She halted her run near the pool, conveniently empty of guests, and muscled him up the stairs to the second level.

"What do you want from me?" Dane whimpered. "If you're going to kill me, get it over with."

"Oh no, I have bigger plans for you, human." She pushed open the door to room twenty and thrust Dane inside.

Coming from the bright Arizona sun, Dane's eyes struggled to adjust to the dark room, but the rank scent of death and decay hit him immediately. He blinked to adjust his vision. When his sight returned, he screamed and backed against the wall.

"Jesus!"

"Not here at the moment," Auriel said. "Haven't seen him in ages."

Flies buzzed around the gray and bloated body on the bed. The obviously dead boy's eyes had glazed over—open, milky, staring toward the door. What had he been waiting for?

"Touch him," Auriel commanded.

Dane glanced at her and then at the dead boy. "No!"

She laughed. "Oh, come on, Dane. Don't you want to meet the new Soulkeeper?"

That brought his head around. Auriel was positively giddy. She'd killed Cheveyo, and now she wanted to torture Dane by making him touch the body. He shook his head and pressed himself against the wall.

Auriel snatched his wrist, squeezed until he yelped in pain, and dragged him toward the bed. "As much as I'd love to play the 'I don't want to' game with you, we are running out of time. Touch him!"

"Please, no." He dug in his heels to no avail. His fingers moved closer and closer to the gray boy's face. The corpse moved. A cloudy eye rolled in the boy's head, and a finger twitched.

Dane flailed, fighting with everything he had. He expected he would pass out soon from fear. Instead, his entire body lurched, and a weird calm gripped him from the inside out. Everything slowed. A fly buzzed by, the wings stirring up dust in the air. His breath came and went in long draws.

She lowered his hand, and his palm connected with the dead boy's face.

Worms. That's what it felt like. The wriggly crawl of a million tiny bugs writhed through his fingers, inside his wrist, up his shoulder, and rooted in his brain. His body shivered. Auriel released his wrist.

It worked, a voice said from inside his head.

"It worked?" Dane repeated, although as a question. He furrowed his brow at the new weight inside his head.

What the hell? the boy's voice said, panicked now.

"Don't be so surprised, Cheveyo," Auriel said. "I told you I would bring you a new body. Now we wait for lover boy and put our plan into motion."

The boy's scream inside Dane's head came on like the worst migraine he'd ever had.

Chapter 15
Bait and Switch

D ane couldn't comprehend what was going on, but based on experience, knew better than to ask Auriel. In the back of his brain, something—the voice, the boy—twisted like a sheet in the wind. The soul screamed painfully loud, but as Dane concentrated, he imagined a door in his mind's eye—a big, heavy, steel door. He imagined himself pulling it closed, and when it was entirely shut, he was alone in his head again. A thought crossed his mind that it was not supposed to be this way, that Auriel had another plan for him gone wrong. But the idea was gelatin, jiggling and formless in his cranium, rendered moot by his pressing anxiety. He would remain silent and play along.

"He's here," Auriel said around a face-splitting grin. "Remember, Cheveyo, follow the plan. I will come to you again before they take you."

The door blew in, torn off its hinges, and slammed against the far wall. Dane shielded his eyes from the resulting barrage of splintered wood. When he lowered his hand again, Ethan stood in the gaping hole, eyes as black as his T-shirt, jaw clenched, and hands balled into fists. A menacing wind coursed through the room.

"I will end you!" Ethan bellowed at Auriel. The splintered wood shot across the room at her along with a barrage of Eden's throwing stars.

With a smirk, Auriel grabbed the dead boy and twisted into a column of black smoke. Boy and Watcher dissolved. The weapons landed harmlessly in the wall behind where she'd stood, cutting through the sulfur stench that lingered there.

"Are you okay?" Ethan was on him in an instant. He ran his hands down Dane's arms, checked his face, his neck. "Did she hurt you? My God, you're pale."

"I'm fine." Dane grabbed Ethan's wrists to ease his inspection. The feel of his hands skimming over his skin was too intense. He couldn't handle it. "I'm okay."

Ghosts fleeted across Ethan's dark eyes, tortured memories or visions gone unspoken.

Before he had time to think what he was doing, Dane pulled his friend into a tight embrace. "It's going to be okay,

Ethan. She's gone." Slowly, the tension bled from his shoulders.

"I thought you were taken, or worse, dead," Ethan muttered. He whipped around toward the bed and grabbed his forehead. "Shit, the Watcher took Cheveyo."

Cheveyo? Dane stepped away from Ethan and rubbed his temples. A splitting headache was coming on again, the voice inside him pounding on the steel door. Maybe this thing, this soul inside his head, *was* Cheveyo, but right now it felt like a tumor. He didn't want to alarm Ethan, but he needed help.

"What's going on, Dane?" Ethan asked nervously.

"I need to see Grace. Now."

"She's patrolling. Can it wait?"

"No."

"Come on, man. What's going on? Don't leave me in the dark here."

The jackhammer in his skull wasn't getting any quieter. "I don't think Auriel took Cheveyo."

"What? But we just saw—"

"He's inside my head!" Dane yelled. Everything sounded muffled by the throbbing pain in his cranium. "Cheveyo is trapped inside my head."

The corners of Ethan's mouth tugged downward into a grimace. "You're slurring your words."

No time to think about that. Dane listed sideways. Ethan lurched forward, catching him in his arms before his head could hit the floor.

"Dane? Dane!"

He couldn't answer. He closed his eyes against the pain and allowed Ethan to carry him from the room.

* * * * *

Dane awoke staring at the stained ceiling of a motel room. His head didn't hurt as terribly anymore, although his mind fogged over like he'd overdosed on cold medicine. He rubbed the bridge of his nose with his thumb and forefinger.

Through the closed door, Ethan's muffled voice filtered in, barely audible. "Grace, you gotta come now. Pull everyone in. We've seen the Watcher. Yeah, I know … Yeah, I know. But we think we've found Cheveyo … No, I can't … Grace, something has happened to Dane. Just trust me, all right? Come back to the motel room."

In his just-woken state, relaxed and renewed, the door inside his mind was easier to see. Well, not *see* so much as sense. Mentally, he pulled the heavy steel back. "Are you still in my head?" Dane said out loud.

Yes.

"Who are you?"

My name is Cheveyo Kikmongwi. The voice sounded tired, resigned.

"We've been looking all over for you, Cheveyo. We're going to help you."

Please don't hurt me.

"I'm not going to hurt you. We've been trying to find you, to bring you home."

What are you talking about?

"You're a Soulkeeper. I should let Grace explain. She's better at this than I am. While we wait for her, care to clarify how you ended up in my head?"

Not supposed to be this way, Cheveyo sobbed. *She's going to hurt me if she finds out.*

"How was it supposed to be?"

No answer.

"Cheveyo?"

She warned me about you.

"What are you talking about? Warned you? About what?"

The boy retreated deeper into Dane's mind. Why was he so afraid?

"What were you doing with Auriel, anyway?"

Auriel?

"The Watcher you were with."

She's a Kachina, a spirit of the underworld.

"You say tomato, I say to-mah-to. She's a Watcher. A demon. Certifiably evil."

Cheveyo twisted at the back of his skull.

"Judging by the way Auriel let us go, I'm guessing you were supposed to be in control instead of trapped inside my head."

No answer, but the slippery twist stilled.

"Don't clam up now. We are literally in this together, dude."

With a click of the key turning in the lock, the door opened, and Ethan entered. "Hey, how are you feeling? You passed out."

"Crowded. Cheveyo is inside my head. Auriel must've poisoned his mind; he said she warned him about me. I think he was supposed to possess me, but instead, somehow, I'm in control. He might be influenced or something. He doesn't know he's a Soulkeeper."

Ethan grimaced.

"You don't believe me?"

"No, I do. I can smell it. You smell different ... like a Soulkeeper."

"I didn't know Soulkeepers had a smell." Dane cautiously sat up, surprised his head didn't get any worse from the change in position.

"Yeah. You know how Watchers smell like sulfur when they're not masked in illusion?"

"Uh-huh."

"Soulkeepers smell like sunlight and honey. You've never noticed before?"

Now that he stopped to think about it, yeah, he had noticed. But the Soulkeepers were his friends and, in Eden, sunshine came with the territory. The aroma was something he took for granted.

"I just thought it was you." Dane smirked.

A hint of a smile teased Ethan's lips, then grew into an infectious laugh. "Yeah, it's my sunlight and honey bodywash."

Suddenly uncomfortable, Dane changed the subject. "Is Grace coming?"

"She's on her way."

"Good."

"So what's he saying, anyway? Why'd he try to possess you?"

"I'm not sure. He won't talk to me. He's fighting me."

"Why? Did you tell him he's a Soulkeeper?"

"Yeah, but he's confused, and like I said, maybe influenced."

The metal on metal clack of the lock opening heralded Grace's arrival. Light washed over the room, carving out her ample silhouette in the opening door. "What's happened? There are policemen downstairs. They've cordoned off one of the motel rooms."

They motioned for her to sit down and told her everything, from Dane's capture to his rescue, his possession, and Auriel's smoky departure. Her frown grew more pronounced with every word. Wringing her hands, she stood and paced the room.

"Ethan, did you touch anything? Any fingerprints?"

"No."

"Good."

"Dane?"

"Just the dead boy and Auriel. Nothing in the room."

"Excellent."

"Did you find out the dead boy's name?"

Dane rubbed a hand over his face. "It never crossed my mind to ask." He closed his eyes, concentrating on the wisp in his head that was Cheveyo. "Do you know who the boy was?" he asked forcibly as if he were shaking the soul at the back of his brain.

His name was Jaden. He worked as a busboy at the Prickly Pear Diner. I didn't mean to kill him. She never told me the risks. I didn't know until it was too late.

Ethan looked at Grace and then back at Dane. "Was that him? Cheveyo?"

Dane opened his eyes. "You heard that?"

"Yeah, and in his voice too."

Grace rubbed her chin. "Amazing. So Cheveyo possessed this Jaden, but when he tried to take possession of you, Dane, he became trapped inside of you."

"Yes."

"And now you've channeled him. His voice came out of you like a medium."

"I guess. I mean, I can feel him in there. I've never had anything like this happen to me before."

"You smell of Soulkeeper."

Ethan nodded. "I noticed earlier. It's how I knew he wasn't delusional about Cheveyo being inside his head."

Grace stood and approached Dane cautiously. She placed her hands on his head and closed her eyes. A smile stretched across her pale face. Removing her hands, she crouched down in front of him. "You're a Soulkeeper, Dane. I can sense you."

"Are you sure the vibes aren't coming off Cheveyo?" Dane mumbled. Even after his conversation with Malini, he couldn't believe. He was afraid to have his hopes dashed once again.

"All Helpers have the ability to sense other Soulkeepers. It's how we find the people we're supposed to help in this big, bad world." She pushed up off her knees and returned to the chair next to the bed. "I don't know if I ever told you, but I sensed Bonnie first. I had no idea what I was sensing of course. We learned together, from the last Healer. But it wasn't until Samantha changed that we knew what they could do together. Before that Bonnie had no power, just the signature of a Soulkeeper, a fingerprint of sunlight and honey. You have it, Dane. Oh, I can sense him too. You might say you have layers, but I sense you the strongest."

"It can't be, can it? All of a sudden? Like this?" Ethan shook his head, eyes narrowed.

Dane reflexively lifted his hand to the stone around his neck, rubbing the smooth surface between his fingers. "Malini thought this might happen. She told me last Friday. She knew I had the potential."

Ethan's mouth dropped open. "What?"

"I think that's why Malini sent me here, to see if I'd trigger the gene."

A sourceless gust blew back Dane's hair. "Why didn't you tell me?" Ethan paced the room. With a high-pitched scrape, the heavy lamp inched across the end table in the mounting interior tornado. "I thought we were friends, and you keep this from me?"

"Ethan, calm down," Grace snapped. She placed her body in front of Dane, breaking Ethan's eye contact. The swirling wind settled, retracting into Ethan.

"I'm sorry," Dane said. "I never really believed it could be true." He reached around Grace and grabbed Ethan's wrist. "I didn't think I was supposed to tell anyone."

Grace looked at him over her shoulder, her red curls framing her quintessential-mom stare. "Well, now we're certain Malini was right. You have power over souls. You've captured another Soulkeeper inside of yourself. I've never even heard of such a thing."

The air-conditioning clicked on, the hum of the unit filling the room as each of them processed this new reality. Ethan's furious glare made it obvious he wasn't happy with this turn of events, but Dane couldn't be sure why. Was it because of the way he found out? Or that he was a Soulkeeper now? Or something else?

Hooking her arm into Ethan's, Grace pulled him toward the door. "You rest. We're going to gather the others. We need to get you back to Eden. Malini will know what to do about Cheveyo."

Chapter 16
Stoned

Malini *would* know what to do, and Dane didn't have to wait for Eden to reach her. He lifted the leather strap over his head and dangled the red stone in front of his face. What exactly was he supposed to do? In the jungle, Malini had said to look into the stone and try to clear his mind. Difficult, considering he had another person inside of it.

For the moment, Cheveyo's presence was hardly noticeable, and he planned to take advantage. He plumped the pillows against the headboard and nestled into them. When he was as comfortable and relaxed as possible, he held the red disc between his thumb and forefinger, closed one eye, and peered through the gem like a monocle. The smooth outside of the stone housed a complex matrix of facets surrounding a darker heart, a rectangle of deep forest green. At the center, something moved. He brought his face closer to the stone to get a better look.

Red glass shingled itself around him, and he tumbled into a dark void. A moment of blackness preceded the reconstruction of his reality, square by square. The surroundings assembled themselves, starting with a pristine blue sky and followed by rolling green hills. Wood planks fashioned a deck under his feet and then a stable with a roof that shaded the walkway where he stood. He blinked once and found the stable full of horses: palominos and thoroughbreds that whinnied when he looked their way.

Footsteps on the floorboards heralded the arrival of a cowboy from the boots up. With skin like tanned leather, he adjusted his pale Stetson. "Welcome. Nice place you brought here."

"I brought here?"

"You created this place. Your subconscious decided this would be the perfect environment to talk." One of the horses nuzzled the man's shoulder, and he scratched the mare behind her spotted ear. "Care to introduce me to your friend?"

"Friend?"

"He means me."

Dane whirled around to face a Native American boy, about fifteen, with an eyebrow piercing. "Cheveyo?"

"Yeah." The boy crossed his arms over his T-shirt and leaned against the entryway to the stable.

Desperate for answers, Dane charged, forearm smacking into the boy's chest and pressing Cheveyo into the wood frame. "Why were you helping Auriel? What were you trying to do to me?"

"She told me about you," Cheveyo said. "How I needed to stop you." He wriggled sideways and shoved Dane away, freeing himself.

"Stop me from what?" Dane backed off, hoping the gesture would encourage the kid to talk.

"She didn't say exactly. She said you were a member of an evil faction called the Soulkeepers."

"You're a Soulkeeper! She's a Watcher. You can't believe what she says. She's working for the devil, Lucifer."

Cheveyo shook his head. "She's a spirit of my people sent to punish me."

Dane's shoulders slumped. "Seriously? You believe that? She stole your body. She killed the boy from the motel."

"She didn't kill Jaden. I think ... I did." Cheveyo scrubbed his face with his hands. "I'm so confused. What's going on?"

"You said you didn't mean to kill him. She tricked you. Because she's evil."

Cheveyo pressed his eyes closed like his head hurt. "Everything made sense before, but now, I don't know what to believe."

"Hold up, partner. I can shed some light on the subject," the cowboy drawled. "Watcher influence is powerless in the In Between. Here, your thoughts are your own."

"How did he get out of my head, anyway?" Dane asked.

"In this place, consciousness is reality." He pointed at Cheveyo. "Separate consciousness, separate reality. In the physical world, all is as you left it."

Disappointment evident, Cheveyo's brown eyes locked onto Dane's. Obviously, he didn't have a clue what to believe. Then again, Dane used the stone for exactly the same reason.

"Do you know where I can find Malini?" Dane asked the man in the Stetson.

The cowboy waved one gloved hand.

"Huh?" Dane scowled.

"I am an echo of the Healer's wisdom in the form you have chosen. You may ask me questions, and I will give you answers."

"Healer?" Cheveyo interrupted. "Like a medicine woman?"

"Exactly like a medicine woman," the cowboy said through a tight smile.

"So I can ask you anything?" Dane glanced at Cheveyo. "We need answers, fast."

"You can. However, I can only answer questions about the future as it stands at this moment. The future is always changing. Every decision is a fork in the road. I can tell you only where the road leads today. Mind yourself, knowledge of the future is a dangerous thing."

"Yeah, okay. I think I understand," Dane said.

"Then follow me." The cowboy led them to a knoll outside the pasture and lowered himself to the grass. He motioned for Dane and Cheveyo to do the same.

"Hold up," Cheveyo said. "What, we lie on our backs in the grass, and this guy answers our questions? What is this?"

"The In Between," the cowboy said. "Your soul is in a metaphysical reality between Heaven and Earth."

Cheveyo narrowed his eyes.

The man folded his gloved hands across his chest, looking up at Dane and Cheveyo expectantly. He sighed heavily when the boys didn't move. "Think of the universe as a football field. The Earth is on the fifty-yard line. Heaven is one goal and Hell is the other. The In Between is on the twenty-five-yard line, Heaven's side."

Dane lowered himself next to the cowboy. "Take a load off, Cheveyo," he said. "We need answers. Both of us."

With a deep sigh, the boy lowered himself to the grass. On their backs in the soft pasture, they had a clear view of puffy white clouds floating like fat sheep across the blue expanse. "Ask your first question, Dane."

"Am I really a Soulkeeper?"

"That's a question about the present."

Dane rubbed his chin. "When we return to Eden, will I be a Soulkeeper?"

The cowboy waved a gloved hand in a wide arc across their field of vision. The clouds shifted, rearranging themselves into symbols then separating again. "Yes."

"So, is this my gift, then? I take souls?"

The cowboy blinked at Dane impassively.

Frustrated, Dane gritted his teeth. How could he learn what he needed to when he had to focus on a future that might or might not happen?

He blew out a deep breath. "How will I help the Soulkeepers?"

Again, the clouds rearranged themselves for the man in the Stetson.

"You will go where they cannot and sacrifice yourself for the greater good. Your power will come from your humility, your deep-seated belief that life is not all about you. But it will be, Dane. Soon the balance of things will depend on you."

Sacrifice yourself for the greater good… Dane didn't like the sound of that. He would, of course, if he needed to. If he were honest with himself, sometimes he wondered if he had much to lose. His family hated him, he wasn't sure what he wanted to do when he graduated, and Ethan … Ethan was the source of something Dane couldn't accept. Yes. It would be better this way, to go out the hero if that was what it took.

Cheveyo slapped the grass and cleared his throat. "Can I ask a question?"

"Yes, Soulkeeper."

"Will … Auriel … or whatever she is, ever give me my body back?"

The clouds moved quickly, as if a storm was moving in. "No. Auriel will never give you your body back. She's using you, as is Lucifer. They expect you will die, and if you don't, they will kill you or worse."

Cheveyo rolled to his feet and paced. "Don't sugarcoat it or anything."

"You've been duped," Dane fumed, sitting up. "I don't know who you thought she was—"

"I told you. A *Kachina*! A Hopi spirit of the underworld. In my culture, winged serpents are extremely powerful, and she came during the Snake Dance, when we open the way to the underworld."

The cowboy cleared his throat. "Did she arrive in the area purified for your ceremony?"

Cheveyo hesitated. "No. She was near a tree down the mesa."

Next to Dane, the Stetson bobbed with the cowboy's knowing nod.

"She took the form that would make you most vulnerable," Dane explained. "She probably couldn't have entered your ceremonial space."

As if the truth hurt, Cheveyo pressed his eyes closed for a moment. "Raine knew. She tried to warn me something was wrong, that the snake woman couldn't be one of our spirits."

"It's not your fault. This is what Watchers do. They are masters of illusion."

"So, if I don't get my body back, how do I get out of his head?" Cheveyo asked the cowboy.

Clouds danced. The cowboy leaned back and adjusted his Stetson on his head. "Your fate is bound to Dane's. His future is your future. More than one road winds before you. One way or another, you will separate."

Turning his head, Dane stared at the cowboy's ear. "Will one of us die?"

Cheveyo grunted from his place standing on the other side of the cowboy. "Hey, maybe I don't want to know."

But it was too late. The clouds were already moving. "It is impossible to know. Every road leads to change, and death is a type of change."

"So, will every road lead to death?" Cheveyo asked softly.

The cowboy rose to his feet. "Death is change, but not all change means death. Something must end for something else to begin."

"Could you be more specific?" Dane asked.

"I think y'all know what you came for." He gave a curt nod, adjusted his Stetson, and moved toward the horses.

"Wait," Cheveyo said, holding out his hands to the man. "That's it? One of us could die, we're both Soulkeepers, and I can't trust anyone?"

"You can trust us," Dane said. "You're one of us, a Soulkeeper."

"Excuse me for not jumping on the next train to nowhere. I don't know you any better than I knew her."

"Well, buddy, unfortunately, you are along for the ride, whether you like it or not."

Hands on his hips, Cheveyo groaned and looked toward the clouds.

The old cowboy glanced up at the sky. The pale azure had gone purple, red at the edges, and the clouds passed in fast forward. "I'm sorry to have to leave y'all so soon, but it appears Dane is wanted on the other side."

Red washed over the landscape and the horizon folded to a pinpoint of light. Cheveyo's body rushed toward Dane's, and slipped inside his head as shingles of red and black light flipped and turned. The stone spit him out on the comforter just in time.

The smell of dark spices whiffed across Dane's nose. He palmed the stone and shoved it into his pocket.

"Alone again," Auriel said from the foot of the bed. "Excellent. We need to talk about the plan."

Dane swallowed hard. If he were to have any hope of thwarting Lucifer's scheme, he had to pretend to be Cheveyo. "What do you want me to do?"

"The Soulkeepers have a place where I cannot go, a place they congregate to do their evil. I think they call it Eden. One of them is named Malini, an East Indian girl, very powerful. Bring her to me. Kill the rest."

"Kill?"

"Do you want your body back or not?" Auriel growled. "Kill all of the Soulkeepers in Eden." She collected herself, lowering her voice to a sweet coo. "It will be easy for you, Cheveyo. In this body, they will trust you. Spare only Malini. Bring her to me. I want her alive."

"How do I find you? After I've done this thing? How do I bring Malini to you?"

A wicked grin spread across her face like a virus. "The body you are in, Dane, he lives on a farm in Paris, Illinois. At the back of his farm is a group of pine trees. I will meet you there in two weeks' time at precisely noon." She reached forward and grabbed the collar of Dane's shirt, pulling him closer to her. "Whether you have succeeded or not, you must meet me there in exactly two weeks. Do you understand?"

"I understand. Go to Eden, kill the Soulkeepers, bring Malini. Two weeks. Noon."

Auriel smiled and shoved him back on the bed, so hard his skull cracked against the headboard. Dane rubbed the forming bump, grateful the hurt wasn't bleeding.

Unadulterated hate clouded Auriel's eyes. "Don't mess this up, Cheveyo, or I will eat your flesh and laugh as you slowly disintegrate inside that borrowed body. And beware of the one called Ethan. He loves this boy. Sickening, pure love. He'll be hard to put off. Kill him first."

Dane nodded. It was all he was capable of. Fear paralyzed him within a mess of shivering limbs. Add that to the revelation that Ethan loved him, truly loved him, and the one-two punch to his psyche left him utterly mute.

If she noticed what she'd done to him, awareness didn't evoke pity from the Watcher. Instead, Auriel released an evil, spine-tingling giggle. With a flourish of her hand, she produced a steaming mug.

"You're afraid," she said, all platinum hair and fluttering blue eyes. "Have some tea."

The smell of cinnamon and cloves wafted over Dane. He accepted the mug, playing along, but of course he wouldn't drink. He remembered the dangers of this particular concoction all too well. With her eyes watching him, he raised the cup to his lips. All the memories of how that elixir had made him feel came rushing back. One taste. One sip was all he needed to feel that rush of power, to make all of his problems go away and lose control. No one would blame him, and he'd be blissfully absolved of responsibility for his future.

"That's it. Drink," she demanded.

Dane pressed his mouth around the rim and tipped the cup. The hot liquid reached his lips but couldn't break through their seal on the glass. He wouldn't drink. He was a Soulkeeper. He couldn't take the easy way out anymore. Lowering the mug, he wiped his mouth with the back of his hand, hoping he'd made a good show of it.

Her lips peeled back from her teeth. "Two weeks, Cheveyo." In a column of smoke, she dissolved, leaving behind the mug, the memory, and the smell of rotten eggs.

Now do you understand what she did to me? She's horrifying. Why couldn't I see it before?

"Oh, I understand more than you know. Auriel and I go way back. I think, maybe, our trip to the In Between and you being inside an uninfluenced body probably has something to do with your sudden clarity. That's why she tried to get us to drink this." Dane rushed to the bathroom and poured the elixir down the sink, running the water longer and harder than he probably needed to in order to wash away every drop. "Auriel befriended me last year, addicted me to this shit, and almost made me kill my friend, Jacob. When I refused, she beat me, almost to death, in the parking lot of my high school."

So, she is the devil.

"Oh no, Auriel is not the devil. I've met the devil too, and he is much, much worse."

Tell me.

And so Dane did, about being captured, taken to Hell, and barbecued inside a ring of fire on a slab of brimstone until he begged for death. He told Cheveyo every detail he could remember and cried from reliving it all.

Stop. I can't hear anymore. I'm in, okay. I'll do whatever it takes to help take Auriel down and Lucifer too if we get the chance.

"Good. Our future isn't set. What the cowboy told us in the In Between … he said there are many roads. If we are going to change our fate and both survive this, we've got to work together."

I agree. Which is why I've got a favor to ask of you.

What he asked for shouldn't have surprised Dane, but it did, almost as much as his sudden compulsion to help him.

Chapter 17

Rescue

At the knock, Dane leapt to his feet and trudged across the beige shag. He released the sliding chain lock, pulling the door open tentatively. Sunlight filtered in, warming his face. Grace and Ethan stood on the other side, more than a little concerned.

"Why was the chain lock engaged?" Grace asked.

Ethan stepped forward, reaching for him. "You don't look so good."

Reflexively, Dane jerked away, like Ethan had a disease or something. He didn't mean to, but his brain couldn't process everything he'd learned today. He needed space.

"What's wrong?" Grace said.

"Uh, nothing," Dane answered, retreating into the room again. "Auriel just poofed out of here. A little shaky is all." *And a little confused about Ethan being in love with me.*

Even now, with the distraction of learning he was a Soulkeeper, being possessed, and knowing he might have to *sacrifice* himself, standing close to Ethan sent a warm current through him. That made him nervous that his body might betray his physical reaction. With his back to them, he pressed his eyes closed and tried to pull himself together. He couldn't be gay; he *refused* to be gay. He vowed to turn whatever this was off and redirect the energy toward something else.

"What did Auriel say?" Grace asked, closing and locking the door behind her.

Dane plunked down on the edge of the bed. "She wants me, well Cheveyo, to go to Eden. Once inside, he's supposed to kill everyone, all of the Soulkeepers, except Malini. Auriel wants us to be her goddamned Trojan horse."

Grace lowered herself to the chair in the corner of the room and folded her hands as if she were praying.

"I used the stone Malini gave me," Dane admitted.

"What did she tell you?" Grace asked softly.

"It's complicated and personal."

She pursed her lips. "Dane…"

"Honestly, the rock wasn't all that helpful. We need to go back to Eden and talk with her in person. Our only blessing in all of this is that Auriel isn't aware I'm pulling the strings in this body, or that Cheveyo is on our side. We've got to make a plan. She's given us two weeks. I'm guessing if I don't deliver, she's not going to let me go away peacefully."

"You're right, of course. She'll hunt you down and kill both of you," Grace said.

Dane nodded.

"The others are waiting in the diner. Let's round everyone up and open the portal," Grace said.

"Good plan." Ethan held the door open for them.

"Wait, Cheveyo needs our help with something."

"And that is?" Grace asked.

"He asked me to find his friend, Raine. I guess he possessed her for a few days, and he's afraid he damaged her like he did Jaden. He wants to know she's okay."

"Absolutely out of the question," Grace said. "We need to get you home. The council needs to know what's going on. And judging by what Cheveyo's possession did to Jaden, I have other concerns."

After what the cowboy said, Dane was painfully aware his relationship with Cheveyo was a deadly one, but he couldn't put the idea of finding Raine aside. He could see her. When Cheveyo thought about Raine, the other boy's memories played out in his head as if they were his own. Beautiful, sweet, innocent Raine. Dane wanted to make sure she was okay as much as Cheveyo did.

"I'm sorry." Dane bolted for the door, much quicker than he'd ever run in his life. He'd heard the Soulkeeper gene made you fast. Boy was that true. He reached the end of the walkway before Ethan's power wrapped around him and squeezed, pulling him up short near the stairs.

"Sorry, buddy. Too risky. If you want, one of us can come back and check on Raine later." Ethan's hands replaced his telekinesis, gripping Dane's shoulders. "Come on."

Ethan's touch brought Dane back into his own head, filling him with a warm electric tingle. "Weird."

"What's weird?" Ethan asked.

"I think that was Cheveyo. It's like I can sense what he's feeling. I have control, but this experience gives new meaning to walking in someone else's shoes. I can feel his memories."

Still gripping Dane around the shoulders from behind, Ethan brought his lips to his ear. "Tell Cheveyo he needs to hold off on those walking shoes until we figure out how to help him get his own body back."

Will you let this guy know I can hear him? Plus, do you mind cooling the internal fireworks?

"Fireworks?" Dane repeated.

"What about fireworks?" Ethan asked.

Dane shook his head. "Er, nothing. Cheveyo says he can hear you."

Ethan sighed, guiding Dane back toward the room by the shoulders. "Come on. Here come the others. Time to go."

On the stair landing, Bonnie appeared with Grace at her side. "I knew it!" she called, catching up to Dane with a face-splitting grin. "I could tell there was something more about you." She hugged him hard, edging Ethan's arm back off his shoulders. She held the hug for an extra beat and then smacked her lips against his cheek. When she finally pulled back, she met Dane's gaze. "I'm so happy for you."

Whoa! Who's the hottie?

"Bonnie," Dane said to Cheveyo, then realized how weird it sounded to everyone else and tacked on, "Thank you. It means a lot to me."

Just then, Samantha and Ghost caught up to them. She pecked Dane on the opposite cheek. "Congratulations, Dane."

"Thanks."

Oh my God, twins! Gorgeous twins. I cannot believe this isn't doing anything for you. Are you dead?

Dane ignored the comment. He'd had about enough of Cheveyo. Reminders of who did or did not "do it" for him were unnecessary. He pulled the steel door shut at the back of his brain, locking Cheveyo out of his thoughts.

As he followed Grace and the others back into the motel room, the desire to find Raine faded along with Cheveyo's presence. Maybe because the desire was actually Cheveyo's. With him locked away, taking action didn't seem as urgent. Still, Ethan stayed close to his side. So did Bonnie. In fact, she couldn't take her eyes off him.

Once behind closed doors, Grace extracted the large geode from the velvet bag and positioned the stone in the empty closet. Then, she punched Jacob's number into her phone. "Yeah. We're ready."

A few minutes later the small space was filled with purple light. "Will we have to ski back up the hill?" Dane asked

Ethan. When the light faded, the closet was transformed into the irregular opening of a deep, dark cave. The ski equipment had been replaced with helmets, headlamps, harnesses, gloves, and carabiners: caving equipment.

"Oh, hell no," Ethan said, backing away.

Dane raised an eyebrow. "Caving not your thing?"

"Claustrophobic."

"Don't worry. I'll help you. This I can actually do." In fact, Dane enjoyed caving and found the thought of being underground a huge rush. He'd spent a week every summer since he was six at a camp in Wisconsin where caving was a favorite activity. Forgetting his previous apprehension about Ethan's feelings, he led the way to the equipment wall.

The others rushed past them and geared up, mounting their headlamps on their helmets and strapping into their harnesses. Once everyone turned their lights on, the cavern gave up its secrets. Under a ceiling of sharp-looking stalactites, smooth, sloping rock gave way to a dramatic drop.

"This isn't about caving at all. No tight spaces. All we have to do is rappel down, same as if we were rock climbing." Dane stepped into his harness and handed one to Ethan.

"Oh, is that all?" Ethan slathered his words in sarcasm.

"We'll take it nice and slow."

"Hey, look," Ghost yelled from the end of the closet floor. "The anchors are already bolted to the rock up here. The ropes are even threaded. Five ropes, five of us. All we have to do is hook on."

Ethan nodded but swallowed hard, eyes widening in the darkness. Dane reached forward and turned his friend's headlamp on, then turned on his own. He slipped on a pair of gloves as they moved to the anchor point.

"This rope loops through the metal eight." He demonstrated for Ethan while the other Soulkeepers locked on and started down the smooth stone. "You let the rope slide through your hands as you go. If you want to slow yourself, you simply clamp down on the rope and move it behind your back like this."

Dane clipped the carabiner on his harness to the small end of the metal eight and watched Ethan do the same, double-checking the clasp. Ghost and the twins had already started down the hill, but Dane didn't care. He'd go as slow as Ethan needed to.

"Ready?" he asked.

Ethan nodded.

Leaning back, Dane allowed the rope to slide through his hands as he backed down the stone ramp. About halfway down, loose pebbles littered the way. He lost his footing and had to catch himself with his hand brake. Like everything Soulkeeper, this was going to be harder than it looked.

"Careful, Ethan," Dane called. "It get's slippery near the—"

His words were cut off by the echo of Bonnie's scream. Quickly, Dane looked over his shoulder and counted the lights up ahead. One was missing.

Smack. The sound of flesh hitting stone echoed through the cavern. Bonnie stopped screaming.

Ethan froze at his side.

"She's hurt!" Samantha yelled from ahead. "There's a huge overhang up here. She lost her footing and dropped her rope. I can't see her over the lip!"

"Ghost," Dane called. "Blink down there, dude, and check if she's okay!"

"I won't be able to stop. I can dissipate and come together at the bottom, but I can't stop halfway. I won't be able to take the rope with me."

"Get on with it," Samantha yelled. "At least we'll know what we're dealing with."

And if she's still alive, Dane thought. One of the lights disappeared up ahead.

"I see her!" Ghost's voice echoed up to them. "She's caught on a ledge. Looks like she fell maybe ten feet, but she's positioned weird. She's unconscious. Crap, there's blood. One of you needs to help her."

"Maybe I should go down and meld with her," Samantha said.

"Have you tried that when she's out?" Ethan asked.

"No," Samantha admitted. "I'm not sure what will happen."

"It's too risky," Ghost called. "What if you pass out too or incorporate her injuries? It won't do any good to have an injured giant on our hands."

"I don't think I can rappel with her added weight without melding," Samantha said. "I've never done this before."

"I'll go," Dane called to Samantha. "I've got the most experience, and I can carry her weight."

"Yeah. Okay. Good idea," Samantha agreed, shakily. She was holding it together, but barely.

Dane nudged Ethan. "I've got to go down and get her. You going to be okay?"

"I think so. You'd better hustle. She's hurt."

Rappelling to the drop-off next to Samantha, Dane took a deep breath. She was right, zero visibility. The lip of the drop masked the wall below. Dane hooked his instep on the edge and leaned back, letting enough rope out so that his body was perpendicular to the wall. He bent his knees and jumped into the abyss. The rope skimmed through his hands for a second before he clamped down again. Like a pendulum, he swung back finding the wall he couldn't see from above. Immediately, he planted both feet and pushed off again.

"You're almost there," Ghost called from below. "One more like that, Dane."

With one more leap, Dane found her. Luck was on their side. The three-foot projection had barely been enough to catch her body, and one leg and arm dangled precariously over the edge. He clamped down and swung in to the ledge, then walked over to her, tying off his rope so he could use both hands.

"She hit her head," Dane called. He lifted her into his arms. The bleeding came from a gash on her head. So much blood. Too much. Her rope dangled next to her body.

"Ghost, I've never done this with two people before. How far are we from the bottom?"

"Only about fifty feet."

"Okay. I'm going to wing it." He unhooked her from her rope and instead locked her on to his harness. He wasn't sure how this would work since his hands and feet had to be free to work the rope. With some effort, he tossed her arms around his neck and wrapped both legs around her abdomen. He braced himself on the ledge with one foot and leaned back until he was perpendicular to the ledge and her dead weight was leaning on top of him.

"Here goes nothing," he said to himself. Dane pushed off. Bonnie's weight was more than he was used to, and he dropped quickly. He swung back into the wall but couldn't keep himself straight. Gripping Bonnie with both legs, he braked hard and took the impact, slamming into the rocky wall, first with his shoulder and then with his lower leg.

He grunted from the pain.

"You're really close. One more like that and I can reach you," Ghost said.

"Okay. I can do this." Only, he was dangling precariously by a damaged arm locked behind his back. Awkwardly, he dropped his legs from gripping Bonnie, steadying her with the arm that wasn't behind his back holding them in place. Then, he wrapped the free end of the rope around his lower leg and used the bottom of his other foot to sandwich the end between the soles of his shoes. Instead of pushing off the wall, he straightened his arm and allowed his feet to do the braking, straight down. The rope burned where it tightened around his calf, and his shoulder bumped painfully down the jagged stone. Somehow Ghost's lamp appeared before him, and strong arms gripped his harness when his feet hit the ground.

"We're all okay," Ghost called to Samantha and Ethan. "Come on down!"

Dane found his footing, and helped Ghost gather Bonnie into his arms, unhooking her from his harness.

"Are you okay?" Ghost whispered.

"Yeah, I think so," Dane said.

Above them, whispering and then the clattering of equipment marked Samantha and Ethan's descent. "One, two, three," Samantha called.

Ethan screamed.

"Are you guys okay?" Dane called.

A laugh echoed through the cavern. "Yeah, we're okay," Samantha said. "But Ethan screams like a girl."

A few seconds later she landed on the cave floor, followed by Ethan. He scowled at her. "Hey, it's only funny until the portal is something you're afraid of, half-pint."

Samantha unhooked herself and raced to her sister's side. "I thought you said she was okay?" She stared accusingly at Ghost.

"She will be. Let's get out of here." He continued down the path.

Now that Dane had the chance to look, he could see a faint light beyond the next turn in the cave. He unhooked himself from the rope and followed Ghost. They all shed their equipment and emerged in the same farmhouse they'd come from, next to a seriously concerned Jacob.

"Holy shit, what happened?" Jacob pulled his phone from his back pocket, thumbs flying across the screen.

"Long story," Dane said.

"Malini's on her way. She'll heal you," Jacob promised.

"Heal *me*? No, it's Bonnie who's hurt," Dane said. That's when he glanced down at himself and saw the blood. His head swam, and he sank to the floor near the wall. Ethan was by his side in a heartbeat.

Ghost unloaded Bonnie on the bed, Samantha swooping in to press a folded T-shirt she'd retrieved from her pack to her sister's head wound.

Hastily, Jacob returned the geode to the velvet bag. "Long story or not, somebody better start talking."

Chapter 18
Revelation

Pain. Throbbing, heated pain. Dane clutched his lower leg.

"What's going on?" Ethan asked.

"My leg."

Blood had soaked through his jeans and was gradually invading new territory. Ethan crouched down and slowly folded Dane's pant leg up off the wound. The cloth clung to his skin, and he hissed through his teeth from the pain of the friction burn.

"Crap, Dane. That rope did a number on your shin. I'm surprised you could help Bonnie like this. What were you thinking?"

A heady presence filled the room, causing Dane to look up to where Malini hovered in the doorway, the afternoon light filling the space around her body so she appeared to glow. "Not to worry, Soulkeeper." She stressed the last word. "I'll fix you right up as soon as I finish with Bonnie. Her injuries are more serious." She moved to Bonnie's side.

The explosive crack of an enchanted staff signaled Grace's arrival, her shoulders laden with everyone's bags. She moved into action, dumping her cargo and fishing out a clean towel from the duffel bag full of weapons. She handed it to Ethan to press on Dane's wound before joining Ghost and Samantha at Bonnie's side. The twin was deathly pale, and Dane said a quick prayer that she would be okay.

"Soulkeeper?" Jacob muttered when the room quieted. "Will someone tell me what's going on?"

With Malini busy healing Bonnie, Grace did the honors. She started by explaining what happened, Dane's newfound abilities, and Cheveyo's presence among them. She tried her best to relay the incredible story in a somewhat believable way. By the time she got to Auriel's demands of Cheveyo, Jacob was nodding with parted lips.

Malini frowned as the details came out and not just because her arm was covered in painful blisters and blackened to the shoulder.

"Auriel wanted to use Cheveyo to kill all of us and capture me? What does Lucifer want with me?" Malini's voice came across high-pitched and innocuous, a much younger version of herself than Dane had grown accustomed to these last months.

"You're the Healer," Grace stated as if the answer was obvious.

"But why wouldn't he want to kill me too, Grace? It's true I can't die naturally until a new Healer is born, but I could be decapitated or dismembered. Why doesn't he want to destroy me?"

Jacob left the room briefly and returned with a jelly jar full of water from the kitchen. Taking her burnt hand in his, he willed the liquid over her damaged skin and then back into the jar. "You know the answer to that. You just don't want to admit it," he whispered to her as her skin pinked beneath his care.

She closed her eyes and shook her head. "Just say it, Jacob. I can't accept it unless I hear it out loud."

Jacob nodded. "If he keeps you a prisoner in Hell, you can't teach or lead the Soulkeepers, including any Healer that might eventually be called to replace you. He'd never let you die, so he'd have the added pleasure of torturing you for eternity."

"Right."

Bonnie groaned and fluttered her eyes. Together, Jesse and Samantha helped her sit up. "What's going on?" she whispered. Grace leaned in to explain what had happened.

Malini walked over to Dane and squatted near his feet, wrapping her hands around his bloody shin. The bleeding stopped, the deep welts filled themselves in, and the purple bruising around the edges of his wound gradually faded. When his leg had healed, she moved to his shoulder. In exchange, Malini's skin blistered and blackened, her grimace telling him all he needed to know. She could heal, but it was painful. Healing came at a steep price. Thank goodness for Jacob, who used his power to flush her wounds with the water she needed to heal.

"Thank you," Dane said.

She nodded and gave him a small smile.

"I think there's another reason Lucifer wants you," Dane sputtered. He wasn't sure if it was his place to say anything, but a thought had been fighting for the surface since Jacob's revelation.

Everyone turned to stare at him. He cleared his throat. "When I was in Hell, in Lucifer's prison, it was obvious that what Lucifer wanted more than anything was control. I think he wants you as a bargaining chip."

"Bargaining chip for what?" Ethan asked.

"Easy access to Earth. An end to his exile below ground." Dane glanced between Malini and Grace.

"Did Cheveyo tell you that?" Grace asked softly.

"No. Auriel posed as a Hopi spirit and told him we were evil. He never knew the truth."

Malini pulled her hair back into a ponytail and tied it with an elastic from around her wrist. Her face hardened, and her amber eyes grew dark with anger. In that moment, Malini returned to the person he knew she was, a warrior, a leader. As her shoulders pulled back, she stood taller, a force to be reckoned with. Dane enjoyed watching her fire ignite. The Healer was pissed off.

"It makes sense." She began pacing the room. "Lucifer thought he'd send Cheveyo to slaughter all of the existing Soulkeepers and imprison me. I can't die until a new Healer releases me. With me in his grasp, I won't be able to train or lead any new Soulkeepers, including any Healer that might replace me. With no one to thwart him, he'll send a contingent of Watchers to influence the most powerful government and corporate leaders. He'll gain control faster than I or any new Soulkeepers can respond."

Dane was confused until Jacob chimed in an explanation. "It's in the water. We found a bottling company in Chicago that's been supplying corporate and government buildings with water tainted with elixir. The most powerful people in the world are already influenced. He just needs to take us out of the equation to move in for the kill. Watchers are cowards. As long as we're around, none of them want to risk staying topside too long."

Malini rubbed her hands together and continued. "Obviously, Senator Bakewell's bill would allow Lucifer to use the corporations to employ slave labor. Food for the next wave of Watchers. The world will keep spinning, but it will be Lucifer turning the crank."

"God will never allow it," Grace said. "The fallen haven't been allowed topside since the flood."

A deep sigh passed over Malini's lips. "Exactly, if the terms remained the same. But as Dane pointed out, Lucifer will use me as a bargaining chip, offering me in exchange for new terms. If God agrees, everything could change. God follows the rules but Lucifer doesn't. The Lord of Lies wanted his Trojan horse to reset the scales in his favor. He's no longer satisfied with Hell. He's making his move."

Stunned, Dane pushed himself to his feet. "Well, seems like Fate wasn't on Lucifer's side. Cheveyo's not in control. I am."

Grace wrung her hands and moved closer to her daughters. "You can't put Auriel off. In two weeks, she's going to come for you. She'll want proof you've killed the others, and she'll expect you to have Malini."

"We need a plan." Jacob rested his hands on his hips. "We can try to take Auriel out, but that doesn't solve the problem, just delays it. Lucifer will know about Dane."

"If what you say is true, and the most powerful people in the world are vulnerable, we are one Watcher away from disaster," Grace added.

"We have three things going for us," Malini said. "Lucifer doesn't know that Dane is in control of Cheveyo, we know exactly when and where Auriel will be next, and we have two weeks to come up with a way to use the first two to our advantage."

"There's one more thing you should know." All eyes fell on Dane. He hesitated for a second, wondering if he should share what Cheveyo told him.

"What?" Malini asked.

"It's very possible that Cheveyo is killing me. The last boy he possessed, Jaden, died from this. A human body isn't supposed to hold two souls."

Ethan, who had been lurking in the corner of the room listening, suddenly became interested in the conversation again. "How long had Cheveyo possessed the kid before he died?"

"Just about two weeks."

* * * * *

The ride back to town was conspicuously void of conversation. Ethan drove mechanically, vacant eyes fixated on the country road as *Florence and the Machine* rocked out of the stereo. Every time the truck hit a bump, one of the speakers would short out. Neither of them mentioned the glitch. Dane had other things on his mind. Like if the silence was due to something he'd said? Or what happened in the cavern? Or perhaps something he didn't say? The last seemed the most likely.

At the back of his mind, Dane checked the steel door that blocked Cheveyo's presence. What he had to say was for Ethan's ears only and hard enough without an audience. "I never fully answered you," Dane began, "about why telling my dad the truth about you was so important to me."

With a startled jerk, Ethan glanced his way and then back at the road, straightening in the torn leather bench seat. "Yeah?"

Mustering his courage, Dane dug down deep, trying to be as honest as possible about what he was going through. He needed to do this, for the sake of their friendship.

"I think, sometimes, people are born a certain way and just know who they are. And other people, well, they're confused about things. Maybe they've been raised a certain way and can't be sure about their feelings because there's too much at stake to be wrong."

"What's at stake?"

"Relationships usually. Important relationships."

"Are we talking about a nameless nomadic tribe here or someone, say, in the cab of this truck?"

Dane took a deep breath. His cheeks burned, and he couldn't look at Ethan without feeling that undeniable pulling sensation. So, he chose to look out the window.

"Look," Dane said toward the glass, "you and I are really good friends. You're my best friend, really. I don't want to do anything to mess that up."

He glanced back to see Ethan nodding, so he continued. "It's important to me that other people give you the respect you deserve, even if it means it makes things harder for me."

"Thank you," Ethan said.

The song on the radio changed, and Dane reached forward to turn the volume down. Up ahead, he recognized the outskirts of Paris. Since he wasn't due home until the next day, he'd be staying in Eden with the rest of the Soulkeepers, which meant sorting this out with Ethan was critical.

"Everything you've said makes a lot of sense," Ethan said. "It's totally understandable."

Dane let out a relieved breath. "Thanks."

"But you need to demand the same respect for yourself that you expect people to give me. That means being true to yourself. I'm gay, and I like who I am. Whatever you tell your family and friends about me, I'm fine with it. I don't need their acceptance."

"Good."

"But I've sensed for a while now you're questioning."

"Questioning?"

"Like, maybe, not sure how to label yourself," Ethan said carefully.

"Yeah." Dane's heart was making a run for it, pounding against his breastbone.

"It's okay. There's no rush. Live your life and figure it out. Or don't. In my opinion, there are too many labels in this world anyway. Like I said, I'm going to be your friend no matter what." Ethan's dark eyes were unguarded, an open window into his soul.

Dane nodded, unable to speak around the lump in his throat. Was he worthy of the kind of unconditional acceptance Ethan was offering?

Too soon, the truck pulled into the service entrance at Laudner's Flowers and Gifts. Ethan parked, but stared straight out the windshield like he was still driving. Gathering his backpack, Dane popped open the door, an action that took more effort than he expected due to the rust on the big blue truck.

Ethan cleared his throat. "One more thing, Dane."

"Yeah."

The full weight of Ethan's dark stare hit him like a blast of heat. "If you do figure it out, promise me I'll be the first to know."

Dane swallowed hard. "I promise."

Chapter 19
Stress Management

Dane exited the cab of the truck and slammed the door against the flood of emotions bubbling to the surface. A resounding crack echoed through the alley, and the distraction of Jacob and Malini's arrival brought him some relief. He approached them, backpack slung carelessly over his shoulder, and tried to bury the conversation with Ethan. Luckily, the bustle of activity behind Laudner's shop didn't allow for much introspection.

Ghost arrived with the twins driving Lillian's new Volkswagen Beetle, something she'd bought with her salary as the new store manager at Laudner's. Of course, it was a convenient position for a warrior responsible for guarding the gate to Eden, which just happened to be under the floor of the backroom. Lillian met them at the service entrance.

"Dane!" She pulled him into a one-armed hug, patting his back on the recoil. "I heard congratulations are in order. I look forward to taking our training sessions to the next level." If the grin she gave him were any indication, she couldn't wait to test Dane's new Soulkeeper abilities, and she wouldn't be gentle. A workout with Lillian hurt a little, Soulkeeper or not.

Ethan growled from behind him. "My God, give him a few days to settle into the idea. He's been through a lot. Barely out of transition."

Laughing, Lillian rolled her eyes. "Oh, please. I haven't killed anyone yet, Ethan. Relax."

"Are we cleared for takeoff?" Jacob asked.

"Yes. John and Carolyn are having dinner at Andrew's Steakhouse and the store is empty." She led them through the service entrance and down the winding staircase to the cavern below.

The old wooden boat reminded Dane of a story he read about Charon, the figure in Greek mythology who ushered the newly dead across the river Styx. Age aside, the architecture seemed held together by magic or faith alone. Warwick Laudner created this portal hundreds of years ago. Now that he was dead, how long would the boat last? Dane took a seat at the stern. The wood creaked under his weight. *Great.* Ethan slid in next to him on the bench, seemingly unconcerned with the way the wood protested. The twins and Ghost sat near the bow, and Jacob and Malini took their usual spots on either side of the mast.

"We can make room," Dane said to Lillian, sliding away from Ethan.

"No need. I have to stay to close up the shop. I'll meet you tomorrow morning, bright and early. We'll get a lesson in before you have to go home."

Hesitantly, Dane nodded.

"Should we wait for Grace?" Jacob asked.

"No," Malini said. "She popped back to Flagstaff to double-check that we made a clean departure."

Can't leave any fingerprints. Dane remembered how Ethan had looked standing in the wreckage of the motel room and was thankful for Grace's help. With how fast everything had happened, a mistake was possible. The last thing they needed was the Flagstaff PD looking for Ethan.

Lillian retreated to the stairwell as Jacob raised the sail, and a spectacular ball of fire barreled through the cavern. Dane braced himself as they rocketed through the cave wall and then slowed to drift toward the burning swords of the cherubim. The ride didn't scare him anymore, not after what he'd been through.

Beneath the eternal flames, the familiar sifting started, his body tested by the magic protecting Eden. Only Soulkeepers, those pure of heart and intention, could enter this place. Usually, the uncomfortable pressure only lasted a moment.

Snap! Something was different. His head pounded as if someone were taking a sledgehammer to the inside of his skull. A scream broke his lips. He sandwiched his splitting head between his hands. It didn't help. Heat blasted from his skin, and poured out his eyes and ears, a sudden and severe fever that racked his body with pain.

"Dane! What's going on?" Malini cried.

Soon, everyone on board understood what was happening. Cheveyo's soul unfolded from Dane's body. Opaque, and with a tortured grimace, the Hopi boy hugged his middle with his ghostly arms. Apparently, the cherubim were weighing his soul on its own merits.

The other Soulkeepers gaped as the boat broke through the invisible membrane, and Cheveyo melded back into Dane, who shivered and heaved onto the floor of the boat.

Ethan caught him as he toppled off the bench. "Are you okay? Dane?"

Lying across Ethan's lap, he blinked at the blue sky above him and the lush green jungle of Eden. By the time the boat docked, he'd caught his breath and righted himself, despite a desperate, primal urge to stay right where he was.

"Yeah. Okay, that's a lot harder with someone else in your head," Dane said, scooting down the bench.

Somewhere deep inside his brain, Cheveyo groaned. Dane slammed the steel door. It was too hard to share the mental space with the other Soulkeeper right now.

Malini breathed an audible sigh of relief.

"So that was him. That was Cheveyo," Jacob stated.

"Yeah," Dane said.

Bonnie piped up from the front of the boat. "The good news is I think we can trust him. If the cherubim let him in, then he's got to be on our side."

Malini nodded.

Ghost blinked out of the boat and onto the dock, then reached over to help Samantha out. "Do I need to remind any of you that there are no classes today? And, I believe, the dining room is still decorated for a party."

To the sound of cheers, Dane exited the boat, positioning himself in the crowd as far away from Ethan as he could get.

* * * * *

Samantha plugged her phone into the speakers at the front of the dining hall, and soon the rafters boomed with Bruno Mars's *Locked Out of Heaven*. Malini yanked Jacob by the arm to the center of the room and started jumping to the beat. It was all the encouragement any of them needed. Dane reached for the ceiling and joined the circle of his friends, gyrating in time. He'd almost forgotten how fun dancing could be, to let loose and not worry about anything.

As the music changed to *On The floor*, Bonnie danced closer, knees bent, hips swaying to the beat, red hair framing her face. Breathtakingly beautiful and totally free, Bonnie came with no complications, no pesky emotions to get in the way. She was a simple recipe: one part fun, one part warrior, one part teenage girl, and she did absolutely nothing for him physically, at the moment a definite plus.

He moved behind her, wrapped an arm around her waist, and fitted his hips into her backside. She placed her hand over his, knitting their fingers, and stretched her other hand up to tangle in the back of his hair. Within the circle of his arms, she turned around, straddling one of his legs and laughing as her whole body kept the rhythm. A sheen of sweat broke out across her skin, glistening in the candlelight.

Dane let himself go, moving with her. He wrapped an arm around her, took her hand, and rolled her away from him. She spun out, and then stepped back in. He placed a hand in her lower back, leading her around the floor, passing Samantha with Ghost, Malini with Jacob. And just like that, he noticed Ethan was gone.

Well, he wouldn't go after him. This was how it should be. Dane would probably die doing this thing he'd have to do, sacrificing himself. It was better this way. His feelings for Ethan were dangerous. What would his mother say if she found out that all of the songs on the radio and all of the stories he'd ever heard about love, wanting, or needing someone, all made sense when he thought about Ethan? He could guess the words his father would use: immoral, unnatural, wrong.

He didn't believe those things about Ethan, of course. Everything about Ethan was right and good. He was who he was. Dane didn't come from the same place, and from where he began there was no place to go. He danced with Bonnie like there was no tomorrow, because the hollow inside his chest made him hope tomorrow wouldn't come. Besides, pushing Ethan away made him brave; he had nothing to lose.

"Come on," Bonnie said, threading her fingers into his. He followed her to the snack table, which had been replenished by one of the gnomes while they were dancing. She poured a glass of blue punch for him, then poured one for herself.

"Thanks," he said.

"You're welcome. Where'd you learn to dance like that?" Her cheeks were still flushed with exertion.

He chuckled. "My sister, Jenny. From the time she could walk, she wanted to dance, and I was always her partner of choice."

"Awww. Cute."

"Well, what kind of big brother would I be if I didn't pirouette on command?"

She giggled, raising her eyebrows.

"Anyway, now that we're both older, she has her own dance partners."

Bonnie's mouth curled into a flirtatious grin. "And so do you."

He looked down into his glass and cleared his throat. "Yeah."

She tucked a strand of hair behind her ear, wrapping the end of the wayward lock around her finger. An awkward silence cut between them. "I haven't had a chance to say thank you for saving me in the cave today. Ghost told me what you did."

"Ah, I'd say it was nothing, but it hurt like hell, so ... you owe me," he teased.

She punched his shoulder. "There. That's what I owe you." She laughed playfully. "No, I suppose I do."

"I'm just kidding, Bonnie. I was happy to do it."

The awkward silence crept back in, and he drank deeply of the blue punch.

"So, what's it like to have another soul inside of you?" she finally asked.

"Weird," he answered truthfully, glad for the distraction of the question. "It's like I have him trapped inside my head, behind a heavy steel door."

"What happens if you can't get him out?"

Dane shrugged. Should he be a downer and remind her he'd probably die? Another wave of awkward washed over them.

After two long minutes had crawled by, Bonnie's face lit up. "Hey, did you know he's not the first Hopi Soulkeeper?"

"No." Dane flashed her a half smile over his cup. "Wait, how would you know he's not?"

"Come on. I'll show you."

Bonnie led him out of the dining hall and through the atrium to the east wing of the school. Glancing over her shoulder, she searched the hallway with a guilty look on her face.

"What are you looking for?" Dane asked.

"Just making sure we're alone. Strictly speaking, I'm not supposed to be in this wing. East is the boy's wing. Us girls sleep in the west wing."

"Then how have you been here before?"

"Ghost showed me when he showed Sam," she whispered. She pulled the door to the stairwell open. "All clear. Come on."

He followed her over the threshold and was instantly stunned by the colors and textures that surrounded them in the stairwell. "What is this?"

"Murals," she said. "By past Soulkeepers."

At the base, the wall was covered in drawings that looked like cave paintings. The art progressed through various time periods and mediums, ending in neon-colored hearts, peace signs, and flowers at the top. Dane gawked at the portrait of an African teen painted in pointillism halfway up the wall. A jagged scar marred the boy's face. Framed by flames composed of red, orange, and yellow dots, the boy's eyes seemed to cut right through him. Who had he been? When had he lived?

"Look here," Bonnie said, pointing to a mural of a Native American boy riding on the back of a spotted pony. Behind him, pueblos topped a red mesa. The boy was depicted shooting light out of his palm at a gathering of Watchers.

"Wow. He's not the first. I need to show this to Cheveyo." With some effort, Dane opened the steel door at the back of his mind. "Cheveyo? Are you there? You've got to see this!"

The other Soulkeeper stirred. *I'm here*, Cheveyo said, after a long pause. *You've got to stop closing the door. Every time you lock me out, it's harder to come back.*

"Wake up. You've got to see this!"

The moment Cheveyo saw the mural, relief and acceptance flowed through Dane's body. Those weren't his emotions. When Cheveyo was loose inside his head, his memories, his thoughts seemed almost as real as Dane's. Now, his fingers stretched toward the drawing, under Cheveyo's control, and the Hopi boy's desire to connect with this place warmed his blood.

"I'm not sure you should touch it," Dane said. "You don't want to damage it."

I'm not the first. How old do you think this is, Dane?

"I have no idea."

"No idea about what?" Bonnie asked.

"Oh, I'm talking to Cheveyo. He was wondering how old this is?"

"I'm not sure. At least a thousand years."

"One thousand years?" Dane turned to face Bonnie on the landing, and hell if Cheveyo didn't see her too. For the first time, Dane was embarrassingly aware of how her jeans rode low on her hip, and he appreciated her snug T-shirt in an entirely new way. These had to be Cheveyo's feelings. Dane had no attraction to Bonnie other than friendship. The allure felt real, though, and familiar. His body reacted to Bonnie the way it always reacted to Ethan, a reflexive comparison that nagged at him like something he'd forgotten to do.

"You're so hot," Cheveyo mumbled through Dane's lips. Luckily, the words came out rushed and hopefully indistinguishable.

"What?" Bonnie asked.

"Nothing," Dane said.

She smiled and took a small step toward him, and didn't that just set Cheveyo off. Dane pinned his hands behind his back on the stair rail to keep from acting on Cheveyo's impulses. He wanted to touch her, and he wanted it desperately.

"Because it sounded like you said I was hot," Bonnie whispered.

Dane shook his head. "Cheveyo— He thinks you're hot."

Another step closer, Bonnie placed her hands on the railing on either side of his hips. Her breath warmed his face. "Thank you, Cheveyo," she said with a lopsided grin.

And then, she kissed him. The slant of her mouth came down hard on his, surprising Dane right out of his head. But that was okay because Cheveyo was there to take over. One hand found the small of her back, and the other fisted into her hair. Dane had a few seconds of experiencing how much Cheveyo was enjoying the kiss before he regained enough control to know he wasn't. In fact, the absolute wrongness of what was happening made his stomach turn. She was too soft and smelled like his grandma. He wrestled Cheveyo for control, trying his best to shut the steel door again. Only Cheveyo refused to go willingly. The mutual attraction between the two was giving the Soulkeeper exceptional strength.

Dane upped his efforts. Planting his hands on Bonnie's hips, he pushed her away. She stumbled back.

Oh, come on! Cheveyo's severe disappointment rattled through Dane's limbic system. He closed his eyes and slammed the steel door. When he opened them again, Ethan was watching from the top of the staircase. How long had he been there? He edged past Bonnie, taking the stairs two at a time.

"Hey!" Bonnie yelled.

Dane ignored her. "Ethan, wait!"

Ethan's black T-shirt disappeared through the door to the second floor. Dane didn't have time to think about the consequences. Free of Cheveyo's thoughts, everything inside compelled him to follow.

Chapter 20
Zap!

"Ethan, stop!" Dane called. "Let me explain!"

Ethan paused in front of the door to his room, staring at the panel of wood as if he could disappear into the grain. "I've stopped. What is it you'd like to say to me?"

"What you think you saw just now, between Bonnie and me, wasn't what it looked like."

He pivoted, brown eyes darkening to almost black when he met Dane's stare. "Really? Because clearly, you were making out with Bonnie."

With a deep sigh, Dane put his hands on his hips. "It wasn't me."

Swaying dramatically, Ethan shook his head. "That's right, your evil twin broke into Eden and shoved his tongue down Bonnie's throat."

"No, listen…" Dane rubbed his eyes with his thumb and forefinger. "It was me, okay, but it was Cheveyo who wanted to do it. I'd given him control."

Ethan groaned and approached his door again. He didn't turn the knob.

"So, ah, are we okay?"

"Why wouldn't we be?" Ethan kept his eyes on the doorknob. "I told you, it's okay for you to be who you are, whatever that is. I'll be your friend no matter what."

A huff of breath broke from Dane's lips. "Yeah, you said that, but your body language says something else. You're acting pissed, Ethan. I want to fix this. Talk to me."

Ethan's shoulders slumped. "Maybe you're right. Maybe I wasn't completely honest."

"Yeah?" Dane leaned against the wall, hugging his chest. Suddenly, he wasn't sure he wanted to poke this rattlesnake. This was dangerous territory.

"Yeah." Ethan turned and paced toward him until the smallest of spaces remained between them. Dane pressed into the wall, heart heading for track practice again. "From the first time I saw you lying in that hospital bed … the way you looked at me as if I could make everything better … you've made me want to *be* better. I've spent countless hours in Lillian's dojo getting stronger, and when I'm tired and think I can't fight her off one more time, I think of you, and somehow I do. I have *feelings* for you. More than friendship. I wasn't lying when I said I'd be your friend no matter what. But it's hard, Dane, because I *am* jealous. I'm jealous as hell."

God, his eyes were stormy, almost feral. Dane swallowed hard, trembling from the intensity of the moment.

Ethan slammed his hand into the wall. "Damn it! I'm sorry. I told myself I wouldn't do this. I didn't want to put you in this position. Forget I ever said anything." He turned on his heel and strode back to his room, this time throwing the door open.

"Ethan," Dane called.

He paused in his doorframe. "Yeah."

"I didn't like kissing her," Dane whispered. "Not at all."

Ethan poked his head back into the hall and raised his eyebrows. "Not at all?"

Dane shook his head slowly. A thick electrical charge pulsed between them. The air seemed to crackle, and for the first time, Dane wasn't afraid of what that might mean.

Just then, the door to the stairwell flew open and Gideon stepped into the hallway, a blanket and pillow in his arms. "Oh good, I was looking for you, Dane. We've got a room for you right down here. Come on, I'll get you set up."

"Okay." Dane's feet wouldn't move, and his eyes were glued on Ethan.

"Ah, this way," Gideon said again.

And just like that, the moment was gone. Dane blinked. "Okay. Um, goodnight, Ethan." He followed Gideon to the last room on the left.

"Goodnight." Ethan's door clicked shut behind him.

* * * * *

"Come on, sleepyhead. Time to train." Lillian's voice was almost as annoying as the way she shook his shoulder hard enough to knock him out of bed.

"What time is it?" Dane blinked his eyes, noting the dim light outside his window.

"Sunrise. Around six-thirty I think. If we start now, we can get an hour in before breakfast."

Dane groaned, remembering the night before, kissing Bonnie, and opening up to Ethan. He wasn't ready to face them again. He plastered his face into his pillow.

"Up, warrior," Lillian scolded. "I want you dressed and in my dojo in ten minutes."

Before Dane could protest, the pillow was yanked from under his head and his blanket from his body.

"Hey!" he said, rubbing his eyes.

"Ten minutes, Dane, or I'll show you no mercy." She left the room, slamming the door behind her. The sound pounded through his brain.

"Hmm. Not sure this Soulkeeper stuff is all it's cracked up to be." He stood, pulled a soft gray T-shirt over his head, and changed into a pair of shorts. A quick bathroom stop and he jogged down the stairs to Lillian's classroom. Briefly, he considered that he should let Cheveyo out. He wasn't sure what kind of damage he caused the guy keeping him locked in the dark recesses of his brain, but after last night, he didn't trust him. Cheveyo was too impulsive. He couldn't risk giving him control again.

He shoved his way through the door, pausing just inside the sanded wood floor of the dojo. Lillian waited, looking impatient.

"You made it," she said. "Showing up is half the battle."

He nodded. "Where do we start?"

"I've already taught you some basic defensive techniques. Today, we are going to practice those techniques with your new Soulkeeper speed and reflexes."

Dane approached cautiously, standing on the spot she indicated. She began with the basics. He swept his arm up to block her punches, or down to thwart her kicks. Aside from a few bruises, he was doing well, or at least holding his own. She attempted a chokehold. He thrust his hands between hers and knocked them away as she'd taught him. All the moves they'd practiced before, she showed him again, only faster, in Soulkeeper speed.

"You're doing very well. I want to take it to the next level."

"Sure."

"I'm going to attack you. Trust your Soulkeeper instincts and defend yourself. No rules, no choreographed moves. Simply respond."

Damn. Not good. Dane was no stranger to a good fight, but Lillian had some mad skills. He wasn't ready.

She showed no mercy. With a low-slung knife, she attacked. He slapped her hand away with his hand and countered with a jab. She ducked and side-kicked his thigh just above the knee. His legs gave out. He rolled onto his back, somersaulting to his feet. Stabbing downward, Lillian's knife plunged straight for his head. He moved to block her, but instead of pushing her away, he grabbed her wrist and pulled her in closer.

Zap! A shockwave traveled through both of them, almost painful, and left a tingling sensation in its wake. The knife dropped from Lillian's hand. With lightning-fast speed, Dane caught the falling blade, flipped it over, and stabbed back at her. His attempt was purposefully slow, meant for her to have time to get out of the way. But she didn't. The blade sank into her shoulder with the sickening crunch of metal on bone.

Her eyes grew wide before a shrill cry navigated her throat.

"I'm sorry, I'm sorry!" Dane yelled. Blood oozed over the hilt, over his fingers. He was afraid to pull the blade out, in case it might do more damage than good. "Help! Someone help!" Carefully, he lowered her body to the floor and bolted into the hall, relieved when Archibald materialized in front of him. "Archibald, I need Gideon or Dr. Silva now! Please. Lillian's been hurt."

To Archibald's credit, mere seconds passed before Dr. Silva came flying down the stairs, Gideon close behind.

"In the weapon's room. She's hurt!" Dane yelled.

He followed them back to Lillian who had pulled the knife out herself and was bleeding all over the floor. She moaned as Gideon pressed his hand over the wound.

"We need Malini," he said. "It's deep."

"Call her. Use the stones," Abigail said. She took over applying pressure to the wound while Gideon raced from the room.

"How did this happen, Dane?" Abigail asked accusingly. Her cornflower blue eyes bore into him.

"We were practicing. She attacked me, and she dropped the knife. I caught it and stabbed at her … slow. She should have been able to move out of the way, but she didn't. I'm so sorry." Nausea swept through him as he thought of the knife sinking into her flesh.

"That's impossible. She's a Soulkeeper; her gift is weapons. She has never, ever dropped a knife."

Dane wrapped his arms around his chest and stared guiltily at Lillian. "Um, well, this time she did."

Abigail must have sensed the honesty in his voice because she frowned as she looked back at Lillian.

"Dane, go wait in my office. I'll take care of this. Malini will be here soon." It was not a request.

He nodded and backed out the door.

Chapter 21
Soul Catcher

M alini leaned over Lillian in the infirmary, pressing a small brown hand against the ugly wound in her shoulder. Worry lines creased her forehead. The burn of healing would pass; Gideon stood by with a pitcher of water. Her concern was for Lillian, and what she couldn't sense under her skin.

The stab injury knit itself closed from the inside out and pinked beneath Malini's touch. Healing was painful work. It never got easier. The results, however, were worth the sacrifice. Lillian's shoulder looked as good as new, although, this time, Malini sensed her cure was only skin deep. She plunged her arm into the soothing water.

"I'm sorry I took so long to get here. Jacob and I went home last night after the party, and I had to pretend to be sick this morning to slip away from my parents."

Lillian nodded. "Thanks for coming."

"How did this happen?" Malini glanced between Gideon and Lillian. She would have liked to ask the same question of Dane, but he was currently in Dr. Silva's office, falling to pieces from guilt.

"I'm not sure." Lillian shook her head. "I've never failed so miserably in a fight, let alone a sparring session with a student. He wasn't even particularly talented."

Malini stifled a laugh.

"I realize, considering the circumstances, that sounds odd, but he wasn't, Malini. He reacted slowly when I dropped the knife. All I needed to do was step out of the way."

"Hmm." Malini tucked a strand of hair behind her ear and scanned Lillian from head to toe.

"Maybe she's getting sick?" Gideon asked. "A Soulkeeper virus?"

Arms crossed over her chest, Malini considered the possibility. "I suppose, but I've never heard of one before." She stared at Lillian for a full minute, tapping her toe on the stone floor before the flicker of an idea raised her eyebrow. Abruptly, she strode behind the curtain that divided the beds in the infirmary. She selected a spoon from the bedside table, tucking it behind her back before she returned to the front of the bed. "Hey, Lillian?"

"Yes."

"Catch." Malini tossed the spoon at Lillian's chest, a soft lob that should have been easy for the Soulkeeper to catch. The utensil thumped against her breastbone.

"I missed." Tears gathered in Lillian's eyes. "Oh my God, what's happened to me?" She looked down at herself as if she wanted to rip her skin off to see the disease within.

"Hold on, Lillian. I want to try something else." She pulled a rough sapphire from her pocket and held the gem out in the palm of her hand. After a moment of concentration, light poured out of the blue stone, and Dr. Silva's face floated before her.

"What is it, Malini? Is Lillian all right?" Dr. Silva's opaque image flickered slightly.

"Can you please send Dane to the infirmary? I need to ask him a few questions."

Abigail nodded. "We'll be there." Her image blinked out, and Malini dropped the stone back into her pocket.

Gideon approached her, narrowing his eyes. "You don't think…"

"Let's not jump to conclusions," Malini whispered.

Lillian sat up in bed. "What is wrong with me?"

Malini approached her, lifting the spoon from the bed and sliding her hand into Lillian's. She concentrated on sending her comfort, peace, and love. The older woman's face warmed at the touch, and she leaned into the pillow, smiling. "Okay. I can wait."

Only a moment later, Dane and Abigail arrived, panting from their run. Dane gawked at Lillian's healed shoulder. "Oh, thank God."

"Dane," Malini called.

"Yeah." Dane looked up at her with tear-stained eyes.

She whipped the spoon as hard and fast as she could at Dane's head. As she expected, his hand shot out, like a snakebite, and snatched the implement from the air.

"Damn," she murmured.

"Huh," Gideon said under his breath.

Dane grinned. "Hey, I caught it! Must be the old football days coming back to me."

Abigail shook her head in time with Malini's.

The light bulb came on for Lillian, and she didn't hesitate to share. "You stole my power!" She bounded out of bed and was in his face in an instant.

"What?" Dane held up his hands. "What are you talking about?"

"He doesn't know," Malini said.

Lillian pulled up short of slamming her hands into Dane's shoulders. Instead, she placed her fists on her hips.

"Your Soulkeeper gift, Dane, is not your ability to trap souls. You borrow other Soulkeepers' powers." Malini approached him with a serene smile.

"Huh?" Dane gaped at her in disbelief.

"The reason Cheveyo is inside your head is because that is *Cheveyo's* power, not yours. He can possess people. Only, he didn't have a body for you to possess, so instead you possessed his soul. But with Lillian, her gift is weapons. You captured her gift."

Dane's eyes darted around the room and then settled on Lillian.

"Give it back," she growled.

Eyes wide, Dane digested the revelation. "I don't know how."

"How did you take it?" Malini asked softly.

"We were sparring, and it just happened."

Lillian shook her head. "You grabbed my wrist. Here." She held out her arm and pointed at the patch of skin.

Forcing a swallow, Dane reached a trembling hand toward her. "Of course, skin to skin. The same as when I took Cheveyo." He wrapped his fingers around her wrist and closed his eyes.

Malini watched the force of will on Dane's features. He was learning, figuring it out. Their bodies jolted and then he let go.

Lillian backed away. "Throw me another spoon."

Gideon obliged, snatching another from behind the divider and lashing the utensil at the back of her head. Without even breaking eye contact with Dane, Lillian's hand seized the projectile from the air, twirled it between her fingers, and pressed it into Dane's neck like a knife. She laughed with delight.

"I'm back! Oh thank God, I'm back."

Malini breathed out a sigh of relief, fixating on Dane.

"I didn't take her power on purpose," he stated firmly.

Malini nodded. "We know that, Dane. It's just going to take some time for us to get used to the idea of what you are."

Abigail folded her hands in front of her. "Yes, and how we can use you."

Dane ran both hands through his hair and blew out a shaky breath.

"Come on," Malini said. "It's getting late. I'll take you home."

* * * * *

Dane waved goodbye to Malini as she backed out of his driveway, so overwhelmed by the weekend he hardly remembered the journey home. She'd promised him she'd check on Raine, the least he could do for the boy trapped in his head. He was a Soulkeeper now, and according to Malini, a powerful one. All the implications of his gift weren't entirely clear. He could borrow other Soulkeepers' powers. What could he do with humans? Watchers? No one seemed to know.

Confusing as his abilities were, Ethan was a close second. He'd left Eden without saying goodbye, easy considering he'd never made it to breakfast. Things were going to be awkward between them. Why had Dane been compelled to admit his feelings? There was no putting that genie back into the bottle. Ethan *knew*. He knew that Dane hadn't enjoyed kissing Bonnie.

He slapped his forehead. How should he play this? He hadn't said straight out he was attracted to Ethan or anything, and he hadn't acted on those feelings. Maybe Dane would be attracted to a different girl someday. Rubbing his chest, he tried to ignore the lingering thought that even if he were attracted to someone else, he'd never get over Ethan. The guy was under his skin. And if he were honest with himself, the thought of Ethan with someone else made his stomach twist.

The screen door squeaked as he let himself into the old farmhouse. "Hello?" he called, wondering if his dad was still of a mind to kick him out of the house, or if the argument had blown over.

Muffled sobs floated out from the dining room. He set his stuff on the table and followed the crying to its source: his mother's hunched body.

"Mom?" He placed a hand on her shoulder. She raised her red-rimmed eyes to his.

"Oh, Dane, thank heavens you're home." She sandwiched one of his hands between her two shaking ones.

"What's going on, Mom?"

"It's your father. He's in the hospital. The sickness is worse. Some kind of crazy virus they don't even have a name for. He's unconscious, and the doctors aren't sure he will ever wake up."

Dane's butt landed in the chair nearest to his mother. "What are you saying?"

"He could die, sweetheart. They just don't know anything about this illness. They're running tests. He has fluids and different medications, but the doctor says Luke's got to fight this bug off on his own."

"What hospital is he at?"

"Terre Haute. Jenny and Walter are still with him. I only came back here to pack some things and meet you. With you coming home today and all anyway, I didn't think you should hear the news over the phone."

Wiping her tears away, Dane took his mother into his arms, rubbing her back and holding her tight. "It's going to be okay, Mom. What do we need to bring back to the hospital? I'll help you pack, and then I'll drive you."

She placed her hand gingerly on either side of his face and searched his eyes. "I can't leave him there alone, Dane. I'm gonna spend the night. Can you bring Jenny and Walter back and take care of things tomorrow?"

Dane nodded. More responsibility. Could he do this? He didn't have a choice; he had to. "Sure, Mom. I'll take care of everything."

She squeezed him hard around the neck, then wiped under her eyes. Absently, she trudged up the stairs to begin packing.

Chapter 22
Spider Woman

Monday morning, Malini plopped into her usual seat in her Themes in Western Literature class, heavy with the stress of the weekend. Dane had texted her that his father was ill, an unfortunate turn of events considering they had less than two weeks to train him to use his new skills *and* make a plan for dealing with Auriel. The easy thing to do would be to heal Luke Michaels so that Dane could get back to work, but what was right was not the same as what was easy. Mr. Michaels's illness had purpose. Natural causes brought him to this place in life, and altering his fate would have negative consequences on the future. Guilt was Malini's price to pay for doing what she had to do in this circumstance, nothing.

"Do we really have time for this?" Jacob said as he slipped into the seat next to her. "What about Dane? Is it safe for him to be at the hospital with his dad when Cheveyo is still locked inside his head?"

Malini scratched behind her ear in such a way that her forearm blocked her lips as she turned her head toward him. "Be careful what you say." It was natural for him to be curious, but school wasn't the safest place to have this conversation. Later, they'd go to Eden and could sort everything out with the council.

Jacob spread his hands and looked at her emphatically.

Right now we need to act as normal as possible, she thought. She'd learned with Gideon last summer she could exchange thoughts with those people who had used her red stone. She preferred not to communicate telepathically if she didn't have to, but today, they couldn't be too careful. *It won't do anyone any good if we get grounded or have Principal Bailey breathing down our necks for truancy.*

But there's so much we should be doing.

"There's time, Jake."

He leaned closer. "Did you see the paper today?"

"No."

Senator Bakewell is all over the headlines. He's back in Washington debating his bill. He's got half the world convinced that S. 5109 will solve our immigration problem and put turbo boosters on the economy.

Great. Too bad it will also give Watchers a legal way to farm their next meal.

"Speaking of," Jacob whispered, "guess whose body they found in the Chicago river, half eaten by animals?"

Malini pressed her fingers to her lips and shook her head.

Our friendly Harrington secretary, Amanda.

When Malini pictured the stunning woman behind the desk at Harrington Enterprises dead in a river, she gagged and had to cough to cover it up. How cocky! After their visit, the Watcher had to have known the Soulkeepers would notice the kill. The only explanation was the demon didn't care. Was it drawing them out, just like in Arizona, or perhaps sending her a message from Lucifer? Was this retaliation for their victory at Fermilab last summer?

"Are you okay?" Jacob whispered.

Mr. White clapped his hands at the front of the room. "Settle down, people. I hope you did this weekend's reading because we are going to move quickly today."

"What was this weekend's reading?" Jacob muttered.

"Beowulf," Malini responded.

"Beo–wolf. Is it about shapeshifters?"

Malini shook her head.

As Mr. White began to lecture at the front of the room, she leaned back in her chair and effectively blocked him out. Fixing her eyes on a spot on the white board, she allowed her vision to blur and her soul to cross over to her spiritual home away from home. She preferred not to do this in such crowded circumstances, but part of her felt like Amanda's blood was on her hands. She'd waited too long to bring the Watcher responsible to justice. The council counted on her for guidance. The Soulkeepers were supposed to protect human souls, to avoid human casualties in this battle between Heaven and Hell, and she was failing. She needed to consult with the immortals for help.

The classroom faded away, replaced by a stucco-walled warehouse full of rolls of fabric. Malini navigated the brightly colored material quickly. She'd been here before, hundreds of times. At the front of the building, in the patch of light filtering through the arched doorways to the veranda, a tall woman weaved new fabric. Her eight arms worked tirelessly, knitting the silk that flowed between her fingers at lightning speed. Malini had seen her use a loom, but today her weaving flowed only from her. The sight of the yarn coming out of her wrists was creepy as was the spiderlike look of her body hovered over her creation.

"Fatima?"

The woman pivoted, giving Malini an unsettling view of her multiple limbs. Her dark eyes twinkled with stars—the light from the past, present, and future of every life on Earth.

"Welcome, Healer," Fatima said.

"Can we have tea?"

"Certainly." Fatima straightened her back and tugged a section of fabric, along with six of her arms inside her torso. The golden dress she wore consisted mostly of beads and clung to her flawless russet skin in a way that defied gravity. She sashayed her perfect silhouette onto the veranda. Malini followed.

"Lucifer is up to something," Malini began.

"Lucifer is always up to something." A pot of tea appeared on the bistro-style table, and Fatima took a seat before pouring two cups.

Sitting across from her, Malini sighed deeply. "Yes, but you must know this is something big or you wouldn't have saved Dane and made him what he is."

Fatima stopped, her cup halfway to her lips. "Fate does not alter the past, present, or future. She simply records the unfolding of the universe."

Malini sipped her tea, a lovely infusion of citrus and oolong. "You're right. It must have been some other woman with eight arms and a web sack full of holy water."

The corner of Fatima's mouth lifted.

"So then, do you have some advice for me as I attempt to thwart Lucifer's latest plan of attack?"

"Of course, it would be against my general prerogative to give you advice, but I've been wanting to tell you a story … for your entertainment."

"Please, I'd love to hear a story." Malini tried not to seem too anxious, although she knew she was pressed for time. Fatima rarely offered help in any form. She'd take what she could get.

"I noticed you recently found the Hopi boy, Cheveyo."

"Yes."

"Fascinating culture, the Hopi. The oldest native culture in the Americas, and still living as they did at the dawn of creation." Fatima sipped her tea.

Malini looked out across the rolling green countryside, where a giant brown animal frolicked in the distance. She smiled. Wisnu. The mongoose had saved her life once. He was too busy catching lunch to say hello. She turned her attention back toward Fatima.

"According to Hopi emergence mythology, in the beginning, the people lived below the earth. The chiefs of the tribe heard footsteps above ground and wondered about the top of the world's crust. They sent up a bird to find a way to the new world.

"The Hopi goddess, Spider Woman, inserted a reed into the earth, allowing the Hopi to climb to what is now the Fourth World. They'd done so before, moving from one existence to the next."

Malini shifted in her chair. "Spider Woman, you say. Interesting."

"Yes, very. Spider Woman created a new world for the Hopi and everything in it. She wove the sun and the moon, corn, adobe. The new world was good, and the people thrived. But the reed remained, and when a Hopi died, some souls chose to slide back down to the underworld."

"Hell?" Malini asked.

"No!" Fatima shook her head. "Not Hell. The Hopi underworld is a good, happy place filled with Hopi spirits. They call them *Kachinas,* the spirits of their ancestors. For the Hopi, there is a thin line between death and life. Their medicine women and priests walk this line regularly with their rituals, and Hopi ancestors are active in the Fourth World."

"I don't understand, Fatima. Is the Hopi underworld the same as Heaven? Are the medicine women Healers like me?"

Fatima laughed. "I forget you are a baby when it comes to the history of the world. Stop trying to fit others into your lexicon, Malini. Heaven? Hell? The underworld? Up, down, over, beyond. You humans try your best to fit things into your construct. True, everything and everyone is connected: Spider Woman's threads crisscross the universe. But connection and truth are very different things. The Hopi truth is different from your truth. Hopi don't go to your Heaven. They don't need to. Their medicine women do not lead Soulkeepers, but their magic is powerful."

"And all is part of the master plan?"

"Yes."

Malini finished the tea in her cup.

"One of the first Soulkeepers was Hopi."

She set the cup down and shot Fatima an inquisitive look.

"Everything is connected."

"Yes, I'm getting that message loud and clear," Malini said.

"Good. Then before you go, Death and I have something to talk to you about."

By the thrumming in her right arm, she could tell he was close. Death, otherwise known as Henry, had given her the skeletal arm that could kill the living with a single touch and raise the dead to do her bidding. When Henry was near, the thing vibrated like a tuning fork.

"Hello, Henry," Malini said, turning around to see him standing behind her.

He bowed stiffly at the waist. "Malini. Nice to see you again."

In the distance, she noticed Mara, astride a black mare. "Will Mara be joining us?" Malini asked.

"She says you won't be here long, and I should get straight to the matter at hand."

"What's going on?" Now Malini was worried.

"We're missing souls," Fatima interjected. Her extra arms pulled her tapestry out and held the weaving up to the ambient light from above. There was no sun in the In Between, but the sky was uniformly bright. A series of red dots appeared in the pattern.

Henry explained. "I feel the death of the body but can't find the soul."

"These red dots are lives that have ended before their time." Fatima ran her hand over the cloth. "Both body and soul, ended."

"What does it mean? Have you ever seen this before?" Malini asked.

"Souls disappear off Fate's tapestry when Watchers take them to Nod," Henry said, "but the body doesn't die. Usually, I can't even see them in Nod."

"So the Watchers are taking more people than usual to Nod but…"

"We think they are killing them there," Fatima said. "Slaughtering them actually, by the numbers."

Malini shook her head. "Why would they do that? I always thought they kept people forever, as servants or pets."

"They can and they used to," Henry said.

"We don't know for sure, but we think Lucifer is doing this to get your attention. He's trying to smoke you out."

"Smoke me out?"

Henry scowled. "Out of Eden. He has wanted his revenge since you fouled his sacrifice, but when you go to Eden you fall off his radar. Lucifer can only be in one place at a time and time is not on his side. Eden is a thorn in his side."

The red dots glowed menacingly. How could she stop this? Lucifer was trying to get her attention, all right. He was goading her. But the Soulkeepers couldn't react fast enough, not with their small numbers. If they could just anticipate where the Watchers would strike next, they could protect the humans involved. They'd gotten by this far because Watcher activity was naturally limited. None of them liked to be above ground for any amount of time; it drained their sorcery and put them at personal risk, a state that worked against the fallen angels' notoriously self-serving nature. But this number of abductions was calculated. This was organized. And the fact that the Watchers were killing them, probably to make room for new abductions, made her nauseous.

"Until next time, Malini," Henry said.

"Wait—" She'd promised the council she'd check on Ethan's thread, but there was no time. The walls blurred, and the familiar stomach-dropping lurch of trading dimensions hit her full force. She wasn't ready. She needed more time, more information. Malini jerked backward, out of the In Between, and landed in her body with a jolt. Jacob was shaking her shoulder vigorously, and Mr. White looked furious.

"Well, Ms. Gupta?" Mr. White folded his hands and stared at her expectantly.

Malini blinked at the board behind him.

He wants to know why you think the author wrote Beowulf.

Malini sat up straighter at her desk. "The author wrote Beowulf because the world needed a hero. He was the first real hero: strong, courageous, self-sacrificing. The author was using fiction to call out the best in people."

"Good insight, Ms. Gupta, as always, and thank you, Mr. Lau, for keeping her with us."

Her face burned from embarrassment. "Thank you," she whispered.

"What did you find out? You look like the sky is falling," Jacob whispered, not taking his eyes off the board.

"Later." Malini squared her notebook in front of her with every intention of focusing on Mr. White's lesson. Only, as she scratched notes on her notebook, none of them had anything to do with Beowulf. Words filled the paper at odd angles. *Hopi. Nod. Death. Souls. Eden. Lucifer. Soulkeepers. Smoked out.* In large letters, she wrote *defend the humans.* She underlined *defend*, then mutated the word to read *defense.* A lightning bolt of inspiration brought her pen back to the paper. She crossed out *defense* and wrote *offense*, underlining the word repeatedly. The part of her that was ancient and immortal kicked into gear. Malini had a plan, and Lucifer was about to get more than he bargained for.

Chapter 23
Medicine Woman

Malini arrived in the Walpi village on First Mesa that evening, having promised Cheveyo and Dane she would check on Raine. While she sensed the girl was still alive, she feared what she would learn from this visit. What was Cheveyo's presence doing to Dane? Oddly jumpy, the loud bang that accompanied her arrival by enchanted staff scared her as much as the native people in the plaza around her. A young boy, shirtless, barefoot, and dressed in a pair of red cotton shorts that seemed out of place with the natural surroundings, widened his eyes at her.

"Who are you?" he asked.

"My name is Malini. I'm here to see your medicine woman."

The boy pointed toward a pueblo to the west, then took off in the opposite direction, no doubt to tell his family about what he'd seen. She wouldn't lie if they asked her who she was or how she'd come, but she wouldn't offer the information either.

Malini knocked on the door of the dwelling and was met by the hunched form of a Hopi woman. Her wrinkled brown skin reminded Malini of Panctu, the Peruvian medicine woman and Healer. She rubbed the ache in her chest; she missed Panctu, especially now when she needed her wisdom.

"Are you Willow?" Malini asked.

"Yes. What are you called?"

"Malini. I am a medicine woman of … my tribe. I'm here on behalf of Cheveyo."

"Cheveyo? Our Cheveyo?" Willow played with the beads that hung around her neck, wrapping the string around her fingers nervously. "Where is he?"

Malini sighed. "Can I see Raine? Cheveyo is concerned about her health."

Willow narrowed her eyes and pressed her thin lips together. "He should be. Very worried. He has made her ill with a sickness my medicine cannot cure. I can barely keep her alive."

"May I see her?" Malini asked.

Willow seemed distrustful but stepped back to allow Malini to enter the adobe house. As soon as her eyes adjusted to the dim light, she could see the truth of Willow's words. Raine lay on a cot near the far wall, her skin tinted gray and smelling of Watcher rot. She remembered that smell when Katrina had been possessed by Cord. The Watcher ate the flesh from the inside out and left behind a black, oily decay. Malini wasn't sure why Cheveyo's possession of Raine had caused the same symptoms as Watcher possession. It was an odd and dangerous gift to have.

"I've come just in time," Malini said. "I can heal her, but I'll need water."

Willow nodded. "I have some here, but I have already purified her body." She pointed at a pot on a wooden table.

Malini approached Raine and knelt beside the cot. She loosened the collar of the girl's tunic, watching her chest rise and fall with each shallow sip of air. Malini placed her left hand on Raine's sternum. The girl's body seized beneath her touch.

"What are you doing?" Willow asked.

The stench of burning flesh filled the room, drowning out the scent of herbs strung drying across the ceiling. Oily black fluid oozed from Raine's nostrils, out the corner of her mouth, and from under her fingernails. Malini's skin blistered.

"Stop!" Willow rattled something off in her native tongue and grabbed Malini's shoulder.

Almost there. Malini sensed Raine's life force flowing back into her. She fought Willow off with her gloved right hand and winced against the burn climbing to her shoulder.

Willow must have noticed the way Raine's cheeks pinked because she mumbled either a curse or a prayer, and backed away from Malini.

Raine coughed and opened her eyes.

"Who are you?" Willow murmured.

Malini removed her hand from Raine's chest and plunged it into the pot of water. "I'm Malini. I'm a medicine woman and a friend of Cheveyo's. He sent me here to heal Raine. He cares for both of you and is deeply sorry for inflicting you with this."

Raine pushed herself up, smoothing her hair back from her face. Willow ran to her side, running hands over her hair, body, legs. "I'm fine, Willow," Raine said. "I feel much better."

Willow handed her a wet rag to clean her face, then turned on Malini. "This is strong medicine. Where do you come from?"

Disappointed that her arm wasn't feeling much better, Malini pulled it from the water. It was healing but not as usual. Slowly. Painfully. And the water was leaving red streaks in its wake on her skin.

"I am a Soulkeeper," she said. "I, and people like me, have been put here to fight demons, ah, bad *Kachinas*. Cheveyo was manipulated by a bad *Kachina*, but he's not anymore. He's with us."

"So you found his body?" Raine asked.

Malini shook her head. "No. Not yet."

"Well then, is he possessing someone? Do they understand this could happen to them?"

"We know. His host is strong and is aware of the risks." Malini hoped her words were true. "Cheveyo will be relieved you're okay."

Malini pulled her arm from the water. It didn't hurt anymore, but the skin wasn't normal. Pinkish streaks scarred her brown skin. "Is this water?"

"Yes, straight from the river." Willow approached her cautiously as if Malini was something from the beyond.

"The scarring isn't normal and the smell..." Malini lowered her nose to her arm. "You're sure there are no herbs in this? Maybe the pot wasn't clean?"

Willow's jaw dropped open as if she were offended. "Of course the pot was clean. I use this only for water."

Raine cleared her throat. "The water does have an odor. You don't notice it as much if you live here, but if you leave the reservation and come back, the scent is awful."

Malini sniffed it again and gasped. Elixir. Watcher elixir was faint but distinguishable. "How long have you noticed the smell, Raine?" she asked.

"For a while ... months. People here think the coal-powered generating station on Navajo lands is polluting the water, maybe dumping or leaking or something."

Icy fingers walked up Malini's spine and gripped the base of her skull. Her scalp prickled. She reached for her staff.

"A coal-powered generating station? Here?"

Raine nodded. "The power goes outside the reservation, of course, but the company pays the Navajo a percentage to use their land. We're downstream. I've joined an environmental coalition at my school to try to stop the pollution and force the NGS to use greener processing methods."

Swallowing hard, Malini pressed her eyes closed. "Raine, do you know the name of the company that owns NGS?"

"Sure. Harrington Enterprises."

Malini stared at the tracks on her arm and groaned. This was so much bigger than she'd thought. Harrington was everywhere, and the elixir was everywhere. How in the world could the Soulkeepers defend against something as ubiquitous as this?

Willow reached out and took Malini's damaged hand in hers. "Thank you for healing Raine and caring for Cheveyo. We are in your debt."

"You're welcome. I need to go, Raine, Willow. As soon as we find Cheveyo's body, I hope to return here with him."

"Healer," Willow said, "I am in your debt. If you need anything…"

Malini nodded.

The old woman sandwiched Malini's healing hand between her own and met her eyes. They shared a moment of connection that transcended the physical world.

"We live in a time of bad spirits. Be vigilant," Malini said.

Willow released her.

From behind her, Raine stood from the cot. "Thank you, Malini, for healing me."

Malini gave the girl a firm hug, then exited the pueblo and tapped her staff on the dirt road.

Chapter 24
Trojan Horse

Dane hated lying to his mother, but he had no choice. Five days had passed, spent in shifts by his father's bedside, eating crappy hospital cafeteria food, and whispering to Walter and Jenny about what they needed to do if his dad didn't wake up. A field of corn would be ready to harvest in a couple of weeks. Someone needed to service the combines, and manage the temporary workers his father had hired to help with their three hundred acres.

What he couldn't tell Jenny and Walter was he wouldn't be around to help them. In a week, Auriel would come for him. Even if he survived her, Cheveyo was dying inside of him. Dane worked harder and harder to wake the guy up each day, and when his consciousness did surface in the back of his brain, his voice was nothing but a whisper. Dane didn't even try to close the steel door any more. He didn't have to. Cheveyo was a limp, wisp of a spirit, and Dane only hoped he'd find some way to save him before it was too late.

He'd told his mother he was going to go home to get some fresh clothes and make some calls regarding the farm. He also said he'd need to stop by the school in the morning to pick up his assignments. In fact, he would do all of those things, eventually, but first he had to visit Eden. Malini's text said a meeting was urgent, and she did not use the term lightly.

He arrived alone and made his way to the conference room on the second floor with haste, pausing for only a moment to greet Archibald, as the garden gnome had developed an affinity for him and snubbing a garden gnome was a particularly bad idea. Outside the door, he halted at the sharp bark of argued words.

"It's insane!" Grace yelled.

"It's our only hope," Malini countered.

"I must agree with Grace. How could you even consider it? Have you stopped to think you are giving Lucifer exactly what he wants?"

A pregnant pause piqued his curiosity. Paper rustled. Someone coughed.

"The surest way to ruin someone is to give them exactly what they want." Malini's voice was crystal clear, firm, confident. Dane had rarely heard such surety in her before.

Abigail piped up. "Malini, have you seen a future where you are successful?"

"I've seen our path but not our success," Malini responded. "You must remember that I cannot see my own future."

"So, you can't guarantee Grace's fears won't become our new reality," Master Lee added.

"In life, there are no guarantees. You know that. We've always trusted in the greater good." A hint of anger or maybe frustration laced her words. "The Soulkeepers had no guarantee Abigail would thwart Lucifer's plan last summer either, but she did. Every path is riddled with choices and consequences. For most of the last week, I've spent every waking hour working this out. I am certain we cannot afford to be reactive any longer. The time has come for us to take up the gauntlet."

Grace made a noise like a cynical grunt.

Eavesdropping wasn't Dane's forte. Time to face this thing head on. He knocked three times.

When the door opened, Gideon stood on the other side, looking tired, as if he was coming down with something. He didn't say hello, but nodded his head slightly before moving out of the way. His eyes shifted downward. Had Dane done something wrong?

Inside, the others acted just as strange. Grace and Master Lee fidgeted, eyes shifting away, fingers knotting together. Lillian's shoulders slumped forward. He'd seen people look like this before, but he couldn't put his finger on when. At the window behind them, Abigail turned to fix him with an almost icy stare, worthy of her days as a fallen angel. Malini, leaning up against the credenza, was the only one to give him a warm, although small, smile. The room was eerily quiet, and he hesitated to say hello, afraid to break whatever spell rendered them silent.

"Hello, Dane," Malini murmured. "I'm sorry for the tension. What we must talk about isn't easy and concerns you."

"This concerns all of us," Grace snapped, shooting daggers at Malini.

Again, the thick silence rolled through the room like a tide.

"Well, if it concerns me, I'm ready to hear it," Dane said.

Malini pushed off the credenza and gestured toward one of the chairs at the table. "Please, sit."

He shook his head. "I prefer to stand. I spent a lifetime in a fetal position on a slab of brimstone. Never again. From now on, I face my challenges head on, standing on my own two feet."

"Understandable." Malini rubbed her hands together in the way she did when she had something difficult to say. Her small brown palms pressed together in front of her ribcage, one slightly on top of the other, sliding back and forth in a slow rhythm.

"Out with it," he insisted, his eyes drilling into her. He didn't have time for this. Not with a Soulkeeper dying in the back of his head and a Watcher coming for him in a matter of days.

Malini nodded. "Your gift is exceptionally powerful, Dane. One I struggled to understand at first."

"Yeah."

"You can borrow Soulkeeper powers for a time, and who knows what else."

"Yeah."

"In seven days, Auriel is going to show up at the back of your property, and she's going to expect you to have me with you. She'll want to take both of us to Nod, where she will likely imprison me and try to kill you and Cheveyo."

"The problem at hand," Dane muttered.

"We've spent enough time reacting to Lucifer's attacks, dodging his advancing trickery. The Soulkeepers need to take the offensive. The time has come for us to attack him where he lives."

Dane placed his hands on his hips and tilted his head inquisitively.

"I want you to be our Trojan horse." Malini took a step toward him, not breaking eye contact. "I want to allow Auriel to take us to Nod and attack the Watchers from the inside."

His mouth dropped open. He closed it. Reaching behind him, he pulled out the chair he'd said he didn't want or need and allowed his knees to give out. He plunked down hard. Minutes ticked by in silence until laughter rumbled from his chest, breaking the spell.

"You must be joking!" he cried.

She shook her head. "You can borrow the other Soulkeepers' powers. Every Watcher we kill is one less in Lucifer's arsenal. He can't make new followers unless an angel is dumb enough to fall from grace. We hit him where he lives and scare the Watchers underground again. It's the only way."

"No ... No ... you must be joking! Having Lillian's weapons gift inside of me for an hour was one thing. Sure, my power gave me her instincts but not her experiences. Who knows if I could actually do anything with her gift in a combat situation? But to hold six separate gifts inside of my head, along with Cheveyo, and somehow use them to our advantage seems incredibly optimistic. I get the Trojan horse thing, Malini, but this is farfetched, even for you."

"Not six. Bonnie and Samantha's gift is shared between the two and wouldn't be useful to you. Plus we need them to carry on the Soulkeeper line should we fail."

"We don't know if I can hold more than one power at a time."

"You had Lillian's and Cheveyo's."

"We don't know how long it will last."

"You've had Cheveyo for a week."

"We don't know if I'm strong enough to wield that kind of power in a battle situation."

"We can practice. We have seven days for you to learn how to fight."

"If I die in Nod, the Soulkeepers could lose their powers."

"Yes."

"And their Healer!"

"Yes."

Close now, she met his eyes with her warm chocolate ones and seemed to look right into his soul.

"I'm not strong enough, Malini."

"You are stronger than you think. The world needs a hero, Dane, and everything in me tells me you're him. Do you think I'd risk my life if I didn't believe we had a chance?"

"A small chance," Grace said. "A tiny chance. You will be surrounded by thousands of Watchers. No matter how many of them you take out, the chances of getting out of Nod alive are next to nothing."

Lillian cocked her head to the side. "Why do you have to do that, Grace?"

"What?"

"Ride Malini like that. Do you think if she saw any other way she'd be putting Dane or herself at risk? You have the least to lose but are making the most noise."

Grace huffed. "Least to lose? If she fails, we lose our Healer! It will be up to the girls and me to continue the fight on our own. What kind of position does that put us in?"

"The only position we have a choice to be in," Abigail stated, turning from the window. "We are Soulkeepers. Malini is right. We have to be proactive. We can't hide safely in Eden while Lucifer has his way with human souls."

"Says the woman who hides safely in Eden," Grace snarked.

Gideon took a step toward her. "Don't you think if we had any power we'd be on the front lines? Administering this school is the best way for us to help right now. Out there, at war, we'd be a liability. Lucifer has spent more than a millennium trying to get his hooks into Abigail, and you know it."

Master Lee leaned back in his chair and threaded his fingers across his stomach. "I think what Grace is trying to say is that all of us are in this together. It is her prerogative to worry for Malini and Dane as much as for her own life and the Soulkeepers in general. We all know this is a long shot, practically a suicide mission. Something this serious is worthy of discussion by the council."

Dane slapped his hand down on the table. Six pairs of eyes swung in his direction. "I'll go first. I can't do this. My father is ill and in the hospital. I have three hundred acres of corn that need to be harvested in a matter of weeks. I've already missed too much school. And there is no way..." He swallowed hard. "There is no way I'm going back to Hell. I'm sorry, Malini. I just can't."

He might have been mistaken, but he could have sworn Malini paled slightly before an emotionless mask snapped into place. She glanced from one council member to the next, but no one, not even Abigail, would meet her eyes.

"Well then, I respectfully request the council come up with a plan to deal with Auriel. While you are at it, you should know that Harrington Enterprises has contaminated water with elixir all over the country. As far as I can tell,

Lucifer is just waiting for the right moment to make his move, and he's primed for invasion."

Dane's head snapped up, and six pairs of eyes locked on Malini.

"How will Dane's likely death and your capture possibly stop that?" Grace asked cynically.

"The Watchers are a self-serving breed. We take out enough of them, and Lucifer will be afraid to put any more of his limited followers at risk. He'll pull the ones who are topside back to regroup."

"You hope," Master Lee chimed in.

Malini nodded slowly. "Oh, and Dane," Malini said, "I worry you won't make it to harvest with Cheveyo rotting inside your head." She didn't say it in a mean way, just matter of fact. And she was right. Dane had forgotten all about the wisp of a soul at the back of his skull. Maybe his mistake was thinking he could go backward in time, to before he was a Soulkeeper. Things weren't so simple anymore.

Breathing deeply in the awkward silence that ensued, Dane spread his fingers on the table. He realized now where he had seen the expressions around him before, the slumped shoulders and shifting eyes. People at funerals acted this way. This was a preemptive funeral ... his.

"It seems my life isn't my own anymore," he said. "Malini is right; I need to get Cheveyo's body back. He's dying inside my head. I can barely wake him up anymore. There's some poetic justice to using Lucifer's scheme against him. We need to send a message that if he messes with us, we'll mess with him. And you're right, Malini, this is our one advantage. Lucifer doesn't know about me or Cheveyo."

"What are you saying?" Grace asked.

Dane sighed. "I'm saying, in the grand scheme of things, three hundred acres of corn is less important than who knows how many souls." He ran a thumb over his eyebrow. "She's right, I'm probably dead anyway if I don't get Cheveyo out of me."

A tear escaped Malini's eye, and she wiped it away. This wasn't easy for her, and it was her life on the line too.

He looked Grace directly in the eye. "I'm saying, I'm in."

Lillian placed a hand over her heart. "Let's put it to a vote. If we are going to do this, I need to start training with Dane as soon as possible. All those in favor?"

A terribly long time passed before the first hand went up.

Chapter 25
Lost

After a surreal moment of watching each member of the council reluctantly agree, one by one, to his mission, Dane found himself in the atrium of the school staring up at the mural of Adam and Eve. Weak-kneed and somewhat dazed, he tried to focus as two words kept crawling through his brain: seven days. A week seemed a short time to live. He'd known something like this was coming since he'd used the red stone. He'd even invited death on occasion to save him from having to deal with his feelings for Ethan and his problems on the farm. But now that a time and date were involved, he was less enthusiastic about the idea of cutting out early on the people he loved.

"Awfully small fig leaf, don't you think?" Beside him, Ethan's mischievous smirk made him seem younger than his nineteen years.

Dane's throat constricted, and try as he might he couldn't return his friend's smile.

"What? What's wrong, Dane? You look like someone died."

Words failed him. Anyway, he wasn't supposed to say anything. Lillian would tell everyone about the council's plan at the same time. But, for reasons Dane didn't want to admit, opening up to Ethan seemed critical in a last-chance-ever kind of way. His pulse throbbed at his neck, and his eyes prickled with the intensity of his need to come clean. With his breath caught in his throat, he just didn't know where to start.

As always, Ethan responded as if hardwired to Dane's brain. He pulled Dane into a hug and whispered into his ear, "It's going to be all right. Whatever happened, I'm here for you. It'll be okay."

Dane hugged him back, hard, thinking he didn't deserve this kind of love. That's what this was, love. He was sure of it now. The way Ethan was there for him unconditionally, knowing his feelings might never be returned and not giving a damn about himself. Auriel found Ethan's feelings for Dane repulsive. What other proof did he need they were true?

"Ethan!" Lillian jogged toward them, tagging his friend's shoulder. "Lecture hall, now."

Meeting his gaze, Ethan gestured in the direction of the room.

Dane shook his head. "Just you this time." He didn't need to go. The other Soulkeepers would need space and time when they realized the repercussions.

Vexed by this news, Ethan trudged toward the lecture hall, eyes narrowing before they tore away. Dane watched the others siphon through the door and decided he couldn't stand to be still a moment longer—not when he wanted to climb out of his own skin. Instead, he decided a long walk in the garden would be the best prescription for his nervous energy.

* * * * *

Jacob emerged from the lecture hall nearing hysterics. Lillian hadn't even finished sharing the council's plan, but he couldn't hear any more. The proposed mission was choking him, and he wouldn't breathe again until he could talk some sense into Malini.

"Where is she?" he demanded from Archibald, almost plowing into the gnome as he rushed from the lecture hall.

"Down by the docks, Master Jacob," the gnome said.

Jacob didn't say thank you. No time for pleasantries.

"Jacob!" Abigail called from behind him.

He shook his head and shot her a deadly glare on his way out the door. "How could you, Dr. Silva? How *dare* you?"

She stopped short as if he'd gut punched her. Well, she deserved that if she'd had any part in this.

Jacob raced for the dock and found Malini sitting cross-legged in front of the water. He should have guessed she'd be here. This is where she came to meditate and contemplate the hard choices she had to make. He didn't even attempt to move quietly into her serene space. He stomped toward her, heart pounding, breath coming in pants, and scooped her up into his arms.

"No, Malini. No. I won't let you do this. Not this time," he fumed. Tears stormed his cheeks unchecked. There was no way she could survive this, and he wouldn't, he couldn't, let her go.

"Jacob," Malini said sympathetically, "this is who I am and what I have to do. A leader has to be the first to serve."

"No." He shook his head. "It would be one thing if I could go with you. We could die together. That's how it's supposed to be. But this is too much to ask of me. I can't sit here, powerless, waiting to find out if you live or die. I *won't*." He sobbed openly.

"You have to, Jacob. There's a chance, if they kill Dane, your power will return to you, and the world will need you even more."

He cupped her face in his hands, running his thumbs along her jawline. "I don't care about the world, Malini! Don't you see how wrong this is? We're supposed to graduate together and go off to the same college, then get married and have a dozen Soulkeeper children. You are supposed to be our queen, our Healer, the one we protect at all costs."

Despondent, Malini wrapped her hands around Jacob's on her cheeks. "It's a beautiful future you paint for us, Jacob, but what if Lucifer decides to set up shop topside? We won't graduate because we'll be too busy surviving, and if we have children someday, we'll constantly live in fear they'll be *eaten* by the enemy. We need to send a message to the devil that if he messes with our world, we'll mess with his."

"It hurts." Jacob rubbed his chest over his heart.

"I know." Malini placed her hand over his on his chest and a wave of warmth and light flowed through him. It was impossible to stay sullen with that type of joy pumping into him, and, even though he knew it was the effect of her power, he wiped his eyes and managed a small, uneven smile.

* * * * *

Dane was lost. He was sure he'd come out of the jungle near the pineapple-shaped palm tree. Only, once he'd taken a few running steps down the white sandy beach he'd happened upon, every palm tree looked like a pineapple. Considering the path he'd traversed from the school was overgrown and barely visible, finding it again without a landmark proved a challenge. So, he ran, panting, until he couldn't run anymore, and then planted his rear on a large piece of driftwood. Who knew that on this side of Eden there was an ocean? Waves rolled in, foamed across the sand to the toes of his shoes, and then receded, leaving seaweed and seashells behind.

"The Divine Sea. So good to see a student enjoying it again."

Dane started at the sight of Archibald sitting next to him, the brim of his pointy green hat rotating through the pads of his meaty fingers. When did he get here?

"Hello, Archibald. I'm so happy to see you." He meant to add *because I'm lost* but stopped short at the gnome's widening grin. He didn't think he should qualify the greeting. It was enough, for now, simply to appreciate the gnome's presence.

"Always happy to see *you*, Master Dane."

"You can call me Dane, Archibald. It's okay with me."

The gnome's eyes widened. If his smile got any broader, his face would split in two. "Oh, thank you. You are very kind to Archibald. Always very kind."

Dane tried to think of something to talk about, to be polite, before he asked for directions back to the school. "So ... did students come here often before the school closed?"

"Oh, yes. They liked to surf and have bonfires. Those were the days when every room in Eden was full, before the war."

"Right. The war. So everyone left Eden to fight, and no one came back. They must have won though because Earth wasn't invaded."

"Some came back, but the school was never the same, and human lives are short anyway."

"Oh." Dane grimaced at the thought of how short his human life had become.

"I didn't mean to upset you, Master—er, Dane. Despite your short lives, you humans are dreadfully important. It's an honor for us gnomes to serve you."

"Uh, thanks."

Dane tapped his feet together, watching sand sprinkle down to the beach. As soon as his shoes were clean, he set them right back down. "I'm going to Nod with Malini to save Cheveyo's body and kill as many Watchers as possible in the process. She's hoping to send a warning, to force the Watchers back into hiding. They're too close to the surface again." He hadn't meant to dump, but the words flowed out like spilled milk. "I'll probably die."

Archibald nodded, keeping his eyes on the ocean. "Soulkeepers will always win against Lucifer because of their self-sacrifice. Watchers find virtue repellent."

"Yeah. I'm hoping."

"You are a powerful Soulkeeper."

Dane turned his head to stare at the gnome's ear. The corners of Archibald's mouth twitched downward.

"How much do you know about what I can do?"

"Gnomes know our Soulkeepers. We have excellent hearing and eyesight. Perceptive too."

"So you know that I can borrow gifts?"

"Yes. And that you are greatly loved."

"Loved?"

"Yes."

Dane stiffened, and tears threatened the corners of his eyes.

"True love is a powerful thing," Archibald said in a low grumble. "Love, friendship, self-sacrifice, kindness, courage, commitment—these are the true gifts of the Soulkeepers. The rest, the power, is just a seasoning to bring out the flavor."

Without thinking, Dane tossed an arm across Archibald's shoulders, disregarding that he'd surely be scuffed with dirt by the action as gnomes were always covered in the garden they tended. He didn't care. Archibald had given him the perspective he needed to do what he had to do. Even if this mission meant his death, stopping the Watchers might be the most important thing he would ever do for the world. This place and these people were worth saving.

"Thank you, Archie," Dane said. "You're a good friend." He released the gnome and stood from the log, resisting the urge to brush off the streak of dirt that had, in fact, gathered down the side of his shirt.

Archibald gave a small smile and nodded, blinking his eyes slowly.

"Can you show me how to get back to the school?" Dane asked.

"Of course, Mast—er, Dane." Archibald flipped his pointy hat on top of his head and led the way into the jungle.

Chapter 26
Doppelganger

Back inside the grand entryway of Eden, Dane was met with a flurry of tears and hugs from the twins and Ghost, and a smattering of ill-aligned anger from Jacob and Ethan. In fact, Ethan looked slightly murderous with his arms crossed over his black T-shirt. He wouldn't meet Dane's eyes, and his countenance was cold as ice.

"Dane, Samantha and I are going to help," Bonnie said. "You can't borrow our power, but we have an idea."

Rending his attention away from Ethan, he looked into Bonnie's emerald green eyes. "What?"

She scanned him from head to toe, stepped back and reached for her sister. He glanced at Malini, but the Healer didn't seem to be any more informed about this idea than

Dane was. She approached to stand next to him as the sisters melded together, their flesh taking on the consistency of worked clay, rounding into a pale cocoon. When they hatched from their metamorphosis, Dane had to catch himself on the jewel-encrusted wall. One of them, he couldn't tell if it had been Bonnie or Samantha, looked exactly like him and the other, Malini's twin.

"We're going to take over your family life while you're gone," they said in unison. "So you don't have to disappear again."

"I'll take care of your mom and the farm as well as I can. And keep you in school," the other Dane said in Bonnie's voice.

"And I'll do my best to blend in with the Guptas," the other Malini said in Samantha's voice.

Malini placed her hand over her heart. "Can you do the voices?"

"Can you do the voices?" the other Malini mimicked, placing a hand over her heart.

"Oh. My. God," Jacob said, staring between the two. "Something about how she moves her hand is slightly different, but I don't think anyone will notice. Believe me, I'm having trouble."

Malini narrowed her eyes at him. "You had better remember she's not me."

Jacob gave her a twisted grin. "Would never happen, but you'd better stay alive to make sure."

"You'll have to help her," Malini said. "She doesn't know my parents or my family history. You'll have to help her be me, Jacob."

"It's a good thing we're inseparable then." Jacob approached Malini, tucking her into his side and kissing her forehead.

Dane was momentarily distracted by the intimacy. No matter how close Samantha resembled Malini, Jacob would never be able to fake the closeness between them. With any luck, their family and friends would assume they were going through a rough patch.

"What about Bonnie?" Ghost asked. "How will she blend into Dane's life? She probably doesn't even know how to drive a combine."

"Maybe I can fake it? How hard could it be?" Bonnie said.

"I'll help her," Ethan interjected.

Dane met his eyes and jerked at the turmoil behind them. His tight throat made a noise like a whimper.

"I'm the only one who can. I know all about your family, I've helped on the farm before, and we're friends so your mom won't be surprised I'm helping you."

"Are you all sure you want to do this?" Malini asked.

"Hell yes. This is the only way we can contribute," Samantha said. "Plus, I need out of this place. I'm going stir crazy here. It makes sense for us to do this."

Malini ran a hand through her hair. "Does your mom know about this?"

Bonnie and Samantha exchanged furtive glances.

"I do," Grace said from the shadow of the hallway. Dane wasn't sure how long she'd been standing there, but surely she'd been in the lecture hall during the briefing.

"Grace," Malini said. All eyes fixated on the redheaded woman.

"I know, I know, I've given you a terrible time lately. I'd say I'm sorry, but I'm not. This work we do deserves scrutiny. The decisions we make need to be challenged. This is our course, and my daughters have been keen to enlighten me on their desire to be of service. I approve, and I will help them for as long as needed."

Malini's eyes darted from face to face, her lips pressing together. She straightened and linked her hands in front of her hips. "Well, today there are only heroes in Eden. Bonnie and Samantha, please proceed with your plan. I believe Dane's mom is waiting at the hospital for some things from home. He can brief you before you go."

Dane nodded.

"We need to get started with Dane's training right away," Lillian said. "I'd like to add one power at a time until D-day. Who wants to go first?"

All eyes turned toward Ethan. Was it so obvious that he was the most likely candidate? The person who wouldn't stall at being the first, the guinea pig.

Ethan slid his hands into the back pockets of his jeans. "I'm ready." His voice broke a little. "Let's do this."

Dane met his gaze and swallowed hard. Good Lord, this was actually happening. His stomach fluttered as he approached Bonnie to tell her the basics about his family, his father's illness, and the hospital where she would find them. And then, his doppelganger walked out the front door to take over his life.

* * * * *

Inside Lillian's dojo, Dane paced with his hands on his hips, avoiding eye contact with Ethan by counting the weapons on the wall. Neither of them could hold still, and nervous energy ricocheted off the walls. The thought of taking Ethan's gift was both exciting and terrible. A Soulkeeper's power was a sizeable part of their identity, a part of their soul, and Ethan's gift had saved his life once when he was younger. He'd been beaten badly for being gay, and his telekinesis had protected him. If Dane took it, he might not be able to defend himself.

"I don't want to do this," Dane said.

Lillian gave him a disappointed scowl. "This isn't the time for cold feet, Dane."

"It just seems cruel, stripping him of his power like this." Dane shifted from foot to foot and crossed his arms over his chest as if his hands might accidentally bump into Ethan and steal his gift.

For his part, Ethan was twitchy and wide-eyed. Dane could practically hear the guy's heart pounding across the room, and despite his recent revelation he might want to be the cause of that particular physical reaction, this was far from the reason he had in mind.

"Just do it," Ethan said. "All of this … waiting is just making it worse."

"I don't want—"

"Dane! Come on. Nothing you can say is going to make this easier. I'm here, and you have my permission, so take my gift."

"Lillian, would you give me a moment alone with Ethan?" Dane asked.

She seemed reluctant, glancing between the two of them, but eventually caved. "Okay. I'm going to go get some water."

Dane waited a moment, watching his friend. Only, *friend* didn't seem like a strong enough word, and in the end, he decided now was the perfect time to tell him so. If he was expected to take his power, it seemed only fair that Dane leave him something in return. He'd known for a long time he had feelings for Ethan; he just couldn't admit them to himself before. But now, faced with his impending and probable death, he didn't have the luxury of denial. If he was going to tell Ethan, it was now or never.

With intensity and purpose, Dane charged forward, jaw tight. He reached for Ethan, sliding his fingers behind the nape of his neck. There was no thinking, no analysis, only feeling as Dane's mouth crashed into Ethan's.

Everything stopped.

For a moment, he thought he might have misinterpreted Ethan's signals. His lips were hard, his body frozen, even fearful. But only for a moment. Ethan responded, his strong hands gripping Dane's hips and pulling him closer, setting the two of them off balance. He retreated, taking Dane with him until his back smacked the wall. With equal parts passion and abandon, he returned the kiss, pressing into Dane's mouth hard enough to leave a bruise.

For months, they'd been friends. For months, they'd carried a torch for each other. Ethan was his other, and his heart almost broke that he'd waited so long to admit it. Ethan shifted against his mouth, completely lost in the kiss, and that was when Dane took his gift.

Under his skin, the power shifted, the telekinesis slipping over his tongue like a hot drink on a cold day. The transfer sent shock waves through both their bodies. The energy of the exchange broke them apart, both panting from the experience. Ethan's eyes shifted to the floor, and Dane realized that he might think the kiss was simply how Dane exercised his power or a clever distraction to numb the effect.

Dane had to set him straight. There was only one thing he could say.

"You're the first to know." He shrugged.

Ethan's face relaxed as the words settled in, and Dane remembered how he demanded to be the first to know.

"You are…?" Ethan prompted.

"Falling in love with you. Yeah. I think that's the only label that matters."

A radiant smile broke across Ethan's face but was soon replaced by fear and dread. "We've got to get you out of here. You can't do this. It's suicide."

"I have to, Ethan." Dane blinked slowly. He'd thought they were beyond this.

"No, you don't. We could sneak away. I've got money on the outside, plenty. You could shove Cheveyo into the first human body we come across, and you and I could leave this place and never look back."

With a shake of his head, Dane cracked a sad smile. "As tempting as that sounds, we both know it's not going to happen."

"Why?"

"Because you're not that person anymore."

To Dane's utter disappointment, Ethan jerked away. "I'm glad you told me first," he said. "But I can't do this now."

Confused, Dane spread his hands. "Right now is all I got, Ethan."

"Bullshit. I fully expect you to kick Watcher ass and come back home ... to me. We're not done with this conversation."

Ethan stormed out the door, passing Lillian on her way back in. She crunched her eyebrows together and turned to Dane expectantly.

"It's done," Dane said. With a little effort, he used Ethan's power to flip a horrifically large knife off the wall and into Lillian's hand.

With an elated wail, she forgot all about Ethan and attacked.

Chapter 27
Transfer

As much as Dane would have liked to spend more time with Ethan before he went to his probable death, Ethan had no interest in long goodbyes. He left the following morning at sunrise, telling only Dr. Silva of his plans. He'd gone to help Bonnie but promised her he'd check in after Dane and Malini began their mission. His absence stung, but Dane understood. Ethan had always been protective, and if he stayed, especially if things between them advanced, he'd never be able to let him go.

Luckily, Dane had enough to keep him occupied from the loss that weighed his chest like a barbed anchor. After Ethan had left the dojo, he'd sparred with Lillian, using his new telekinesis until a migraine hit him so fast and hard he thought he might die. He'd been able to sleep the pain away, but a new day meant a new gift. Time for him to continue his training.

Ghost volunteered to go next. He blinked into the dojo without notice and scared Lillian half to death.

"Damn it, Ghost! I hate when you do that!" she yelled.

He chuckled and pointed his chin toward Dane. "Hey, he doesn't have to kiss me for this to work, right? Because from what I saw yesterday, I don't think I could handle the heat."

Embarrassment flamed up Dane's cheeks. "You friggin' eavesdropper!"

"It's what I do." Ghost's smug attitude filled the room.

Lillian ignored the exchange. "Let's hustle boys. Dane and I need time to practice after the exchange."

"My pleasure." Dane struck quickly, snatching Ghost's bare wrist and yanking his power from him in the metaphysical equivalent of arm wrestling. Compared to Ethan, whose gift had tasted like a hot beverage, Ghost's was all grit and ice. The flow chilled his fingers, and Dane released him promptly as soon as the transfer was complete.

"Oh." Lillian gaped in their direction.

Ghost's eyes were blue, instead of their usual purple, and his dishwater blond hair was now honey brown with platinum highlights. He was tan, and the red Quicksilver shirt he wore stood out against the wood grain and white rice paper of the dojo. Ghost was no longer a ghost. He was *stunning*, more than noticeable.

"Huzzah," Dane said, allowing his mouth to drop open.

"What you said," Ghost murmured. "Lillian, do you think the Watchers will notice his eyes?"

Eyes? Dane leaned left to see his reflection in the wall mirror. His body looked blurry, nondescript even, and his eyes were … purple.

Lillian shook her head. "I'll ask Grace to get him some contacts to be sure. He's forgettable this way."

"True." Ghost smiled. "Hmm. Gives me an idea of showing Samantha how unforgettable I really am." He made a face like he had to go to the bathroom.

"Are you okay?" Dane asked.

"Yeah, it's just been a really long time since I had to walk out of a room the old-fashioned way." He cleared his throat. "Old habits." He nodded his goodbyes and made a hasty retreat.

Dane spread his hands and looked at Lillian, who seemed slightly taken aback by his appearance. She composed herself and retrieved a bladed staff from the wall.

Her eyes flashed. "Don't die."

* * * * *

"You'll need to be aware of her," Jacob said the following day.

Dane had been practicing in the lab, manipulating the water in ever more creative ways while Jacob coached him with tips and advice. They'd decided to take a break when Dane's head started to throb, a sure sign he was pushing his limits again. Every day he'd added a power, but every day the length of time he could wield them grew shorter. He felt stretched to the limit, and although he wanted to listen to what Jacob had to say, he struggled through the pounding hammer in his brain.

"Say again," he slurred.

"You'll need to be aware of Malini. She won't be careful with herself. Your job, well, my job through you, is to care for her. Use the water to heal her if she burns herself."

"I'll do my best." Dane cradled his head in his hands.

"No," Jacob insisted, yanking his arm so that his head jarred painfully. "Do better than your best. I'm not fooling around here, Dane. You've got to be willing to die for her."

Dane turned his head to scowl at Jacob.

"I'm not kidding. It sounds harsh, and I'm sorry your life is on the line. I'd go in your place if I could, believe me. But she's more important than you or our powers. Do what you have to do to get her out alive."

What did he think, anyway? Dane wasn't doing this for his health. He'd resolved that he would die on this mission. Of course he'd give his life for Malini if he needed to. He took a deep breath and nodded for Jacob's benefit.

"Cool. Maybe you should go lie down or something. You don't look so good."

"I don't feel so good."

"Do you think … Is it Cheveyo?"

"I don't think so. I haven't heard anything from him in days, but he's still alive in there, at the back of my head. He's just too weak to communicate with me anymore."

"What happens if he dies?"

"No one knows."

Jacob swallowed. "Everything will work out," he said, but he didn't look like he believed his words. Not at all.

* * * * *

Dane wasn't sleeping well. All the stuff he had going on in his head, the new powers and Cheveyo's soul, fought for room against the synapses and neurons keeping his body running. Dark circles had formed under his eyes, and his training sessions had grown shorter and shorter. He'd tried his best, but there was only so much he could give before his body quit on him.

As Friday grew closer, he became competent with each of the skills provided him. Lillian, as head of field operations, had given up her gift last, and with some reluctance turned his training over to Master Lee. The man was older but spry. Though Dane would never admit the truth to Lillian, Lee was a more empathetic teacher.

"Your nose is bleeding," Lee said, grabbing a towel from the stack near the door of the dojo and tossing it to him. They'd been training for only three hours, but Dane's body was already breaking down.

"Yeah, my head is pounding too. I've got to sit down."

Master Lee helped him to the floor.

"I'm not getting stronger, Lee. I'm falling apart. I'm not sure I can do this."

Lee took a seat next to him on the wood floor. "Breathe with me, Dane, in and out, in and out. Life is breath."

Dane did as he suggested, closing his eyes and opening his lungs.

"What you have to hold inside yourself is greater than your human body can handle. You have pieces of four souls and Cheveyo caught inside the web of your mind. The mind is a powerful thing, tightly connected to the heart and soul. If you survive this, it will be by the power of your spirit, not of your body. Your spirit is bigger than your body."

"No offense, but I feel like even my spirit has a nosebleed these days," Dane said, mopping his face.

Patiently, Lee sat in silence until the bleeding stopped.

"Should we practice some more?" Dane asked.

"Not fighting." Lee shook his head. "Sit like this, cross-legged."

Dane obeyed, mimicking the man.

"Relax your head, your arms, your neck, your shoulders, and try to clear your mind."

"Clearing my mind isn't easy these days. It's pretty crowded in there."

"Breathe," Lee said again. "Relax. Clear. Close your eyes."

Again, Dane tried, and this time pictured the web of his mind and the five souls caught in the crisscrossing fibers. The spider woman climbed into his thoughts and began to weave, expanding the network of threads. His body was weak, but this part of him, heart, soul, and mind, was limitless. Red and pulsating, the web expanded beyond the confines of his skin.

Inside this inner world behind his eyelids, he simply stopped thinking, stopped worrying about how he might die tomorrow, stopped beating himself up about not pursuing Ethan when he had the chance, and stopped dreading what might happen if he did live and had to deal with his family and the farm. He just stopped.

Spider Woman smiled.

When he opened his eyes, the room was dark, Lee was gone, and Malini was standing in the doorway.

"Lee told me you'd be here," she said softly. "I hope I didn't disturb you."

He stretched his arms above his head and cracked his neck. "How long have I been sitting here?"

"About twelve hours, I think. It's after midnight. I had a sense you were coming out of it. With all of those pieces of Soulkeeper inside of you, the Healer in me can smell you a mile away." She smiled.

"Sunshine and honey, I hope."

"Absolutely."

He stood and walked to her, the wood boards creaking in the quiet room.

"We leave tomorrow," she said. *Are you ready?*

Dane heard Malini's thoughts in his head as clearly as if she'd said them out loud.

I'm not sure a person can be ready for this. But I'm not backing down.

Good. She led the way into the hall.

"So, what's with the telepathy?" he asked.

"I can communicate with the thoughts of anyone who's used the stone. I wanted to test my connection with you. I have a feeling we'll need it."

"Almost guaranteed," Dane responded. He offered her his elbow, and she hooked her hand inside. "I'll be honest, Malini, the thought of facing Auriel, after what she did to me, is horrifying. My time in Hell—"

"I know, Dane, you don't have to say it."

"But I'm glad I can do this. I've never been so proud to be a Soulkeeper." He cleared his throat. "If we pull this off, Nod will be my revenge. I'm not looking forward to seeing Auriel, but I am looking forward to killing her."

Malini smiled. "That's the spirit! Now, let's get some sleep. Tomorrow is going to be a very big day."

Dane agreed, releasing her arm to move toward the east wing. Truth was he didn't feel tired anymore. If he could describe what he felt at the moment in one word, it would be *vengeful*, and although it surprised him to no end, he was almost anxious to exercise that particular emotion.

Chapter 28
Into Shadow

Friday, high noon, Dane led Malini across his parents' property with a knife in her back. It helped that his doppelganger, Bonnie, had confirmed she was with his family at the hospital. He was confident they were alone.

"I thought Archibald might not let go of your hand this morning," Malini whispered in an obvious attempt to lift the mood.

"Yeah, about that…" Dane stopped talking when he saw *her*. Auriel waited by the clump of pine trees where he'd met her multiple times sophomore year. A vortex of fall wind billowed her platinum tresses as if the air around her was a different density than the rest of the atmosphere. What might have been natural if she'd been underwater, here gave away her inhumanity.

Auriel's wicked grin preceded a laugh that made Dane's skin want to climb off his body.

"You did it," she seethed, inhaling deeply. "I can smell their blood on your hands."

"You'll never get away with this," Malini sneered.

Even though Dane knew her venom was an act, her accusing stare made him squirm.

"Shut it, Healer. Be a good little monkey and put on your collar." She held up a chain with a metal ring for her neck. "I'd prefer not to touch you."

Malini didn't move. Dane made a show of pressing the knife into her back.

"Cheveyo, sweetheart, would you do the honors?" She held out the chain.

With all his will, he demanded his hand's compliance and took the leash from Auriel, fastening the collar around Malini's neck. This is what they'd signed up for. They had to allow her to take them to Nod.

Auriel brought her lips to Malini's ear. "See? Cheveyo knows how to follow a basic command. You'll learn too, even if breaking you takes Lucifer a century. Frankly, I hope I get to watch him try."

With a twist of her head, Malini slapped the side of her face into Auriel's lips and cheek. The Watcher screamed when their skin touched, Her flesh burned and bubbled. She backed off.

"You bitch!" Auriel patted her blistered skin. She gave the chain a hard yank, causing Malini's head to snap back. Dane winced. Luckily, Auriel wasn't looking at him to see his reaction.

"Come, Cheveyo, let's take this one where she belongs." She eyed Dane with disgust. "Remember, no skin to skin. I don't want your smell on me." Grasping his elbow over his gray plaid shirt, she wrapped Malini's chain around her wrist. Then, she reached for a nearby pine tree.

The pine bark shingled Auriel's arm, up over her head, and extended its wooden grip toward Dane and Malini. Everything in him begged for an escape from the advancing threat.

Relax, Dane. Breathe. This is how it works.

Even Malini's voice in his head wasn't enough to calm his panic as the tree swallowed him. He descended into the earth, pulled down through the roots of the tree, through the soil where every creepy, crawly thing seemed to sift through his cells. Relief came in the form of a bed of filthy sand in the middle of a garden of thorns. He coughed and spit from the squirming nausea.

Auriel leaned over his prone body. Her wings were out, two pearly white numbers that arced over her shoulders and swept down to her ankles. Of course, her beauty was an illusion. She was made of evil, snakeskin, and black leather. With one hand, she lifted him to his feet by the back of his shirt. The motion pushed his stomach over the edge. He puked near her feet.

"Gross," she deadpanned. As if he were contagious, she released him and backed away. "Come on, my pets. Lucifer is waiting."

Amazingly unaffected by the trip through the tree, Malini passively allowed Auriel to lead her by the neck. On the other side of a central fountain in the shape of an angel, Dane followed as Auriel led the way down a narrow path. They walked single file, twisting thorn bushes reaching for him from the sides of the trail, as well as the occasional skull.

Discretely, Malini reached back to squeeze his hand. *Just stay with me. The darkness will break when we reach Nod.*

Darkness?

She squeezed his hand again. *Dane, can you see here?*

Clear as day.

How? It's pitch black.

Archibald? He gave me something, a gift before we left. That's why he held my hand for so long when we said goodbye.

If we ever get out of this mess, I'm going to give that little guy a medal. Do you know if he gave you anything else?

Not a clue.

They walked in silence through the desert of death. At times, Dane wished he couldn't see. Dead plants, dried tangles of thorns, bones, skulls, decaying things. What would the inside of the city be like? Eventually, a fluorescent blue glow lit the horizon. Nod. The skyline was boxy and plain— steel and wood designed with all the artistry of a dog kennel. Malini's eyes blinked to adjust to the burgeoning light.

With a flick of her hand, Auriel opened the gate, dragging Malini forward by the neck. A delta of sand led to a central street area. The pavement was potholed and filthy, with all manner of junk congesting the lane. He had to work to keep from stepping in filth or on something sharp. But the Watchers seemed to take this for granted, kicking aside what they couldn't walk over. On foot, or by human-drawn rickshaw, they picked their way through the mess.

Tall buildings reached toward a skyless darkness, windows emitting the fluorescent blue that lit the city. The place smelled like a sewer, but then, with all the rotting refuse near his feet, that was no surprise. As Watchers moved between the buildings, they kicked up a dusty, dirty fog. Ironically, Nod was at odds with the appearance of its inhabitants. Watchers were illusionists and their collective beauty momentarily stunned Dane. Each one looked as if they'd just walked off the pages of a designer underwear catalog, tall and thin with perfect hair and fluffy angel wings.

For a moment, he wondered why creatures with wings didn't fly where they needed to go. All of them walked or rode to their destination. But then he remembered the number one rule Abigail had taught him about Watchers; they were lazy. Slothful was the word she'd used. Watchers didn't fly if they could walk and probably didn't walk if they could sit. What a disgusting waste of wings.

Auriel kept Malini close but seemed indifferent to Dane's presence, maybe because she believed Cheveyo was influenced and would follow along like a trained puppy.

Whatever the reason, from behind he had a panoramic view of the moment the city of Watchers noticed them. When the crowd turned, one by one, to see Malini on the end of Auriel's chain, the menace on their faces was far from beautiful. The bustling city of Nod stopped. The street became as quiet as a tomb.

"All hail, the great and powerful Healer!" Auriel bellowed sarcastically.

The crowd whooped and howled. They approached tentatively, circling Malini, taunting her, eyes wide and unbelieving. Dane stepped back, using Ghost's unique ability to blend into the crowd while staying close enough to keep an eye on her. He wasn't invisible, just easily forgettable, which made it difficult to be brave as they closed in around her.

A blond male picked up a piece of garbage from the street, a bone Dane preferred to imagine was an animal's, and hurled it at Malini. The heavy object struck her in the chest. The impact must've hurt, but she didn't call out or struggle. Malini gave no reaction at all.

Others joined in, fueled by each other. They pummeled her. Watchers couldn't touch Malini without burning their skin, but that didn't stop them. All manner of rotting trash, thorny sticks, and the bones of the dead became her affliction. Dane couldn't take it anymore. Calling Ethan's power, he deflected the worst of it from her face.

Not yet, Dane.

He had to look away to obey her.

Finally, Auriel put an end to the attack. "To the throne room! Lucifer will want to play with his prize." The crowd cheered, moving as one to an exceptionally tall glass and steel monolith on their right. He thought the taunting would stop, but it didn't. His heart sank as a thick lock of her hair drifted through the crowd and landed near his shoes. Had they ripped it out or cut it off?

Malini?

Find Cheveyo. Then, come back for me.

Even her thoughts sounded miserable and resigned. The horror in his chest turned to anger. He dropped back, allowing the Watchers to swarm around him, pushing and shoving toward the glass doors.

"So we meet again, Cheveyo," a voice said from beside him. A redheaded Watcher with an evil grin looked at him through suspiciously long lashes. One of her wings was crippled, smaller, hanging limp at her back. He thought this odd considering the Watcher's illusive abilities but tried not to seal his death sentence by staring.

Cheveyo! Cheveyo! Who is this? He mentally shook the wisp at the back of his skull.

No answer came to him. But then, Cheveyo hadn't woken up in days. He was on his own.

"His Royal Darkness has asked me to give you your reward," she said cynically, "while everyone else gets to celebrate. Come on."

Obediently, he followed her through the city to a train, the likes of which he'd never seen before. Transparent, made of glass or some other such material, the passengers and their human slaves were clearly visible as the train came to a stop on the platform. Dane cringed at the sight. Evil. That was the only word to describe the behavior within. The doors opened. Watchers lashed at their human slaves to get them to move. Some did. Others, too bloody and broken to obey, were dragged, half-conscious, from the train. Their blood smeared the street.

Dane wanted to fight. He lowered his head and stuffed his anger down deep. Soon. Very soon, he'd show these demons exactly what he could do.

He allowed the redhead to lead him to an empty car. Dane supposed the other Watchers had exited to join the celebration of Malini's capture. He attempted to sit down on one of the empty seats, but she tugged him to standing by his hair.

"Humans don't sit," she hissed.

The rumble of movement had him reaching for the pole at the center of the car. Luckily, she didn't say anything else as they advanced, or tell him where they were going. Dane took the opportunity to close his eyes and focus on his breath as Master Lee had taught him. He needed to hold it together if he was going to save Malini.

Talons dug into his shoulder. "Come. Now."

Off the train and up a dirt path, she led him under an archway. With a little help from Jacob's power, he read *zoo* in the symbols above him. He'd heard about this place, the human zoo. This was where Lillian had been held captive for a year before Dr. Silva, Jacob, and Malini had rescued her. But none of the stories could prepare him for the grisly sight. Inside their filthy prisons, the humans were tragically beautiful. Every race, every color … Dane never appreciated before the art that was humanity. But here, in this ugly place of cages and rags, the souls shined like candles, even in their somewhat catatonic states.

"Here you are," the redhead said, pointing into a cage labeled Native American. "Your body."

The heap of brown flesh on the floor behind the bars stared with dead, unblinking eyes. The body looked nothing like the boy he'd seen in the In Between when he used the stone. But then, the thin, drawn shell was soulless. Dane reached for the body.

Powerful hands yanked him back. "Oh no." She laughed. "You don't get to touch it. You just get to watch it rot." With a giggle, she dragged him across the central pathway and tossed him forcibly into an open cage.

He crashed into the concrete. "Ugh!"

She slammed the door and locked the cage. "Enjoy the view. Maybe in a few weeks you'll be able to smell your own decay."

Curled on his side, Dane clutched his throbbing shoulder as she skipped away from his cage and exited under the archway.

Chapter 29
Temptation

In Eden, Dane had trained in all manner of weaponry, hand-to-hand combat, and of course using the gifts he'd borrowed. Nothing could prepare him for the despair inside his prison. Painfully, he used the bars to pull himself to a standing position. Strapped to his ankle was a flask full of holy water. All he had to do was use it to spring the lock, just as Jacob had taught him. Or he could use Ghost's gift to spread his molecules and sift through the bars. Lillian's power could kick the door open, or Ethan's could slam a rock against the lock.

But every muscle in his body ached with fatigue. He belonged here. He'd been a terrible person. He'd bullied Jacob and Malini mercilessly and almost got them killed helping Auriel. He'd led Amy Barger on, when deep inside he knew he didn't like girls. Plus, there were his parents. He was such a disappointment to his family. What would they think of him when they found out he was gay?

If he wanted to help things, he should collapse on the floor this minute and stay there. He dropped to his knees and allowed his head to loll to his chest. In this position, he couldn't help but notice a green smudge on the tail of his gray plaid shirt. A small thing, a simple thing, dirt and something green. A vivid memory of Archibald's face, his chubby hand staining the material weeks ago, filled his mind. It had been a kindness to allow him that. What had the gnome said? The mark of a Soulkeeper wasn't the power he possessed but the true gifts of kindness, loyalty, friendship, courage, and love.

The stain on his shirt reminded him of his true power. Dane raised his head to look at Cheveyo's body. He thought of Ethan, the way he'd volunteered to help Bonnie fill in with his family. Malini needed him, too. Yes, he'd done some things he wasn't proud of, and this cage was good at reminding him of those things, but his true gifts shone like stars against the backdrop of his past. Right now, he couldn't waste another minute on the darkness.

Fortunately, the zoo was empty of Watchers; he supposed they were all distracted with Malini. Channeling Ghost, he blinked through the bars and into Cheveyo's cell. With conviction, he pushed aside the neck of the rag sack the boy wore and lowered his hand to his bare chest.

"Come on, Cheveyo. Wake the hell up! It's time to go home," Dane said. He pressed his palm over the guy's heart.

The tiniest niggle wormed at the back of his skull and then stilled.

"No way, my friend. I feel you back there. You can't die on me, dude. Get the hell out of my head." Dane reached deep inside and dragged the slip of a soul out, psychically tossing Cheveyo into his own body. The flesh jerked beneath his palm and the boy gasped a bit, but nothing more. No matter how hard Dane shook Cheveyo or thumped his chest, he was unresponsive. Cheveyo's soul had entered the body. He wasn't dead. His heart beat steadily under Dane's touch, and his chest rose and fell with every breath. But something was wrong. The Soulkeeper wouldn't wake up.

"Damn. Looks like we do this the hard way." Using Jacob's water trick, Dane popped the lock to Cheveyo's cell, careful to return every drop of the precious water to his flask. With brute strength, he heaved Cheveyo over his shoulder and stepped out of the cage. At the sight of the unguarded gate, compassion for the other prisoners got the best of him. Setting Cheveyo down, he bolted from cage to cage, unlocking the doors. Even with Soulkeeper speed, it took several minutes to reach them all. Of course, none of the prisoners moved. Based on how the cage had affected Dane, he suspected the long-term residents were permanently damaged. He didn't have time to help them, but was comforted by the thought they might, somehow, be able to free themselves.

"Let's go save the princess," Dane said to Cheveyo's limp body. He rolled the boy onto his back and started walking toward the entrance. "It would be a big help if you could carry your own weight. I mean that literally. Wake the eff up and give me a hand."

Cheveyo didn't even twitch in response.

"You weighed a lot less inside my head," Dane said. He stepped into the empty train car, dumping Cheveyo's body on the seats not meant for humans. The thought made him laugh. Nod was about to learn just how many rules he intended to break.

* * * * *

"Oh, darling, I can replace this for you if you swear your allegiance to me." Lucifer pulled at the roots of Malini's hair. All that was left were the roots. They'd cut the rest off in jagged chunks. Malini didn't answer him or make eye contact. She knew better. Giving the devil the use of your words or your attention was never a good idea.

"I have to say, I'm disappointed." Lucifer paced away from her, toward Auriel, who sat on the throne rubbing her fingertips together. "I'd have thought you would fight harder. I overestimated your intelligence. Auriel and I had a bet on whether or not you'd fall for the Trojan horse routine. It's been done to death, after all. But then, you're young. You don't remember, do you?"

He returned to her in a rush and ran a long fingernail up the side of her jaw. Lucifer was a blond Michelangelo's David in a three-piece suit, attractive in a worldly way but equally deadly. He leaned his face in close to hers. "Do you know what Auriel wins for being right?" he whispered. "She gets the first taste of Healer flesh, your flesh."

The smell of death surrounded her like a fog. He might look like art, but he smelled of decay. She closed her eyes and turned her head.

Auriel cackled from the platform. "Is it too early to indulge? I bet her blood is ambrosia."

Lucifer grinned. "I'm afraid your prize is worthless. She's extra spicy."

"Oh? You think her insides will burn me the same as her outsides?" Auriel rose from her throne, adjusting the train of her gold dress behind her. She sighed and cocked her head. "What shall we do with her, if we can't eat her?"

"I think our bird deserves a gilded cage." He snapped his fingers and a gold birdcage formed around her. "We leave her in the street and go about our business while she slowly goes mad."

Auriel circled her, dragging her fingers across the bars. "Won't she die, Lucifer? We don't want another Healer to be called because we didn't feed her."

He grabbed her by the chin roughly. "Not to worry, my sweet. Healers are ultradurable and, just to be safe, I've enchanted the bars to keep her alive without food, water, sleep, or anything else for that matter. Just alive, forever."

Malini's breathing quickened. Power or no power, the thought scared her. He was effectively burying her alive.

Lucifer inhaled deeply. "Mmmm, do you smell it, Auriel? Nothing is as intoxicating as a Healer's fear."

"Yummy," she said. "But since I can't eat her, I want something else."

"What, my dear?"

"Her humiliation."

"Done."

Lucifer snapped his fingers and Malini was suddenly thankful for the cage. In the middle of Nod, thousands of Watchers closed in around her. And there was something else. The laughing and pointing wasn't just about the cage or her shorn hair. Her clothes were gone. He'd left her naked inside her gilded tomb.

Lucifer had given Auriel exactly what she'd asked for.

Chapter 30
Revenge

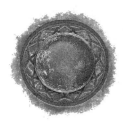

Luck was on Dane's side. The train car he'd chosen remained empty, and the few Watchers he spotted through the transparent walls seemed too distracted with their own business to notice him. Part of that could have been Ghost's gift but, considering Cheveyo was laid out on the seat, he was apt to call it good fortune. But the real test of destiny was about to occur as the train stopped in the heart of Nod, and Dane exited near the back of a swarming mass of Watchers. Fortunately, they were swarming away from him, toward something in the street.

Holy shit! Malini, in a cage! What had they done to her? Her hair was gone, and she was naked.

Dane? Dane? Oh, God, please help me.

I'm coming, Malini. Hang on.

One good thing about Malini's situation, the Watchers were completely distracted with her predicament. Dane dodged behind a building on the edge of the platform, wedging himself and Cheveyo between steel and a mass of thorny bushes. He jammed the boy's body under the branches. "Sorry, buddy. You're going to have a few scrapes, but it's my best bet for saving you. Unless you'd rather wake up and help me kill these sons of bitches?"

Cheveyo stared, unblinking.

"Okay, but you're missing all the fun."

As Jacob had taught him, Dane removed the flask from his ankle and poured the water into his hand, freezing it into the blade he was most comfortable with. Unlike Jacob's favorite broadsword, Dane, who was taller, found the long, curved blade of a katana more to his liking. He walked toward the crowd quite boldly, thinking he had one thing going for him that not even Lillian had predicted; the Watchers underestimated him.

His first strike sent two heads flying at the edge of the crowd of thousands. Destroyed, the Watchers crumpled to the sand, reduced to bubbling black pools. The other Watchers turned, panic erupting as they understood what was happening.

"Soulkeeper!" a female screeched.

"That's right," Dane growled. "Holy water. Now who's next?" He circled right, moving along the edge of the crowd to put the city wall at his back.

Red fire rained in his direction, Watcher sorcery. He used Ethan's gift to gently deter its course. It exploded harmlessly in the sand behind him. This small taste of success drove him forward into the slashing talons. Lillian's gift surfaced as he spun and delivered a roundhouse kick to an attacking Watcher's chest, flipped his sword under his arm, and sank his blade into the heart of another. The holy water did its duty, acting as an infection that spread from the inside out. The pierced Watcher imploded into ash. Dane flashed deeper into the crowd, avoiding a shower of cursed fire. He circled his blade, slicing three Watchers in half and blinking into thin air before the crowd could redirect their attack.

Watcher sorcery didn't just burn. The fire would spread in him the way his holy water blade spread through them. But thanks to Ethan, he used his mind to push and shield while attacking with his katana. Control of the ice came from Jacob, but the art with which he wielded it was all Lillian's. Wildly, he kicked, sliced, stabbed, and pushed until he was covered in black blood. He broke apart again, coming together even deeper inside the scrambling crowd.

"Dane! Behind you!" Malini yelled.

He dodged the spray of fire and relieved an ebony-haired Watcher of his head and then another of her wings. When he was knocked down, he stabbed and kicked his way back up. If he was attacked, he broke apart and came back together where they least expected. Lillian and Master Lee had taught him well. Pure instinct drove him on. The street ran with black blood.

How many had he killed? Twenty? Forty?

However many it was, the Watchers noticed, their self-serving natures kicking in. The circle around Dane widened as the fallen ran for safety, unwilling to risk their existence for each other. He made short work of the few who stayed behind. Driven by anger, they made rash errors and posed less of a challenge. He'd killed another half dozen by the time he reached the golden cage. With his back to the bars, he circled her.

Out of the corner of his eye, he saw Malini shiver. "Are you okay?"

"Dane, Lucifer is here, inside the building. You're in great danger."

Dane slashed another Watcher in two. And then, the challenge ended. None of them dared come within fifty feet. A few had flown to the tops of buildings, scanning the scene like vultures waiting for their prey to die. Others dodged inside, faces pressed to the windows. For a moment, Dane allowed himself to hope he might survive this suicide mission.

Like a wrecking ball, something big and black plowed into him, hauling him backward in the grip of a sulfur-smelling fog. When the haze settled, he was trapped behind glass like a bug. His catatonic body lay in a heap near his feet. Dane banged against the glass, but his ghostly hands were useless against his prison.

"No," he cried, as the last frozen bits of the katana melted from his body's hand into the streets of Nod.

Lucifer strode forward and delivered a kick to his lifeless ribs. "Didn't remember I could do that, Dane?" Lucifer hissed. "I've tasted your soul. I can demand it at any time." His black eyes took in the ruined streets of Nod, the black blood, ash, and writhing pieces of his army of darkness.

"You can't hold him forever," Malini said.

"I don't need forever. Just long enough to tear his body apart." Lucifer whistled. The nearest Watchers stopped their retreat and responded to his presence.

"Lucifer, how can we please you today?" a dark-haired Watcher said from a safe distance. His tone was disingenuous, and his eyes darted fearfully between Malini and Dane's soul.

"All of this trouble must have left you quite hungry. Please." Lucifer pointed a hand at Dane's body. He brushed his wavy blond hair out of his blue eyes and smiled at his minions with an artificial radiance.

Slowly, the Watcher approached. He licked his lips. Another female stepped carefully behind him.

Lucifer tapped on the glass around Dane's soul. "Enjoy the show. I know I will." With a wave of his hand, two comfortable-looking chairs appeared outside the closest building, and Auriel materialized at his side. He kissed her cheek and made himself comfortable. The Watchers took this as a sign and came out of hiding, cautiously closing in around them.

Dane stared across the mound of his body at Malini, still trapped inside her gilded cage. What was her plan? She was the Healer. She was supposed to know what to do. Right now, she just looked hopeless, collapsed in on herself in the center of her cage. Maybe it was what they'd done to her, the nudity and her hair. Or maybe the cage was like the one in the zoo, draining the hope from her. Decidedly, it didn't matter the cause; as the two Watchers closed in and more filled the street around them, he needed her to snap out of it.

Malini, come on, he yelled inside his head. *Snap out of it. Don't you want to get out of here and show Jacob that sassy new haircut?*

With her back turned to Lucifer, she began to weep. Her shoulders bobbed with each high-pitched sob.

"Malini. Don't give up on me," Dane pleaded.

The dark-haired male Watcher reached Dane's body first and used his talon to strip a patch of skin from the shoulder. He slurped it down with a smack of his lips. The female caught up to him, hissing, "Save some for me."

"Hey!" Dane yelled. "I have to live in that."

Malini's sobs picked up intensity. She stood, turning so he could see her face. She wasn't crying at all, but laughing. "Leave the boy alone, or else."

Her skeleton arm extended toward them, fingers bending, beckoning.

"Or else what? Your gift from Death can't hurt them, Healer," Lucifer said, rolling his eyes. "They're not alive."

"Neither are the people you've killed and buried here." Malini's husky voice had a badass quality worthy of her buzzed head. Dane's heart leapt in his chest. She hadn't given up. She'd simply stalled for time.

A heavy trudge came from the direction of the train, the sound of an advancing army. Thankfully, it was enough to make the Watchers look up from their meal. Dane tried to get a better look at the damage to his body from within his glass prison.

"Fu—" Lucifer's curse was cut off by the howl of a Watcher at the back of the crowd.

Chaos broke out. Watchers scattered. At the edge of the crowd, unholy screams preceded geysers of black blood. Trapped under glass, Dane couldn't see Malini's army of the dead behind the crowd, but he could guess the damage. A head rolled near his feet, and a disembodied arm made an awful splat near Lucifer's head.

Lucifer charged into his minions. With a powerful sweeping motion, he parted the crowd and sent Malini's zombies tumbling like bowling pins. Dane had a clear view of the dead, mostly bones and half-eaten flesh. Was this the end? Had Lucifer destroyed their last hope of escape?

Slowly, the bones stood back up. They kept coming. Lucifer ripped more apart, only for the bones to come back together. The other Watchers joined in the fight. Even Auriel got off her chair and attacked the dead. The two crouched over Dane's body mercifully became distracted by the fight. They abandoned their meal to watch the dead be dismembered by the Watchers who'd filled the street— burned with sorcery or pulled limb from limb.

Dane cast a worried glance toward Malini, whose skin had begun to blister. She bared her teeth. He turned back toward the battle. Another wave of dead joined the fray. Black blood sprayed across his glass enclosure.

"It's working! Keep 'em coming, Mal!" Dane cheered.

Auriel panicked, wielding a terrible flaming sword at the dead, and grinned broadly as they burst into flame. The burning dead didn't run. Bones blazing, they continued forward, skeletons of death, tearing apart anything in their path. A few desperate howls rose up from Watchers who'd failed to escape in time, including the dark-haired Watcher and the female. They sizzled in the unholy flames before being shredded by the crowd of undead.

"My lord, perhaps we should take shelter inside," Auriel said, pulling on Lucifer's elbow.

He cast her off of him, his fury filling the streets of Nod. Pivoting, he glared at the source of the army of dead, Malini. "Enough." The force of his attack was so great that he dropped the spell around Dane, who slammed back into his body just in time to see the gilded cage ignite into green flames.

"Lord God, NO!" he yelled.

Chin to his chest, Lucifer spread his lips from his multitude of sharp teeth. He turned back toward the army of the dead. "Auriel, take care of our pest."

Dane didn't hesitate. He rolled to the nearest piece of junk he could use as a weapon, a section of metal scrap with a jagged edge. Flipping to the balls of his feet, he faced Auriel head on.

She laughed wickedly. "Oh, Dane, are you some kind of hero now. Please. I own you. I've always owned you. You are nothing, NOTHING, but a country bumpkin with a thing for boys." She swung her sword of fire at his torso.

With Soulkeeper speed, he dodged her attack, stabbing toward her abdomen. He missed.

"The problem, Auriel," he said, dodging her attack, "is you never really knew me at all." He somersaulted backward. She drove him toward the wall of the city. "If you had, you would know not to underestimate me."

He opened himself up, and she stabbed toward his torso. But just as her fiery blade threatened to skewer his heart, he used Ghost's power to break apart and form behind her. He stabbed the chunk of metal through the center of her spine and twisted. The junk wasn't blessed. It wouldn't kill her. But Dane was sure it hurt.

Her scream ripped through the crowd.

Boom! Dane crashed into the wall of Nod and crumpled to the dirt.

Lucifer caught Auriel's body in his arms, yanking the metal fragment from between her wings. His eyes drilled into Dane's. "This isn't over, Soulkeeper. Not by a long shot." He snapped his fingers. Lucifer and Auriel disappeared, as did the Watchers circling above them and those running from Malini's zombies.

As soon as they were gone, the undead collapsed. The zombies fell apart, one by one. Bones and flesh were sucked back to their burial places.

"Malini!" Dane yelled. He dragged his broken body from the street. The cage blazed higher. He reached for Jacob's power, but there wasn't a drop of water anywhere to put out the flames.

I'm alive. Her voice was strained but sure.

"Malini?"

The fire lowered, and Dane glimpsed her small form curled on her side in the center of the cage. Badly burned, her entire body was blackened and blistered. She shouldn't be alive. Dane remembered the ring of fire where Lucifer had imprisoned him in Hell. He'd tried to kill himself in it and couldn't. The sorcery kept him alive no matter what. Maybe, the enchantment meant to contain her had protected her.

He rushed forward and stomped out the remaining flames. The cage didn't have a door, but he circled the bars and delivered a front kick to the flimsiest looking section. The assault of Lucifer's own sorcery had weakened the cage. The section crumbled. He rushed to her side.

Almost burnt beyond recognition, her amber eyes rolled back in her head. He unbuttoned and removed his plaid shirt. Carefully, he dressed her in it, then scooped her into his aching arms. Her head lolled against his chest. Dane swallowed, hard. Without the enchantment of the cage, would she die?

"Malini? Malini? Stay with me."

"Where the hell are we?" Dane jerked at Cheveyo's voice. The Hopi boy wobbled toward him in the abandoned street.

"So now you decide to wake up!" Dane spat. "Thank you, mister ten-minutes-too-late."

"Uh, sorry, but not really sure how I could've helped anyway. I feel like I've been hit by a truck."

"Perfect—" Dane was cut off by Malini's rattling breath.

"Get. Out. Of. Here."

"Gladly." Dane repositioned her in his arms, causing her to grunt from the pain. "Sorry, Mal, there's no other way."

The gate to Nod could only be unlocked by a Watcher, but as fate would have it, the heavy doors had been left open. Dane didn't question why. He strode through to the thorn-lined path with Cheveyo hobbling behind him.

* * * * *

Alexandra watched the one called Dane leave Nod with the Healer in his arms. She was the reason the gate was open, having escaped from the walking dead minutes before. If she'd been loyal and brave, she might have destroyed the Soulkeepers right then. But Alexandra was not loyal or brave. She was a Watcher, and a crippled one at that.

She flexed the wing Lucifer had torn off. The appendage was growing back slowly but still mostly illusion. Normally, healing would be quick and easy, but Lucifer's touch had cursed the wound and left her with this. No, she wasn't going to risk a single feather for anyone but herself.

After the boy was well out of sight, she slipped back inside the gates of Nod, seeing the remnants of the Watchers killed in battle. The street was coated in black blood. Still, they couldn't all be dead, although she couldn't find a single one. The click-clack of her stiletto boots echoed on the street.

Her fate was evident in every empty building she searched. Lucifer had taken the survivors but left her. His action was the ultimate slap in the face. As an angel who had followed him at the fall, Lucifer had an intimate knowledge of the stuff she was made of; all of the fallen were tied to him on a metaphysical level. She wasn't merely forgotten. She was abandoned.

Watchers didn't cry. They couldn't. The stuff they were made of wasn't capable of the full spectrum of emotions, but rather hovered in the vicinity of the seven deadly sins. In this case, Alexandra's pride and sense of self-preservation fueled the anger that drove her from Nod, and raw jealousy of Auriel's position hastened her pursuit. She'd kill the Soulkeeper, recapture the Healer, and, with any luck, she'd be sitting in the throne room tomorrow. Maybe, if she did well, the evil one would even fix her wing.

Chapter 31
Fourth World

By the time they reached the underground garden, Dane was falling apart. His nose was bleeding furiously, and his brain throbbed like it'd been bludgeoned inside his skull. By the rattle in Malini's breath, he was pretty sure she was dying.

"This is the tree," he said to Cheveyo. "We touch it, and it will take us home."

He leaned his shoulder onto the bark, and then repositioned Malini to place his palm flat against the trunk for good measure. Nothing happened.

"Malini, it's not working."

"Too late. Need sorcery," she rasped.

"I'm fresh out of sorcery. How the hell do we get out of here?"

Malini didn't answer. She went limp in his arms, her breath shallow.

Cheveyo stared at him blankly.

Dane closed his eyes in frustration. He had to think of something, but who could think with this pounding? Strange, it almost seemed like…

"Do you hear that?" he asked Cheveyo.

"What?"

"It's like …drumbeats."

"No. I don't hear anything."

"Do you think it's the Watchers?"

Cheveyo shook his head. "Judging by the looks of that place I wouldn't say they were into music or the arts. Where I come from, drums are sacred."

"Follow," Malini rasped.

Dane widened his eyes. "It's as good a hope as any. Let's go." Wiping the blood from his face with the back of his sleeve, he led the way toward the rhythm of the drums. He had to go slowly because Cheveyo couldn't see in the dark and the path he took snaked through the thorny landscape. Between the blood loss and Malini's weight, he was incapable of speed anyway.

"I hear them," Cheveyo said, squeezing his shoulder. "Those are Hopi drums, Dane. This is the way out!"

Dane tried to walk faster, but every step brought pain. The path widened and the thorn bushes became sparse, replaced by juniper trees, cactus, and deep green shrubs. Soon, the landscape was bathed in a bright, warm glow from ahead.

Cheveyo released his shoulder. "Come on." He jogged toward the light.

Step by labored step, Dane caught up, the drums growing louder and louder as he approached. When he reached the source, his jaw dropped. He'd entered a summer land of sun and sand, in a circle of pueblos and smiling Native American faces. Cheveyo stood at the center of the community, arms open.

A man with a heavily lined face and a small animal skin kilt approached Cheveyo and spoke to him in a language Dane didn't understand. He didn't have the strength to call up Jacob's gift to translate, and he didn't have to. Cheveyo understood what he was saying. The exchange was warm and ended in a familial embrace.

When it was over, Cheveyo rushed to Dane. "We have to hurry. The way is only open during the ceremony, while the drums are still beating."

Dane followed Cheveyo's lead to a tall and worrisome wooden ladder. Would the ancient wood hold? Could he carry Malini and climb to the top? And for that matter, where was the top?

"Give her to me. I feel strong." Cheveyo pulled Malini from Dane's arms and rolled her over his shoulder, holding her legs against his chest with one arm, he began to climb with the other.

Dane didn't argue with the plan. He had enough trouble pulling himself up the rungs.

"Where does this lead, Cheveyo? Are you sure the man can be trusted?

Cheveyo didn't pause his slow and steady ascent. "That man is my great-great-great-great-grandfather and long ago chief of the Hopi tribe. This is our underworld, the land of our dead."

"What? Here?"

"Don't judge what you don't understand."

"Who's judging?"

Fog rolled in, blocking out the light until even Dane couldn't see a thing but the rung ahead of him. Over the sound of the drumbeats, another more soothing rhythm met his ears.

"I hear rain!" he said.

"Yes. We're close," Cheveyo said excitedly. His feet disappeared into the fog.

A wet clump of red hit Dane in the face. With one hand, he wiped it from his forehead. Mud. He climbed faster, into the muck, holding his breath as he plowed through a particularly thick stretch of wet dirt. When his head broke the surface, he gasped for breath, rain washing the remnants of earth and blood from his face. He thrust his hand up and, mercifully, Cheveyo clasped it between his own and hauled him up.

They were in another, more modern Hopi village, at the center of some type of ceremony with dancing and drums.

Dane didn't pause to appreciate the staring faces. He rushed to Malini's side. The rain was helping wash the burn from her body, one drop at a time, but he knew he could help things considerably. Lifting her head, he called Jacob's energy and directed the rain to wash over her more thoroughly. A flinch. A sputter. Finally, she opened her eyes.

He lowered her head.

"Dane!" Malini yelled. But there was nothing she could do. He'd used up everything he had. Exhausted, he toppled toward the mud but wasn't conscious long enough to feel the fall.

* * * * *

At the center of the Hopi ceremony, Cheveyo found it ironic that he'd ended up exactly where he'd begun. While Dane helped Malini, long fingers reached for him from the red mud. Bewildered, he grasped the hand and pulled.

"Stop! Cheveyo, don't help her!" Malini screamed.

He yanked his hand away, but it was too late, the red-haired Watcher, Alexandra, clawed her way up from the hole. Her illusion melted with the rain, or maybe the power of the sacred space, and she stretched her hideous leathery wings.

"You're mine, Healer," she hissed through elongated fangs. Completely focused on Malini, the demon didn't give Cheveyo a second glance. Her black scales twitched with rage.

Dane couldn't help. He lay in a heap at Malini's side. Cheveyo wasn't sure what he could do to stop the Watcher from hurting his new friends or his old ones. But he had to do something.

Alexandra lowered her head and charged for Malini, talons flashing as lightning and thunder rocked the mesa.

"No!" Cheveyo yelled and thrust both hands into the Watcher's scaly torso. He meant only to push the demon, to give everyone enough time to run, but from the very beginning, nothing had happened as Cheveyo expected. His soul transferred into the Watcher, his body dropping to the mud. From inside, Cheveyo felt the demon clutch its throat, then shake its head frantically. Alexandra clawed at her face until the black skin was sliced to ribbons. Through bulging eyes, Cheveyo watched a scaly hand swell bigger and bigger. Unable to contain him, the Watcher's body finally popped. Black blood and chunks of scaly flesh showered the plaza, staining the walls of the surrounding pueblos and everyone in between. And Cheveyo, freed from his enemy, slipped back into his body.

The drums stopped. The rain stopped. The clouds moved aside to reveal a bright sun that contrasted sharply with the horrified faces covered in black oily splotches all around him. A large snake slithered across his toes.

Cheveyo took a deep breath and rolled up to a sitting position, wiping black gunk from his cheek. He turned toward Malini.

"Well, that was a hell of a thing," he said flatly. "You know, I don't think I'm supposed to possess humans at all."

Malini nodded, then began to giggle. She turned her face to the sun and raised her arms to the sky in a gesture of intense gratitude. Cheveyo couldn't help it. He began to laugh too. They laughed until they could hardly breathe and the stares of the people around them became too intense.

At her side, Dane groaned, and Malini turned her attention to him.

Cheveyo glanced around the Hopi tribe, meeting the eyes of Willow, Raine, and his father. Would they be angry that he'd brought this evil upon them? Now, more connected to his roots than ever, he desperately wanted their acceptance. How could he help them understand?

What happened next made his heart swell. As a tribe, the Hopi people bowed. Even his dad. The look on his father's face was not horror; it was pride.

Chapter 32
Coming Out

Exhausted, Malini borrowed a phone to call Jacob to come and get them. When Lucifer took her clothes, he also took Warwick's sapphire, her only means of communication with Eden. The Hopi were unbelievably accommodating, especially the medicine woman. Willow explained that Spider Woman came to her in a dream and commanded the Hopi to perform the Snake Dance at the highly unusual time of year.

She'd have to thank Fate later for saving her life. Of course, Fatima would deny everything. Technically, the immortals weren't allowed to interfere.

Cheveyo borrowed his father's Jeep and helped carry Dane down the mesa. Working together, they transported him back to the Desert Days Motel, where they procured a room and propped Dane's limp body on the bed. His nose was still bleeding, and his skin was doing a good job of matching the sheets.

Malini tried to heal him but healing wasn't the problem. He needed to unload the gifts he'd been carrying before they ate him alive from the inside out. It was like any of their powers. If Malini healed for too long, she burned. If Ghost dispersed for too long, he ached all over like he had the flu. For Dane, if he held onto a gift for too long, it ate him alive.

With a crack, Samantha arrived in the room, staff in one hand and geode in the other. She gasped when she saw Malini and then Dane, a storm of emotions: horror, anger, and pity flitting across her face. She didn't say a word, just walked to the closet and set up the portal. A few minutes later, Jacob emerged from a tunnel of purple light, T-shirt and shorts dappled with wet spots.

"Surfing," he said to Samantha. "It might take the others a few more minutes."

She nodded.

The second Jacob saw Malini, a growl breached his throat from deep within. "What happened?" His eyes wandered over her chopped hair, her borrowed T-shirt and shorts.

"Believe me, Lucifer got the worst of it." She reached for his hand.

He pulled her into his embrace, running his hands through her hair and whispering sweetly in her ear.

"Um, I'm Cheveyo, but people call me Chevy." Cheveyo's mahogany hand extended toward Jacob awkwardly.

Jacob stepped back from Malini and shook the boy's hand. "Nice to meet you in the flesh."

Any further greeting was cut off by the sound of the ocean and a spray of seawater. Bonnie and Ethan stepped from the closet.

Ethan didn't even look toward the small group of Soulkeepers near the window. He rushed to Dane's side, lowering himself to the edge of the bed and leaning over his body. Carefully, he placed a hand on his cheek. "What's wrong with him? He's burning up."

"He needs to give you all your gifts back. They're killing him," Malini said.

Ethan tapped Dane's cheek and shook his shoulder gently. "Dane. Dane. Wake up, buddy."

Dane's eyes fluttered open.

"Good morning, Hero. You need to give me my power back, now."

A pinched smile spread across Dane's face. "So, take it," he drawled.

Ethan lowered his mouth to Dane's.

"Whoa." Malini forcibly turned Jacob and Cheveyo toward the window. Bonnie turned too, raising an eyebrow.

"So, ah, you were right about that one thing we talked about before," Malini said to Jacob.

"And don't you forget it. You know, just because you're the Healer doesn't mean you know everything."

Samantha cleared her throat from her place in front of the closet. "Yeah, it kinda does, Jacob."

"Definitely," Bonnie agreed. She pressed her eyes closed and smacked her forehead with her palm. No one needed to ask why.

"Huh. Well, I'll always have this." Jacob pulled Malini into his side.

A loud pop behind them welcomed Grace and Master Lee to the room, each arriving by means of their own staff.

"Oh!" Grace said when she saw the kiss. She joined the others at the window while Lee made himself busy helping Samantha. "So ... that's happening."

"And it's about time," Malini added.

Grace smiled warmly in response. "Maybe we should leave them alone?" she offered.

"Not until you get your damn powers out of my boyfriend," Ethan said. "He's not doing so good over here."

"Happily." Jacob turned from the window and reached across the bed for Dane's hand. With a jolt, his eyes took on the sparkle of a Soulkeeper.

Lillian arrived next through the closet, followed by Ghost, who seemed like he'd enjoyed the journey all too well. He whooped and gave Samantha a peck on her cheek.

"We just got the message from Dr. Silva— shit, Dane, you look like Hell."

Concerned, he walked over to the bed, slugging Ethan in the shoulder in lieu of a hello.

"He needs to dump your power," Jacob said. "It's giving him a headache."

"It's probably the smell," Ethan added, rubbing his arm where Ghost had punched him.

"Ha, ha. More like he can't handle the magnanimous power that is me." Ghost clasped Dane's arm at the elbow.

Dane returned the grip, flipping him off with his other hand. "Oh, I handled it. I just know you need it more than I do," he said, passing the power back.

Malini rolled her eyes. "Do you guys ever stop?"

Ghost's electric violet eyes fluttered in response. "Whatever do you mean?"

"One more," Lillian said, grabbing Dane's hand. Malini watched her power return to her like a long lost friend.

"How are you feeling now, Dane?" Malini asked.

"Much better. My headache is gone." He accepted Ethan's help and sat up on the ugly brown bedspread.

"Excellent. We'll help you back to Eden to unload Archibald's gift."

"Archibald? He gave you something?" Ethan asked.

"Yeah, super sight and hearing. It saved our lives."

"No shit?" Ghost grinned incredulously.

"No shit," Dane said.

At the serious glare Dane gave him, the smile melted from Ghost's face and he nodded.

"Malini," Lee said. "We'd better go. I don't think it's safe for all of us to be here."

"Absolutely," Malini said. "Not to mention, I've got to do something about this before my parents see me." She pointed to her head.

Grace and the girls lowered their eyes, as if they couldn't stand the sight of her talon-shorn hair. Even Lillian looked like she might cry. But Jacob rubbed her head with his hand. "Looks tough. Very G.I. Jane."

* * * * *

While the other Soulkeepers discussed the mission and how they were all going to get back to Eden, Dane smiled weakly at Ethan. "So, I made it home, as promised."

"Knew you would." Ethan shrugged.

"Right. You thought I was Watcher fodder."

"But you weren't." Ethan's dark eyes lit up, and he wove his fingers into Dane's.

"So, I guess we should come out to my parents," Dane suggested, suddenly serious.

Glancing away, Ethan played with the corner of the pillowcase.

"What?" Dane asked.

"Might not be the best time," he said. "Your dad is still in the hospital. He hasn't gotten any better."

"How long were we gone?" Dane asked.

"Weeks. It's October fifth."

Stunned, Dane glanced at Malini. She didn't look much better than he felt. This mission had ruined both of them and she'd missed her birthday. But he would never forget how it felt to plunge that metal rod into Auriel's back. They'd attacked Lucifer in his own backyard, and they'd lived to tell the tale.

"Well, I guess life-changing conversations can wait 'til everything is back to normal."

Ethan nodded. "We've got nothing but time."

"Yeah. I guess we do."

* * * * *

After some discussion, the Soulkeepers divided themselves into groups of two for the trip home, deciding to take turns with the enchanted staffs rather than chancing the challenge of a new portal with Malini and Dane in their weakened condition. Since the staffs were limited to two Soulkeepers at a time, Jacob, Ethan, and Jesse volunteered to stay back for the second trip.

Cheveyo balked. "What about me? This is my home. What about my mom and dad? Raine?"

Malini placed a hand on his shoulder. "Your father, Willow, and Raine were there today. They understand exactly what you are and why you need to leave. Our Helpers will come up with something to tell your mother."

"I want to stay." Cheveyo shook his head. "My dad says I can complete the Hopi coming-of-age ritual. I never thought I wanted to before but I do. I really do."

Bonnie, Samantha, and Grace glanced at each other, and then eyed Cheveyo empathetically. They knew all too well what sacrifices becoming a Soulkeeper required.

"I'm sorry," Malini said. "There will come a time when you can go home. But not now. It's too dangerous. Lucifer could retaliate and you're too vulnerable here."

He opened his mouth to argue but Malini grasped his hand, giving him a heavy dose of her healing power. Understanding softened his shoulders, and eventually he nodded his acceptance.

They agreed to meet behind the flower shop. Lee helped Dane into position, and Malini joined Lillian at the staff Lee had brought for her. Bonnie and Samantha huddled around the one Samantha had used, and Grace offered a kind hand to Cheveyo. They tapped the staffs on the shaggy beige carpet and began their journey home.

Epilogue

Abigail waited in her bedroom in Eden for any word from Malini or the rest of the council. Jacob's call had been brief and hurried with little details other than Malini's location at the Desert Days in Flagstaff. She'd passed on the urgent request for help to the other Soulkeepers but hadn't heard anything since. Were they alive? Dead? Captured? If Dane didn't survive, the other Soulkeepers would be without the benefit of their gifts. They'd be sitting ducks.

She wrung her hands and wished Gideon would return from the library. Something was wrong; she could feel it in her bones. And she couldn't shake the feeling, not by reading or working on potions in the lab. Anxiety made her queasy and tired, but she couldn't sleep. Restless, she paced the floor in front of the four-poster bed until a vibration in her pocket made the breath catch in her throat.

She pulled out the sapphire and allowed the blue glow to etch out Malini's transparent form in the space before her.

"Malini! Where are you? Are you okay?"

"Abigail, I need your help. I can't give you the details now, but you have to meet me." Malini brushed her long brown hair behind her shoulder before clasping her hands together in front of her lips.

"You need me to leave Eden?" Abigail asked.

"Right away. It's an emergency." Malini sighed heavily. "You are the only one who can help us. You must come right away."

"Of course. Where are you?"

"Meet me in the maple orchard, behind your old house. Come immediately, Abigail. You are our last and only hope."

The blue stone flickered and Malini's hologram was gone. Abigail wasted no time. She scratched Gideon a hasty note and left it on the bed. Then, she raced from the room, asking the nearest gnome to call the boat that would take her out of Eden.

* * * * *

Lucifer quivered from head to toe, shaking Malini's illusion from his black, double-breasted suit. He flipped the blue stone into the air, caught it, and slid it into his pocket. Imitating Malini's appearance had been easy. He had her clothing. He had the stone.

"Do you think she bought it?" Auriel asked, adjusting the tortoiseshell glasses on her nose. Dressed in a gray suit with her hair styled in a blonde chignon, she presented a sophisticated demeanor at his side. Her back had already healed, thanks to Lucifer's sorcery.

"I am the Lord of Illusions, Auriel. Of course she bought it," he said. The wall of windows in Harrington's office gave him a panoramic view of Lake Michigan, one piece of the world he would own soon enough.

She glanced at the crumpled, bloody mess in the corner. "What should I do with him?"

"Eat him for all I care." The look he gave her burned, and not because of the flames that flickered in his pupils. Lucifer was angry, so angry he was calm and cold. Auriel hoped to never be on the receiving end of that anger, which was why she didn't rush to the human snack that bled in the corner.

"How many did we lose?" she asked.

"Including this summer? Thousands. Our minions are less in number but no less powerful. Those who were destroyed were weak and disloyal."

"Yes."

Lucifer approached her until she could feel the heat of Hell blasting through his Armani suit. "We are not going to run or hide this time, Auriel. The stage is set and that little twit and her team of birthday party magicians aren't going to get the best of us."

A heavy knock rattled the door. "Come in, Cord," Lucifer said, unlocking it with his will.

Cord entered, twirling the gold, lion's head ring on his finger.

"I have a job for you," Lucifer said.

"Yes, my lord."

"Retrieve Abigail." Lucifer scowled at Cord's reaction, a subtle cringe that betrayed his fear of the former fallen angel. "Oh, I think you will find that Abigail has become much more amicable, Cord. She'll be waiting for you in the maple orchard, behind her old house."

Cord nodded. "Of course. As you wish." He remained fixed to the spot.

"You're not leaving."

"My illusion is weak, my lord." Cord glanced toward the body in the corner.

Lucifer motioned toward Mr. Harrington's body. "Well? Help yourself. Lunch is getting cold."

With an unholy growl, both Watchers swooped in and began to eat, fighting over every scrap.

Lucifer lowered himself into the executive's leather chair. He grinned as the evidence of Mr. Harrington's murder was conveniently ingested. "Enjoy. Consider the meal an employee benefit." Fingers laced behind his head, he leaned back to prop his feet up on the mahogany desk.

"Harrington Enterprises is officially under new management."

Other Books in The Soulkeepers Series

Lost Eden (Book 5)
Rules. Balance. Consequences. War.

When Fate gave Dane the water from Eden to drink, she did more than save his life. She changed his destiny. Since the beginning, a covenant between God and Lucifer has maintained a tenuous peace, balancing Soulkeepers and Watchers and the natural order of things. Dane upset that balance the day he became a Soulkeeper. Fate broke the rules.

Now, Lucifer is demanding a consequence, requiring Fate to pay the ultimate price for her involvement. God intervenes on the immortal's behalf but in order to save her soul must dissolve the covenant and with it the rules, order, and balance that have kept the peace. A challenge is issued. A contest for human souls begins. And the stakes? Earth. Winner take all.

The Soulkeepers are at the center of a war between Heaven and Hell, and this time nobody, anywhere, is safe from Lucifer's reach.

The Last Soulkeeper (Book 6)

The end is near.

Just when the Soulkeepers think they've established a foothold in the war between Heaven and Hell, the playing field shifts. Enraged by Cord's disappearance, Lucifer replaces his right-hand man with the Wicked Brethren, three Watchers so formidable even their own kind fears them.

The Soulkeepers struggle to survive in an increasingly deadly world while continuing to defend human souls. How far will they go when saving the world means sacrificing their most precious team member?

Other Books By G. P. Ching

Grounded

A seventeen-year-old girl discovers she's the product of a government experiment, when her father's illness causes her to leave her isolated community.

Lost Eden (Excerpt)
Book 5 in The Soulkeepers Series

Chapter 1
Consequences

Balance. All life, the world's very existence, hinged on perfect balance. Rain and drought, work and play, love and hate, good and evil, each in measured quantities, rising and falling in a constant struggle for equilibrium. Balance bolstered the natural order of things, and Fatima's job was to record it all. Record but not change.

As Fatima, or Fate to those who would call her by her title, stood barefoot on packed dirt, her eight arms weaving the fabric of human destiny, she carried a heavy weight within her bosom. She bent her knees to counteract the encumbrance of the yards of shimmering cloth made by her hand, but the heavy burden of a secret bothered her most. Fatima had broken the rules—rules put in place to maintain balance. She'd taken an action, saved a boy named Dane from certain death by giving him a sip of water. A simple, compassionate gesture meant only to counteract the devil's unjust deeds.

But small deeds could have big consequences.

In the process of saving Dane, she'd made him a Soulkeeper. Fate understood the implications all too well.

You did not drop a pebble into a sacred pool without causing ripples. All she had to do was read this particular stretch of fabric emerging from her hands—red, pink, and yellow threads, bright and hot colors—that spoke of increased metaphysical activity on Earth. It stung her fingers. Things were heating up down below. How much had her crime cost humanity? She crumpled her forehead and wove faster to alleviate the burn.

Movement caught her eye near the bolts behind her. Without pausing her work, she twisted her neck, and shuffled her feet to see who it was. Perhaps Malini was back from Nod with news of the Soulkeepers' latest mission. For a moment, she was blinded by the sparkle from the fabric, the woven destinies of billions of souls, their light seeming to collect at the center of the room. Like a mirror, it reflected her image back at her, sleek black hair, smooth russet skin, graceful limbs and eyes …

Fate halted her weaving. Her lips parted. Her reflection did not share her black eyes or the dancing lights of souls within them. The reflection's eyes were hazel, as Fatima's had been when she was human. Other differences prevailed. The image did not bear the burden of her weaving or the frown that Fatima was sure she wore now. This reflection was a perfect Fate.

Light. Warmth. Joy. Fatima's doppelganger exuded peace and love. When she realized who had come to see her, she put aside her work and dropped to her knees, both honored and terrified by the presence before her. As a kindness, God always took the form of the person present, a concession meant to keep the soul from going mad.

"M-my lord, to what do I owe the honor of your visit?" Fatima stuttered.

"Rise. We have only moments. I've come to warn you."

Fatima scrambled to her feet, unable to take her eyes off the beauty of the being in her own image who floated to her side.

"There is sin between us, Fatima. I feel a blockage, an invisible wall, keeping me from connecting with you. Tell me so we can move beyond it." God moved closer and met her eyes.

"When Lucifer freed Dane from Hell, he left him for dead. Abigail delivered his body to the gate of Eden. She didn't know any better. In her fallen condition, she'd never been allowed close enough to learn he'd be cast out. The injustice of it all would have tipped the balance in Lucifer's favor. I had to do something. I visited the boat and gave the boy the living water to drink."

"You took his destiny into your own hands." God widened her eyes.

"Yes."

"And your actions produced greater consequences than his admission to Eden."

"He became a Soulkeeper."

God turned away then, clasping her hands behind her back. Fatima shuddered at the elimination of the light and warmth of her attention. "Not just a Soulkeeper, Fatima.

Dane's power, along with his personal characteristics, allowed him to slay over a thousand Watchers in Nod. He broke the terms of my compact with Lucifer."

"I don't understand."

"Nod is off-limits to Soulkeepers as the In Between is off-limits to Watchers. He will demand a consequence for the infraction."

"But...but...he broke the compact first! Watchers live among men even now, permanently! They taint the water. He'd planned to use Cheveyo to destroy Eden. Not to mention, Auriel took Malini and Dane to Nod in the first place. The two Soulkeepers simply fought their way out."

God's still, small voice was in direct contrast to Fate's panicked one. "All valid points, Fatima, but you must see how your actions have forced my hand."

Fatima did see. The rules existed for a reason. Even though other immortals had taken similar actions to keep Lucifer at bay, it didn't excuse her. She'd given the devil an opening, and surely it was just a matter of time before he took full advantage. She fell on her knees again, tears forming in her black eyes. "Please forgive me. Tell me what I can do to make this right."

With a smile that spread a tangible joy across the villa, God turned back to Fate, and motioned for her to rise. "All is forgiven, Dear One, but now we must manage the consequences, and unfortunately the cure for the world's ills will be more than either you or any of the immortals can achieve."

As Fatima rose from the dirt, she noticed a patch of black mold where the ceiling met the front wall in the upper corner of her stucco manse. Her home was a product of her consciousness, constructed of her thoughts and will, but this was not hers. She did not invite the darkness. This was something other, something dangerous. The black mold spread down the corner of the wall to the floor, and then mushroomed, reproducing to the size of a grapefruit, a bowling ball, a bush. Fatima backed away, taking her place behind God who held Her ground faithfully.

With a final sprout of growth, the black fuzz paled and hardened, and a man in a shiny gray business suit stepped from the darkness. His blond curls set off his lapis eyes, and the perfect smile he flashed took Fatima's breath away. But his expression was icy and his posture arrogant. *Lucifer.*

"I see you are expecting me," he rasped. His voice held the sizzle of Hell and his breath the hint of brimstone. Fatima covered her mouth and nose with her hand.

"Say what you came to say," God said. Her glow increased, pressing his darkness back toward the wall.

He blinked rapidly, and then shifted his eyes downward, smoothing his perfectly tailored suit. "I demand a consequence."

"State your reasoning."

"Your immortal has broken the law. She has created a Soulkeeper of her own will, and disrupted the balance by sending that soul to attack me in my own dominion."

"Were you not also to blame, Lucifer? Did you not break our agreement first? Even now, I sense your minions on Earth, in clear violation."

He gave a half smile and slid his hands into his pockets, pacing toward the archway to the veranda. "No. I did nothing of the sort."

"You lie."

"Yes, I do. It is my nature, and as such, it should be expected. I am entitled to a consequence, and I will not back down until I have my just due."

God approached him, the air crackling with her presence. The back of Lucifer's head glowed brassy in her light. "Very well. What is your suggested price?"

"My price is Fate. She has been in her position far too long. I will choose her replacement, and she will step down."

"No!" Fatima yelled, her hands flying to cover her foolhardy mouth. Why had she allowed her true feelings to show? Now he'd be even more likely to use those feelings against her.

He turned the force of his stare on her, laughing through a toothy half smile. "Oh yes, Fatima. Perhaps, I will not only choose your replacement but take your soul as my own." In a blink, he was in her face, his hand on the small of her back. Her skin squirmed beneath his touch. "You are a beautiful sinner. Hell could use an ornament such as you."

"Let her go." A wash of cool light poured through the room, and Lucifer retreated, joints folding unnaturally in his haste for the shadows. "The Watchers who reside on Earth negate your ability to make such a demand. You are in breach of the law, Lucifer. You must return your minions to Nod or Hell."

"Or what?" Lucifer carefully slithered into the shadow of a bolt of fabric where his eyes could open fully.

"Or the compact is rendered null and void."

"War." The word rolled off his tongue, smooth as melted butter.

God rubbed her chin. "As ever, you are cunning, Lucifer, and perhaps it is time that your superior intelligence is rewarded." She circled right, eyeing him from head to toe as she passed the upright bolts of woven human history. "Instead of exacting your revenge on a peasant girl turned Fate, would you consider a wager for something more?"

"More?" Lucifer narrowed his eyes and licked his lips. His Adam's apple bobbed as he swallowed again and again, salivating at the thought of *more*.

"Our covenant is ancient and worthless, but human hearts must be ruled. Do you agree it is time for a new covenant?"

Lucifer rubbed his hands together. "How will the terms be decided?"

"By human hearts." God snapped her fingers. "If you will follow me outside, I will propose a change."

Fatima and Lucifer trailed the supreme deity out onto the veranda and then into Fate's yard. Above the swell of a grassy green knoll at the back of her territory, an angel descended from the heavens. A blinding aura surrounded the winged woman, her dark hair rippling against her white toga-like dress. When her toes touched down, her flesh hardened from the feet up, white marble swallowing her to the tips of her outstretched wings. The angel looked familiar to Fate, like Themis, a human depiction of justice embodied, only this living statue had wings. Blindfolded, the angel held scales in one hand and a crystal model of Earth in the other.

"We need witnesses." Another snap of God's fingers and Henry and Mara appeared beside Fate, flustered and confused. When they saw the second Fatima, realization dawned slowly, confusion followed by terror. They fell to their knees in the grass.

"Rise, Mara. Rise, Henry. We need your help."

Henry nodded, staggering to his feet. Mara reached for his hand, and he helped her stand.

"Lucifer," God said, turning her full attention on the walking stain on the countryside that was the devil. "This scorekeeper holds in her hand a model of the world. Stare into the depths of this crystal, and tell me what you see."

Lucifer approached cautiously and stared into the translucent orb. "Pinpoints of light and darkness."

"You see human hearts. Some are aligned with me, appearing as points of light, and some are aligned with you, appearing as points of darkness. As you can see, at the moment, the scales are slightly tipped in your favor." God flourished her hand in front of the dark plate of the left side of the scale.

"They appear to be. Get to the point, Oppressor. What is your wager?"

"First, we abolish the compact."

Fate, Time, and Death gasped at the thought. Fatima reached for Mara's free hand, her other firmly in Henry's grip. All three immortals stood connected in their horror. Fatima trusted God, but this was terrifying. None of them had lived in a world without an agreement between good and evil. Her stomach twisted. Lucifer already had the advantage. The scales tipped in his favor. Without the compact, what would keep him at bay?

"And then?" Lucifer prompted.

"We compete for the hearts of men," God said.

Lucifer narrowed his eyes against her light. "Compete how?"

"You release six temptations unto the world, and I release six gifts." She held out her hand toward the statue. "The scorekeeper will record human alignment with good or evil. When the last gift or temptation has come to pass, the challenge will be over and whomever has won the most souls will rule Earth."

"And the other?"

"Banished from contact with humanity for one thousand years. Hark, Lucifer, there will be no cheating this banishment. Should you lose, you will be sealed within Hell for the entire epoch."

Lucifer began to pace in front of the scorekeeper, checked her crystal, and then checked again. "It's a trick. You would not risk so many souls."

"No trick. Six temptations verses six gifts. You have the advantage. A few of your minions are already living among men, men they've influenced to do your will."

"If the compact is dissolved, all of my Watchers can remain above ground?"

"Of course! If the compact is no more, they can journey wherever they wish."

Lucifer tilted his chin up and smiled viciously. "What's the catch?"

"No catch. But the Watchers are still bound by the natural order of things. The sun will dull their powers. The night will strengthen them."

"They will kill to remain strong."

"No compact. No rules."

"Besides the natural laws," Lucifer lamented.

"Yes. All humans have free will. Earth's natural resources have limits. Sunlight gives my souls an advantage, darkness, yours. I can be everywhere at once; you can only be in one place at a time. This is how it has always been and always will be."

Lucifer gave a small, almost imperceptible nod of agreement.

"And one more thing, humans must choose you of their free will. I know you've poisoned the water. Influenced humans are incapable of choosing. They are merely your puppets. If we are to do this, any souls you or your Watchers influence will be deemed neutral."

Lucifer scowled. "Only six temptations and no influencing free will? *Bah.*"

"Only six gifts and you already have the advantage."

While Fatima held her breath, Lucifer stared at the scales, slightly tipped in his favor. She couldn't decide which was worse, a Fate chosen by Lucifer or the potential to have a world ruled by him. The devil seemed to be weighing his options.

"Are you afraid, Lucifer? Should I take your hesitation as an admission of my greater power?" God's voice echoed with a deep hollow tenor that didn't fit her current appearance.

Lucifer growled, his face reddened with anger. "I am the more powerful! I accept your challenge and claim the right to go first. Do you agree?"

God beamed, flooding the hillside with light. "I do agree." She offered her right hand. "In the presence of these three witnesses, the challenge for human souls begins now. Winner take all for one thousand years."

"Agreed." Lucifer slapped his hand into God's. The connection created a sonic boom that flattened Fatima and the other immortals to the grass. The sound rippled outward, visible in the blue sky of the In Between, and a shockwave plowed through the cells of her body. *No*, she thought, *not just my body but also my weaving.* The future had changed. The universe had changed. She was witness to an agreement that might end life as she knew it.

God retracted her hand. She turned toward the crystal Earth in the scorekeeper's grip. "The world awaits you, Lucifer."

He backed up a few steps, a wicked laugh bubbling from deep within. "This is going to be fun." He came apart in a rush of black fog that passed over them and straight into the villa. *Where was he going?*

Fatima jolted at a strange and painful sensation in her abdomen. A thread had been plucked from her body and her weaving. Frantically, she patted her stomach, retrieving her work from deep within. He'd taken something from her. When he'd blown out of the In Between, he'd taken *someone.* Yes, that was it. A soul was missing. But who? What human being was important enough to steal from the fabric of history?

"You know who," God said, as she broke apart and blended into the light.

Fatima scrambled to her feet, Mara and Henry cursing at her side in their own pursuit of vertical. One by one they stepped to the scorekeeper and watched the light and the dark dance within the globe.

"Who did he take, Fatima?" Henry asked.

"I can't be certain. There are so many souls."

"You know," Mara said. "She said you know."

Fatima swallowed and raised a hand to the base of her neck. "There is only one person I can think of who is a constant reminder of Lucifer's failures. She is the only one who has denied him time and time again. Her life is a testament to God's grace and mercy."

Henry glanced at Mara, who looked off into space as if reading the stars. The immortals said the name together, in perfect unison. "Abigail."

About the Author

G.P. Ching is the bestselling author of The Soulkeepers Series and Grounded. She specializes in cross-genre YA novels with paranormal elements and surprising twists. The Soulkeepers was named a 2013 iBookstore Breakout Book.

G.P. lives in central Illinois with her husband, two children, and a Brittany spaniel named Riptide Jack. Learn more about G.P. and her books at www.gpching.com.

Follow G.P. on:
  Twitter: @gpching
  Facebook: G.P. Ching
  Facebook: The Soulkeepers Series

Sign up for her exclusive newsletter at www.gpching.com to be the first to know about new releases!

The greatest compliment you can give an author is a positive review. If you've enjoyed this title, please consider reviewing it at your place of purchase.

Acknowledgements

Soul Catcher took some bravery to write. My vision for Dane and Ethan was always that they end up together. But we live in a time when homosexuality is an emotionally charged and controversial topic. The Soulkeepers Series is fantasy with religious elements, and when I introduced Ethan in the third book, I received some backlash from a small but vocal minority of readers who didn't like his sexual orientation. At that point, I considered not writing the fourth book.

I'm happy to say that thanks to a number of people in my life, I found the courage to continue the series as I'd imagined it. My husband for one, along with fellow authors Karly Kirkpatrick and Angela Carlie, helped me to remember that the Soulkeepers has always been about self-acceptance. Writing about Dane's relationship was necessary, more than ever in this time of divisive politics, because the world needs a hero who, like so many teens today, is struggling with his sexuality.

Thanks also to Adam Bedore of Anjin design for coming through for me on the cover once again. Finally, thank you readers for coming along on this journey with me.

Book Club Discussion Questions

1. The Hopi Snake Dance at the beginning of the novel is based on an actual ceremony. Do you feel that preserving cultures like the Hopi's is important for our future?

2. Adults don't always take Malini seriously as a leader. Why do you think this is?

3. Grace says that the Soulkeepers' work deserves scrutiny. Do you agree that it's better to debate important decisions from both sides before adopting a change? Or should people simply follow a leader's direction?

4. Is Malini a good leader? Why or why not?

5. Dane shows small kindnesses to Archibald throughout the book. Do these things matter?

6. Compare and contrast Ethan and Dane's relationship with Lucifer and Auriel's. Which do you think is the healthier relationship?

7. Did anything about the progression of Dane and Ethan's relationship bother you? Did you think Ethan should have been more direct?

8. Dane never labels his sexuality in this novel. How would you characterize him based on what you know? Do you think how Dane is portrayed is realistic?

9. Eden is perfectly safe. Some people would call it paradise. Would you want to live there?

10. Bonnie has a misaligned attraction throughout most of Soul Catcher. Why do you think girls sometimes obsess over what they can't have?